Oh Lord, Won't You Steal Me a Mercedes Benz

Also by Steve Liskow

The Kids Are All Right

Postcards of the Hanging

Blood On The Tracks

The Night Has 1000 Eyes

Run Straight Down

Cherry Bomb

The Whammer Jammers

Who Wrote the Book of Death?

Oh Lord, Won't You Steal Me a Mercedes Benz

by

Steve Liskow

Jim + Rob

Enjoy!

Thanks —
See you soon

Steve Liskow

Cover art and design by Peter B. Riley

Image of woman by bg_knight/Shutterstock

ISBN: 978-1511686402

For Barbara

1

Chris Guthrie couldn't remember when he first met Hot Rod Lincoln. He knew he was with the Detroit Police, and he thought he'd busted Lincoln for stealing a car owned by somebody who was friends with somebody he knew in high school. And that guy dated somebody who slept with someone who went through the Police Academy with Guthrie, and who was once married to somebody else who knew somebody who had played on a recording session with Megan Traine, Guthrie's girlfriend. Or something like that. Kevin Bacon had something to do with it.

Now, ten years later, Hot Rod wore what might have been the same denim shirt and faded jeans from when Guthrie last saw him. He still resembled an out-take from *The Dukes of Hazzard*, his pompadour and 70s porn-star sideburns the color of furniture polish, but wrinkles ringed his eyes as though he were staring into the sun.

Unless Guthrie could help, he was really staring at twenty years to life.

"Why do they think you did it, Hot Rod?"

"Mr. Fillmore was miles away at the time," the attorney said.

Guthrie remembered William "Billable Hours" Powers, too, the most expensive defense attorney in Detroit. They were on the same side now but Powers's type A-squared personality would make espresso beans twitch.

Powers forged ahead in a theatrical baritone. "He and the victim never laid eyes on each other. Ever. So there's no motive, either."

Guthrie glanced at Hot Rod, who studied his coffee, kahlua hazelnut because Guthrie refused to serve instant or decaf. He told himself his clients remembered the little touches. Besides, he hated instant and decaf.

"What's the victim's name again?"

"Fortunato," Powers answered. "Anthony Fortunato of Fortunato, Montesori and Klein, LLC. They're CPAs in Grosse Pointe."

Guthrie's office was in funky Ferndale, north of Detroit. Grosse Pointe was east and still housed money from the dawn of the auto industry.

"Counselor, should I repeat my original question?" Guthrie kept his face neutral and his voice soft, but he visualized Powers's fingers in a shredder.

Powers kept his face even more neutral. "Fortunato was found in the trunk of his Mercedes."

Hot Rod Lincoln earned his nickname by stealing high-end vehicles. Like, say, a Mercedes. If it had wheels, he could get it open and start it up.

Powers glanced at his client and back at Guthrie. "Of course, Lincoln's...reputation certainly didn't help."

Guthrie shook his head. "Hot Rod was already a legend when I was on the force, but everyone knew he wouldn't hurt a rabid rat if it was chewing off his big toe. How do the cops connect him with a murder?"

"Obviously, they want an easy fix. If the man was found in the trunk, he couldn't drive, so someone must have stolen the car. Ergo, a car thief. But my client hasn't boosted a car in years. He's worked hard to turn his life around and become a solid member of the community."

Guthrie sipped his own coffee.

"Billable, I get the feeling you've left something out."

"Don't call me that." The lawyer pushed out his lower lip and it took thirty years off his age. "I've told my client not to answer any questions in a way that might incriminate himself."

"We're on the same side here, remember?" Most of the world's problems wouldn't be problems if people could just sit down and talk, but now there were so many lawyers that there weren't enough hours in the day to kill them all. Guthrie reminded himself that they also brought him a substantial amount of his business.

"If my understanding of privileged communication holds true, anything Hot Rod tells me is protected just like anything he says to you. Or a priest."

"I'm not Catholic." Hot Rod's voice rolled out smooth as Kentucky bourbon, at least ninety proof.

"I'm just making a point, Hot Rod."

"Oh."

"Lincoln has every reason to walk the straight and narrow now." Even in the horrible August humidity, Powers wore a three-piece suit that bore not one single wrinkle. He made Guthrie think of a game show host. "He has a good job and a fiancée. He has a happy and meaningful life ahead of him and certainly wouldn't throw it all away for a car."

Powers looked out the window beyond the hanging plant. "You yourself pointed out that Lincoln has no history of violence. And his record goes back...a long way. Not that any of that has a bearing on this case."

Guthrie saw Hot Rod's lower lip move.

"Hot Rod, where was the car?"

"Near the river," Powers answered. "Behind the old Grande Ballroom. A couple of kids saw it, wanted to check it out. When they got close, they smelled something and called the police. They found the body in less than pristine condition."

"I almost hate to ask. How long?"

"His wife reported him missing eleven days ago. The kids found the body in the car five days later. The ME thinks he was dead for most of that five days."

Summer in Detroit. Five days in the trunk. Guthrie tried not to imagine the stench.

"Hot Rod?" Guthrie watched the man's head rotate toward him. The wrinkles surrounding his eyes seemed deeper than a few minutes before. "Anything you can tell me?"

Powers spoke up again in a voice that needed a reverb unit to get the full effect.

"Lincoln has turned his life around and has become a valuable member of society."

"Yeah, you've said that." Guthrie wanted to slap him. "But you're both here because the police think he killed somebody. And perceptions matter."

Guthrie looked at his cell phone and hoped the others thought he was typing notes. He was really texting his secretary:

"Whn lwyr cms out keep hm busy."

He hit "send" and the reply came back in mere seconds.

"I dnt do lp dnces NEmr, mr G."

"I no," he typed. "gt kreAtv."

He looked back and forth between the men again.

"Billable, I'm willing to take this case, so why don't you go out and fill out the paperwork with Valerie. We've got a boilerplate contract you might want to amend a little."

Powers stood and glanced at Lincoln, but Guthrie motioned for him to stay seated.

He pointed to Hot Rod's mug. "You want more coffee?"

"Sure."

"Billable, why don't you ask Valerie to make a fresh pot while you go over the contract with her."

Powers took both his own and Hot Rod's coffee mugs. As he opened the door, Guthrie heard Valerie's lilt. She had butter-blonde hair, sky-blue eyes the size of dimes and a near-genius IQ. Guthrie figured he had a good fifteen minutes.

"Hot Rod, how did you get Billable as your defense? He charges more an hour than you could've sold that Mercedes for, if you took it, of course, which we both know you didn't."

Hot Rod leaned forward and stared at the carpet.

"He's taking me on pro boner. Says he's got to do some of that."

"Pro bono."

"Yeah, that." Hot Rod locked his fingers in his lap. The nails were huge and lined with black. He stared at them until Guthrie wondered if he remembered the original question.

"They say they found my fingerprints in the car."

"Could it be true?" Guthrie heard Valerie's voice working her magic outside.

"Um, maybe. See, I...found that car somewhere else and decided to, um, see how it ran."

"Hot Rod, work with me here, OK?"

"OK, it was over on the Cass Corridor. About eleven-thirty, maybe a little later."

The Cass Corridor was Detroit's porn district. "What night?"

"Um...Thursday? I guess the same day the guy went missing. But I didn't know he was in the trunk, honest."

"So you took the car. But you didn't kill him."

"No way. I'd cop to the car, but they like me for the killing, too."

"I'm guessing you dumped the car when you found the body?"

"Well...something like that. See, Billable's right, I'm getting married—but the diamond my girl picked out is a biggie, and my credit rating's not exactly what the banks are looking for, you know?"

"Whose is?"

"Right. So anyway, I saw this car and I figured, who'd leave a nice car like this in a place like that, you know?"

Hot Rod ran his tongue across his lips.

"I figured nobody in his right mind would do that unless he wanted it to go away, maybe insurance or something, so I thought I'd help out a little, you know?"

Guthrie bit his tongue.

"Uh, I figured the guy gets his insurance, I can sell the car for the parts, put the cash toward the diamond, everyone makes out."

Guthrie had to admit that once you got past the stealing part, it sounded pretty good.

"How was I supposed to know the guy was in the trunk?"

"When did you find him?"

"At the shop. I pulled in and we started going through the car to see if there was anything else we could...sell. So we popped the trunk..."

Hot Rod closed his eyes. Guthrie watched him replay the scene.

"The chop shop told you to dump the car somewhere else so they didn't get stuck with the body, right?"

"Yeah." Hot Rod looked out the window at the restaurant across the street. "We go back a long time, this is the kind of thing that can ruin a good relationship, you know?"

"I'll bet." Guthrie waited for Hot Rod to look at him again. "Have you got the ring yet?"

"Uh-uh. Haven't boosted another car, either. Finding a body, that really dents your karma, know what I'm saying?"

"I guess." In the outer office, Powers's voice sounded like he was falling into a trance. Even fully clothed, Valerie had the beauty and the people skills to enchant anything with a pulse. "So you dumped the car by the river. That same night? What time?"

"Late, around three."

"And nobody saw you, right? Or the cops would be leaning heavier."

"Yeah." Hot Rod shook his head. "I'm losing my touch. Leaving a print somewhere. Can't believe I'd do that."

"But you usually sell the parts, so you don't have to worry about that, right?"

"Well, yeah. But still..." Hot Rod shook his head again. "Getting old. Time to settle down."

Guthrie hated to point out that wanting to settle down got him into his this mess. When Hot Rod stood, he had nearly six inches on Guthrie's five-ten, but they probably weighed the same.

"How did the guy die?"

Hot Rod shrugged.

"Where's the chop shop? And who's in charge?"

"Over in the Northeast off McNichols. Just tell them you know me and ask for Frankie. They had a cow, told me to dump the friggin' heap somewhere far away. So here I am with a stiff and a hot car."

Guthrie thought about the car again. "You said the car was in the Cass Corridor when you found it? A Mercedes?"

"Yeah. Vanity license plate. TONY F" Hot Rod's eyes widened. "Hey, I just thought of something. The keys were in it, right in the ignition. And it wasn't even locked."

They understood at the same time.

"Someone wanted that car stolen, all right." Guthrie said. "But screw the insurance. They wanted someone to help them get rid of the body."

"Shoot," Hot Rod said. "So now they'll want to make me an accessory."

"Not if we can help it." Guthrie ushered him to the door.

In the outer office, Valerie Karr wore a linen tee with a tasteful v-neck and a skirt that showcased the second-best legs Guthrie had ever seen. Her delft blue eyes held Billable Hours Powers in thrall.

"We'll need a retainer, of course." Her voice had enough texture to stroke the beads of sweat off the lawyer's forehead. "Three days' fee up front for initial expenses. Should I bill your office electronically or by regular mail?"

Powers handed Valerie a business card and she leaned forward to type the address into the invoice on the monitor. Powers's eyes almost rolled back in his head.

Valerie turned to Guthrie and Hot Rod.

"Mr. Lincoln, what's your full name? I need it for the contract."

"Um...Lincoln Jefferson Fillmore."

Everyone stared. Hot Rod shifted his weight from one foot to the other. "My father was a history teacher and my mom had a sense of humor."

Valerie gave him a smile that could make plants grow.

"It's a good thing your father's last name wasn't Davis, isn't it?"

2

Everything about 1300 Beaubien, Detroit Police Headquarters, gave Guthrie flashbacks, from the faded snot color of the walls and worn tile floor to the stale coffee and BO smells pervading the squad room. He still noticed the vestigial scent of tobacco, too, even though nobody'd been allowed to smoke for years. It was embedded in the walls and tiles, probably even in the streaky glass of the windows. It helped obscure the mildew from the leaky roof and ceiling. No place like home.

He recognized a few faces from when he'd used the desk in the far corner, but if anyone recognized him, they didn't show it. Except Shoobie Dube.

She and Guthrie walked beats in the Northwest before he made detective, and now she carried the same badge. She cleaned up better than he did, aging like a good wine. She wore her strawberry blond hair short now with skinny jeans he suspected were really painted on. They were both approaching forty, but she could pass for ten years younger. It was probably those jeans.

"You're looking good, Woody."

"You too, Shoobie. Life treating you well?"

"Off and on." She shrugged and he could tell this was an "off" day. "I'm guessing you're not here for the reunion. We're not having one."

He settled into the chair across from her. "They tell me you caught the Fortunato body last week."

She rolled her eyes. "The guy'd been rotting in his trunk until some kids caught wind of him, if you'll excuse the expression. They used dental records to identify him, the rest of him was pretty much soup."

"Any idea how he died?"

"You're going to love this. He lost his front teeth in an accident in high school and had a bridge. Somehow, he swallowed it and choked to death."

Guthrie struggled to keep a straight face. "You're kidding."

"Scout's honor." Shoobie wore a pale pink tee with those jeans that made her legs look tall enough to need rungs. Her accessories included a plain gold band, a Mickey Mouse watch, and a 9mm Sig Sauer under her left arm. A beige blazer draped over the back of her chair. "The ME thinks someone punched him, knocked the plate loose. He found it lodged in the guy's throat."

"Was the guy a fighter?"

Shoobie shook her head. "Only about five-eight, scrawny. His wife says he was always pretty quiet and meek—well, it goes with a numbers cruncher, doesn't it?"

"So what do you think happened?"

Shoobie swiveled her chair and rested her feet on her desk. "We think he caught Fillmore trying to steal his car and the guy slugged him. Then he dumped the body in the trunk and ditched the car."

"But why bother to steal the car at all then? Why not leave the body right where it was and take off?"

"Maybe he panicked." She studied Guthrie. "You wouldn't be here if you didn't already know we tagged Fillmore for it, right? He may be a genius with cars, but outside of that, he's not that far up Darwin's ladder. I'm betting he's still got a prehensile tail."

"But he's never hurt anyone, even going back to Juvie. Nothing worse than smoking in the boys' room."

Shoobie shrugged again. The sun through the smudged window behind her gave her an aura the color of her tee.

"The guy's been under the radar for awhile. I figure he must've needed money bad enough to fall back on old habits. And when he got caught, everything turned to shit."

"But..."

"Woody, give me a break, OK? I just catch them, I don't psychoanalyze them. That's someone else's job."

Guthrie looked around the place again. The sludge in the coffee maker looked darker and the tile looked even more worn, but the clock was the same and the beat-to-shit chairs and desks almost called out to him.

"Sounds kind of iffy, though, doesn't it?"

Shoobie recrossed her ankles so the other foot was on top. "We got a fingerprint. That puts the guy in a car that wasn't his with the owner dead in the trunk. KISS. Keep it simple, stupid."

"But..."

"I hear you're seeing someone from here, Woody. A lady in IT?"

"You've been talking to Max and Lowe, haven't you?"

"Word gets around. Especially when you and she saved that stripper's ass, no pun intended."

Guthrie remembered the heavily censored news footage of Valerie in a g-string and stilettos with a gun pointed at her head. He was a captive, too, but the cameras paid no attention to him. Sexist pigs.

"We're still working things out, but...yeah."

"What's she like?"

Guthrie remembered how he and Shoobie flirted shamelessly in the academy, but never followed up.

"She's a lot like you. A little shorter, but..."

"Then we'd probably hate each other's guts."

"Yeah, good chance."

The elevator doors swooshed open and a man strode across the room, khaki linen blazer over a white shirt and black slacks. Even his shoes gleamed. His dark brown cheekbones belonged on a ship's prow and his energy level made Guthrie sweat.

Shoobie did the introductions. "Grady Hall, my partner. Grady, this is Woody Guthrie. He used to be one of us until he went over to the dark side."

"Lawyer?" Hall didn't offer to shake hands. Neither did Guthrie. He figured Hall was about ten years younger than he was.

"Close enough," Guthrie said. "Private investigator."

"Uh-huh." Hall's eyes grew another layer of skin.

"I got wounded." Guthrie wondered why he felt he had to explain. "When I came back, they said I was disabled and offered me a desk job. Take it or leave."

Shoobie's eyes moved down toward Guthrie's leg and jerked up again when she caught herself. "How's..."

"I can tell when it's going to rain, but other than that, no big deal."

He returned to his original point. "You found the Mercedes where, down by the Grande? Did the guy die there?"

"Can't be sure. His wife said he was out that night, but she didn't know where. She got home from a meeting of her own, he wasn't there yet. They've got a nanny, looks after the two kids, so she didn't think anything about it until about midnight. Then she called here."

"And the car wasn't found for a few days, right?" Guthrie watched Shoobie and Hall trade looks. "Where did you find the print?"

"Back of the rearview mirror. Hot Rod remembered to wipe the seat adjustment lever, but he forgot the mirror."

"But the print is all you have, right? No real motive, no connection between the two guys?"

Hall stepped in like the alpha dog he had to be.

"That print trumps everything, Guthrie. You know that."

Shoobie stuck her tongue into her cheek the way he remembered. It made her cheek puff out like a chipmunk. Cute as hell except for the Sig Sauer, which nullified the effect. Her nails were trimmed short. Guthrie guessed Hall wouldn't want a girlie-girl riding with him even if she could kick his ass.

"How old are the kids, if they've got a nanny?"

"Boy and a girl, ten and eleven. The nanny's a college kid, off for the summer."

"Insurance?"

"Yeah, but it's not going to let the wife pay off the house and move to the Bahamas, that's for sure. Hell, they were both still in their thirties."

Shoobie looked across the room. "Younger than we are."

She rummaged in her drawer and found a tin of Altoids. Hall flopped into the chair at the next desk and put his feet up. The soles of those shiny shoes showed almost no wear.

"I guess you're working with the lawyer." The word sounded obscene in his mouth.

"It pays the bills," Guthrie said. "And helps me spoil my girlfriend."

Shoobie popped the mints back into her drawer.

"Lucky broad."

3

Constance Fortunato lived in a house that clashed with every other house on the block. Most of the neighbors were gray stucco, but the Fortunatos had a venerable brown brick with a wide plank fence surrounding the back yard. A two-car garage held a basketball backboard that gleamed with disuse and a maple tree that looked like the original builders might have planted it after World War II shaded the front porch.

Guthrie tried the doorbell twice then wandered around the side of the house and studied the fence, slightly taller than he was. He heard water splashing: a swimming pool. The accounting business must do better than he would have expected, especially in Detroit's depressed economy. He rapped his knuckles on the wood.

"Hello? Anyone out here?"

"Wait a second." A woman's voice. "There's no gate. Go around to the front."

The door opened with a whoosh that released a burst of air-conditioned chill.

Guthrie knew the woman before him was in mourning because she wore a black bikini under an open terry cloth robe that barely reached her crotch. Her hair was pulled back into an elaborate twist and her sunglasses were slightly smaller than hubcaps. Her deeply tanned skin gleamed with moisturizer.

"Ms. Fortunato? My name is Guthrie, and I have a few more questions about your husband's death." He showed his license just long enough for her to see something official.

"You from the insurance company? I sent the death certificate Saturday."

Guthrie put Connie Fortunato at his own late thirties, but years of sun had aged her skin ten years beyond that, and her hair style and the bikini both suggested younger. He wondered how many people he was really talking to.

"Well, there are a few loose ends I'm trying to tie up. May I come in? This should only take a few minutes."

When the woman removed those sunglasses, her eyes held the vaguely stunned look Guthrie called "next of kin." His own eyes probably looked the same when his wife served him with the divorce papers.

He followed her into a living room where a leather sofa and three matching armchairs faced an HDTV. The woman motioned him to a chair. The coffee table had clawed feet and a shine that could scorch his retina. Sympathy cards and flower arrangements in discolored water filled the coffee table, both end tables and the mantel.

"What more do you want to know?" The woman pulled the robe down, but it couldn't cover much. "That lady cop seemed to think you've got the man who killed my husband."

"Yes, ma'am, they think so." Guthrie was careful not to say "we."

"So what's...?" The woman's hands tangled in her lap, her manicure perfect.

"Well, nobody can find a connection between your husband and the man in custody. Do you know if they knew each other? Was the man one of your husband's accounting clients, for example? Or maybe they played golf or went fishing together? Something like that?"

The woman shook her head.

"Tony doesn't—didn't do a lot of outdoor stuff. He really had the personality to be an accountant, you know what I mean? Nice, but kind of shy. And not very athletic."

Guthrie wondered how the woman and her dead husband met. Even in her grief, she pulsated with vitality he could feel across the room. He remembered being a point guard in high school and still being shy with girls. How would a nerd like Tony Fortunato have caught this girl's eye, helping her with her math homework?

"Hmm. Was he in any clubs or anything like that where they might have met?"

The woman shook her head. "Just a couple of accounting organizations. And they didn't meet. They posted—post—newsletters online, stuff like that. Tony loved numbers more than people. Except the kids...and me."

Guthrie watched the woman's lip suddenly wobble.

"No outings. Bus trips, tours—maybe with you and your children—nothing like that?"

"No. And I thought you said the guy who killed him was a mechanic or something like that. He wouldn't have come to Tony for his taxes. Tony and his partners do corporations' accounting, not people."

"I understand that, Ms. Fortunato. But right now, there doesn't seem to be a motive, and the police aren't sure where your husband might have been before he died. Do you remember his having any appointments or errands the night he disappeared?"

"Wait a minute." The woman's eyes narrowed. "You're not police?"

"No, ma'am, but I used to be. I'm trying to fill in some of the blanks."

"Like what?"

"Well, without a motive, the police can't really figure out what happened, and that will make it hard to go to trial. They need a lot more details, and I'm trying to supply them."

Connie Fortunato reached out and picked up one of the sympathy cards from the coffee table to fan herself.

"It's hot enough to melt the change in your pocket. You want something to drink?"

"No, thanks, but I appreciate it."

"You mind if I get something? This heat knocks me for a loop."

She stood and vanished through the doorway to the kitchen. From the back, her robe was even less decent. Guthrie stood and examined the flower arrangements to see if the cards had names. Most of the messages were as generic as the cards they were written on.

Connie Fortunato returned with a wineglass so full that only surface tension kept it from spilling.

"Sure you don't want any?" She settled to the couch again and the robe rode higher. Her strappy sandals matched her bikini and may have used more material.

"No, thanks again." He kept his eyes on her face.

"Do you remember where your husband was going that night? You told the police he was home for dinner, is that correct?"

"Uh, yes. He went out, he didn't say where he was going. I supposed he was just meeting someone on business. I mean, it was a Thursday, he did that sometimes, you know? Met clients, or people he wanted to bring in as clients. We went out weekends a lot, but that's a dead night..."

Her eyes filled with tears. "Shit, I didn't mean..."

"I'm sorry." Guthrie watched her swallow a substantial portion of the wine. "How often did he meet people at night?"

"Well, enough so I was used to it. I mean, he and the others did a lot of business, you know? You have to get it where you can, so sometimes he'd meet someone."

"But I thought most of the clients were corporate, so wouldn't he do that during his usual working hours?"

"I don't know, I guess." Connie finished her wine and held up the glass to Guthrie, who shook his head.

"I need another." She vanished into the kitchen again. Guthrie wondered if the children knew anything about Dad's comings and goings. He wondered at how quiet everything was, even out by the pool. Then he remembered that the children had a nanny. Maybe they were away somewhere with her.

Connie returned and plopped down on the couch again. The wine almost splashed over her hand and Guthrie wondered if she'd chugged another glass in the kitchen.

"You were out that night, too, am I right?"

"Uh-huh. My book club. We meet every two weeks. And I'm out Tuesdays for my art league. Tony was out a lot, I figured what the hell. As long as we've got someone to look after the kids..."

"Are your children around, by the way? Would you mind if I talked to them?"

The woman put the glass down with an audible clink. "They aren't here. They're at the lake with Tobi."

"Tobi?"

"The girl, the what-do-you-call her. Nanny. Tony always had some name for her, o pear, something like that. I thought he was talking about her rack, I told him not to talk dirty, but he said it's French."

"Au pair," Guthrie said.

"Whatever." Connie looked at the glass. "No, I been trying to keep them busy, not let them think about...this. The funeral's gonna be Thursday, the cops say they'll be finished with...everything...by then. I'll have the kids at the funeral..."

Guthrie wondered how they were really taking this and how much damage control a nanny could do.

Connie gave in to the inevitable and picked up the glass again.

"We've got a cottage, and I figured they'd be better off there for a few days. They come back at night."

"How long have you—they—had a nanny?"

"Just for the summer. She's a college kid, a theater major who's been trying for parts around here. She's wonderful with the kids, though, so she's staying here for the summer."

"Were you looking for a nanny? Or did someone recommend her, or what?"

"I...guess Tony saw her name and number on a board somewhere. I don't remember. Grocery store, something like that. She had her number and email, so I got in touch."

"It was you who called her? Not your husband."

"No, me." The woman finished her wine in two long swallows. "Who are you again?"

"I used to be a police officer, Ms. Fortunato. Any detective on the force has twenty or thirty cases at a time, but I only handle a few cases at once, so I can give them more careful attention, make sure everything really fits."

"This fits. The bastard tried to steal my husband's car and Tony tried to stop him. The bastard killed him."

She raised her glass. "Sure you don't want another?"

"No, thank you." He could see that Connie Fortunato was rapidly out-drinking her ability to help him.

"Well, you mind if I get back to my swimming then?" She stared at the glass. "Exercise helps. Keeps my mind off this."

"Does it?"

"Yeah. Whole seconds at a time."

Guthrie felt the humidity slam into him again when she closed the door behind him. He knew the path to the swimming pool led through that kitchen again. And another glass of wine.

He walked back to his car, blessedly parked in the shade.

4

Hot Rod refused to name the chop shop that rejected Tony Fortunato's Mercedes so Guthrie spent the afternoon touring East McNichols and checking out a succession of auto junkyards and body shops. They all looked pretty much the same, chain link fences surrounding stacks of tires, bumpers, and car bodies in varying degrees of distress. Even in the former automotive capital of the world, it amazed Guthrie how many dead cars still begged for resurrection.

REAL DEAL AUTO PARTS lay not far from the Detroit City Airport, the usual dilapidated building with dirty windows—most of them open—inside the double-wide gate. Both the gate and the hanger door on the building gaped open, too. Inside, Guthrie saw movement and heard the sounds of tools overwhelming a boom box tuned to heavy metal.

He parked inside the gate, carefully locking his car so nobody would try to strip it by mistake. A Rottweiler with eyes the color of a worn bumper sat near the door and stared at him, what might have been a human femur between its paws.

Guthrie meandered inside to inhale the smells of oil, rubber and a welding torch. Eventually, a few men in coveralls noticed him and one sauntered over, wiping his hands on a filthy rag.

"Help you?" The patch on his coveralls read "Frank." His nose seemed to point in three different directions.

"I'm looking for a fuel pump," Guthrie said. "For a Mercedes E320."

"What year?"

"Oh-six."

The guy looked beyond Guthrie at his car by the gate, a four-year-old Accord.

"Won't fit the vehicle out there."

"I can't drive a car without a fuel pump." Guthrie pointed at the lift. "You've got a Mercedes right there, maybe you've got what I need around somewhere."

Frank tucked the rag into his back pocket. "Could be. We can look around, see."

Guthrie fell into step behind him. "A guy I know told me you might have one."

"Lots of guys come in here. He a regular?"

"Maybe." Guthrie followed the man into a maze of tires and fenders. He recognized hood ornaments from BMW, Mercedes, and Porsches, but cars had never interested him as much as sports and cheerleaders.

"Skinny guy," he said, "bushy sideburns."

"Got a name?" Frank slowed down and surveyed a rack of parts that looked like they belonged in Frankenstein's laboratory.

"Lincoln. Some guys call him Hot Rod, I think."

The man shook his head, too quickly. "Don't think I know him."

"He says he knows you."

"Don't think so." Frank took in Guthrie's tee shirt and jeans under a worn blazer and seemed to decide that he was a cop and that he wasn't carrying.

"Really good mechanic," Guthrie tried again, "especially with ignitions. Car alarms, stuff like that."

Frank's eyes turned blank as a windshield.

"There's a guy a mile or so up Van Dyke, maybe he can help you."

"Hot Rod told me to talk to you. He's got kind of a problem, I'm trying to help him."

"That's real kind of you, Guy, but I'm busy."

"So am I. I'm trying to help Hot Rod."

Frank put two fingers to his mouth and a piercing whistle cut through the pneumatic screw gun, the lift, and the music. Guthrie's ears were still ringing when the Rottweiler appeared in the aisle. Now that Guthrie saw it standing up, he wondered if it came with a gear shift. Frank pointed toward Guthrie's car.

"Get your ass gone or I'll let the dog carry you out in pieces. Whatever he doesn't swallow."

"Beautiful dog." Guthrie grew up with dogs. Even if he'd had a gun, he would never shoot one, and this one was just doing its job.

"Yeah. And loyal. He remembers who feeds him."

Guthrie kept his eyes on the dog's face and walked through the far side of the door with his hands in sight. He could feel the dog and all three men watching him until he buckled himself in and started up.

He drove through the gate and turned right at a gravel road, slowly circumnavigating the entire lot, all of it behind chain link and razor wire, two or three acres of rusting car parts.

He got out and leaned against his Accord to study the terrain. A plane roared overhead and the smells of dust and August humidity filled his nostrils.

There was no other gate in back, which didn't surprise him. This was definitely the place Hot Rod had brought the car, but so what? He'd moved the car with the body still in it, and there was a good chance that the guy he'd talked to never touched anything—if he was even the one Guthrie met.

Frank definitely had something to hide, though. If he was dealing in stolen parts, that could be enough, and seeing a dead man in a Mercedes would qualify, too. Either way, what more could Guthrie ask now that he'd found the place?

The Rottweiler appeared on the other side of the fence. Its eyes were still the color of a bumper. If Guthrie came back, he'd have to deal with the dog after he got over the fence.

He climbed back into his car and drove away.

5

Shoobie slammed her car door and the garage echoed to remind her that she had the whole two-car space to herself now. She dropped the mail on the dining room table and made her way to the kitchen with newly-bare counters and extra shelf space. The refrigerator held the remains of Saturday's take-out and she told herself she should finish it up before it got strong enough to fight back.

She went upstairs to shower and change, sliding her holster and badge into the drawer by what she still thought of as "her" side of the bed. She knew at least twenty other cops who were working on second or third marriages—a badge was like a dowsing rod for divorce lawyers—but she still thought of herself as married even though Brian left five weeks before.

She forced her mind to focus on work because murder sucked less than her own life now, but even the hot needle spray that steamed up the bathroom couldn't help.

Now Hot Rod Lincoln's lawyer was bringing in reinforcements.

Shoobie walked a beat with Chris Guthrie back before everyone called him "Woody." He'd been a good cop before he went over to the dark side and become a PI. If he was looking at Hot Rod Lincoln, he had to think there was something to find.

She hated to agree, but he had a point: a guy with no history of violence isn't going to kill someone who catches him stealing a car. He'll take off on foot. Something was missing. They found Hot Rod's prints, but they didn't find any connection between him and Tony Fortunato, and they'd been looking hard.

So go back out and look harder.

Hot water cascaded between her shoulder blades and down her back, the way Brian used to touch her. They used to shower together sometimes, using up most of the hot water before they finished. And the nights in bed when they'd take turns eating strawberries and cherries and pineapple off...

The soap thumped against the bottom of the tub and Shoobie snapped back to the present. Her eyes burned and so did her throat.

Now's the time to cry, she told herself. *Nobody's around to hear you, and you're already wet.*

No. She wouldn't be that weak. She was tough, she was strong, she was still beautiful, and she was going to win him back. He was just going through some weird pre-mid-life crisis. She even liked his parents, they liked her cooking—such as it was—and they liked the same sports teams. Except golf. Shoobie still didn't quite see the point.

She picked up the soap and slowly slid it along her stomach, then up higher. She rubbed the back of her neck and rolled her head around, slowly under the water. She turned the nozzle to a pulsating jet and let it slap her like gentle karate chops. Her tension slowly dissipated until she didn't feel grating when she turned her head. She picked up the conditioner and rubbed a dollop into her scalp, cocoanut filling her nostrils and suds filling her fingers.

She dug in with her blunt nails and worked the lather into her scalp, hard enough to bruise her brains, then rinsed and let the suds wash down her body.

When she finally pushed back the shower curtain, steam packed the bathroom thick as cotton. She let the whine of her hair dryer fill the space, her short hair only needed a few seconds to dry. When she wore it long, Brian used to run his fingers through the waves, wrap it around his fingers, pull her face close to his when they...

She didn't sleep her way through the dorms, but she'd had enough experience to know that Brian Trask rang all her bells when they went to bed the first time. And the second. And...

Oh, stop it.

She returned to the bedroom and looked at the King-sized bed again. Any bigger, she could plant wheat. Or corn. Whatever farmers planted in Lower Michigan. If there were any farms left.

She picked out a Detroit Tigers tee shirt, cargo shorts and sandals. She wasn't going anywhere tonight. It was too hot to go out, especially alone, even more so on a Monday night. How lame was that? Brian used to take her to the good places, show off his hot wife and threaten to order champagne, but only if he could drink it from her stiletto. She pointed out that she wore open toes, which would kind of defeat the purpose, and he said he didn't care.

God, it seemed like another century.

She studied her face in the mirror. Was that a new wrinkle by her mouth? At this rate, she'd have jowls by Christmas. She was pushing forty harder than she dared to admit. Woody was about her age, and he looked great, maybe because he was getting laid.

She went downstairs and opened the fridge again. Yeah, Chinese take-out, she didn't even remember what it was, but it was spicy. She didn't have beer, which was probably a good thing. Put on weight to complement the new wrinkles. She poured a glass of water. There was frozen yogurt in the freezer. In college, she remembered her ice cream binges when a boy dumped her. Not now, not at thirty-nine.

She spread the shrimp and veggies in peanut sauce on a plate and put it in the microwave. She should get to the health club early tomorrow, her jeans felt tight.

Her hip vibrated and she pulled out her phone: Emily Stoddard. *When social workers call you at suppertime, it can't be good.*

"Eleanor, good, got you. I left a message awhile ago, but you didn't get back."

Emily Stoddard was one of two people Shoobie could think of who called her by her proper name. Brian called her "Ellie." And lots of dirty things with the right encouragement.

"I just got home. I might have been in the shower."

The microwave chirped. She turned the plate a quick one-eighty and closed the door again.

"Maybe. Anyway, I'm calling because Brian cancelled out of tomorrow's session."

"Again? Shit."

How was she going to get things back together when her husband wouldn't even talk to her except in counseling sessions—which he'd missed twice already—and now a third?

"Yeah, he left a message and I called him back. I only reached his voicemail."

Shoobie remembered the night he told her he couldn't do this shit anymore. She knew he'd been seeing someone else, but hoped it would blow over, so to speak. She'd tried sexy underwear and surprises in bed, but her weird schedule made it hard to connect, which was a big piece of the puzzle in the first place. Another reason so many cops ended up divorced. Citizens didn't understand what it was like out there.

But she was a cop. By now the job was part of her DNA. You couldn't get her out of the force with a hydraulic press and a court order.

"At least he called you. He hasn't talked to me outside your office in...weeks." Shoobie looked at the calendar by the key rack: "ES 4:00" in green marker.

"I know. But can you try calling him again? I've left a message. Maybe he's had enough time to cool off."

"He was never upset, Em. At least not like you and I mean it. He said he was tired and moved out. I'm willing to change shifts, see if I can take a desk..."

Her eyes and throat burned again and she felt snot dripping from her nose. *Dammit.*

"I want him back here. I love him."

"I know. And I want him to hear you say it. Help you work things out. But he's not on the same page."

She hadn't told Em or anyone else about Brian's affair. She was pretty sure it was over, though. If he was moving out anyway, why would he lie about that?

How do you meet someone new and start all over again when you're almost forty? Dating was crazy enough when she was in high school. Learning new rules and trying to read what guys wanted again made her taste bile in her mouth.

But Woody Guthrie managed to do it somehow, didn't he?

The microwave beeped again. Shoobie put the plate on the counter, steam shimmering off it and the smell making her mouth water.

She tried to picture Emily Stoddard behind her big desk, with a computer and stacks of files and a pencil stuck into her coal-black bun. If she unrolled it, her hair probably fell clear to her waist. Emily looked barely old enough to stay up without a nap, but she had degrees on her office wall and a funky wardrobe. And those cute little gold glasses that made her look like she could drink without a sippy cup. Well, we all have to start somewhere.

Shoobie remembered the first time she put on the patrolman's belt with the mace and the flashlight and the radio and the handcuffs and everything else. It took her a week to learn to walk with that extra thirty pounds.

She chewed through the micro-waved Chinese without tasting a single bite. The sun drilled through the kitchen window, hot enough so she thought she'd turn to ashes. She wiped her hands, then walked into the living room and pulled out her phone again.

She punched in Brian's number and waited through the first few bars of the "William Tell Overture."

"You've reached..." That mechanical female voice, the same one Shoobie had on her GPS. "At the tone, please record your message. When you are finished, you may hang up, or press the pound sign for more options."

Beep.

"Brian, this is Shoobie—Ellie. Em called to say you've cancelled again and I'm wondering if there's some way we can reschedule, or maybe get together over the weekend or sometime and work some of this out. I'm trying really hard, but I need you to carry some of this, too. Please. Call me back, OK?"

She ended the call before she whimpered "I miss you."

6

Danny Hammersmith slid the glass of Bud across the bar to the dude with the nose ring and felt his pants vibrate against his left hipbone. He let it go to voicemail while he scooped up the guy's twenty and made change. Monday was deadly slow— a lot of the strip joints closed that day—so he made a point of coddling anyone who showed up, especially a decent tipper.

His break came twenty minutes later and he stepped out from behind the bar. The music felt like a body punch and Rita Moneysworth swiveled her hips on the platform to his left, the lights turning her hair the color of blood while Danny checked his phone

Number blocked.

He'd been waiting all day for this, but he still crossed his fingers and tapped his knuckles on the doorframe before he hit "return."

Someone picked up on the second ring, like they'd been waiting.

"How are you progressing, Daniel?"

If things were going well, Danny wouldn't be getting this call in the first place, and they both knew it.

"I'm still working on it."

"Work faster. People are saying bad things."

"Look, I'm doing—"

"Bad things about you."

Shit, shit, shit.

Danny strode outside into a summer night that felt like soggy flannel and smelled equal parts car exhaust, hot pavement and cigarette smoke. Behind him, the music pounded into the back of his head and he heard a voice introducing the next girl. Monday night, the lot was only half-full, the girls were probably doing better for tips, but only barely.

Barely. In a strip club. Ha fucking ha.

"Listen, I've got a couple of ideas, let me see how they pan out."

"When you say 'ideas,' that is not the same as 'leads' or 'clues' or 'information,' is it?"

"Well, no, but—"

"Daniel, you were hired to do a job, and you did not do it. That puts me in a bad position."

From the voice, Danny pictured a turtle crawling over rocks. A huge turtle with jaws that could snap his head off.

"I understand. I'm working on it, all right?"

"All right is a poor choice of words. You were hired because things were not all right. And you have made them worse. You know what happens to independent contractors who fail?"

Danny watched cars roll along 8 Mile, the night almost as clammy as his armpits. "I've got a reputation to keep up here, too."

"Forget your reputation. Worry about your head."

He shouldn't have hit the guy so hard. How'd he know the asshole had a glass jaw, or a weak heart or whatever the hell it was? Actually, he didn't really hit the guy that hard at all, just enough to get his attention when he started yammering, and the next thing he knew the little dweeb was choking and wheezing and turning blue and his eyes were rolling up. Stopped breathing so quick Danny barely got him out of the car before he messed himself. That's when he dumped him in the trunk.

"Listen, I told you, I've got a couple of ideas, let me get back to you."

"When?"

"I'll call you when something turns up."

"Exactly when do you expect that to be?"

The neon sign with its orange, red, and blue circles suggesting breasts blinked over the road and bathed the cars in the lot. Nips Ahoy! Danny wondered who named the place.

An SUV rolled into the lot and four guys rolled out, clowns from a circus car, their voices young and excited, all wearing Tigers' caps and laughing about some stupid shit, bragging about how they were going to score big with the broads in here. Yeah, right. If they dropped enough money, one of the girls might treat them to an extra smile.

"It's hard to say..."

"No, it is easy to say. Tomorrow. Saturday. Six hours."

"I'm not sure. Probably another day or two."

"What do you have in mind?"

Danny held the phone away from his face and watched the jocks disappear inside.

"If I tell you, you won't need me anymore, so then where do I stand?"

"Where do you think you stand now?"

"Listen, I know, it's been crazy. I didn't expect the guy to—"

"You were supposed to get information from him, not kill him. We've been through this. You are on my shit list, and moving close to the top. You know what happens if you reach Number One?"

Another car pulled into the lot and Eminem blasted across the gravel.

"Yeah. Yes. I'm working on it."

"Do you need some motivation?"

"No, I'm good."

"Another unfortunate choice of words."

The phone went dead. Danny stared at the screen and resisted the urge to crush the fucker in his hand. Traffic surged by on 8 Mile Road, nobody giving a shit about him. In a few minutes, he'd be back behind the bar serving drinks to the assholes who came to watch the girls. A year ago, he'd been one of the bouncers, now he'd moved up to bartender. Six months ago, this place had been called G's Spot, too. Things change.

Danny knew he had to find that money soon or he'd be SOL. Shit out of luck.

Three Buds, you got it. Red wine, coming up. Jack, straight up. Right away. On the far platform, Misty Meaner was drawing horndogs like sugar draws flies. Misty'd hooked up with some guy, said he might be able to get her into modeling, maybe even into movies. Yeah, right. Had to be DIY porn, but hey, she said she wanted to get away from all this, live like real people.

Danny figured he was a working stiff, which made him real people.

But he wanted to get away from all this, too.

7

Guthrie locked his car under a streetlight and spent the next four hours touring the Cass Corridor, the section of Detroit he'd heard some of the vice cops call "Pussyland." He'd walked a beat in the area nearly twelve years ago and learned that when people want to buy something badly enough, you can't stop them, no matter how good your intentions or how pure your heart.

The area hadn't changed much since then. The papers and bottles lying along the curb and clogging the sewer drains might be new, and the cars bore different bumper stickers, but that was about it. The buildings alternated between old stone from a century before or faded wooden buildings in danger of collapsing in on themselves. The setting sun and faint streetlights gave everything the hue of ashes. The vibe matched it.

The humidity faded after the sun went down, too, bringing out the locals whose limited social skills often involved money and hourly rates. Guthrie strolled closer to a woman carrying a huge purse and pretending to study a magazine.

"Hey." The woman wore a denim skirt and strappy sandals with six-inch heels. Her tank top was thin enough so passing headlights silhouetted her nipples. Her heels put those nipples nearly level with Guthrie's eyes, adding a whole new meaning to product placement.

"Hey," he replied. "I'm wondering, were you here twelve days ago?"

"You serious? You want me to check my time sheets?"

"It was a Thursday. That help?"

"Not much."

"I'm looking for a guy," Guthrie said. "He would have been driving a—"

"I don't know from cars. Someone slows down, we chat a little. I see their big bright headlights, show 'em my own big bright headlights, we take it from there."

She flashed a smile that didn't reach above her upper lip.

"Not a problem." Guthrie could feel a dozen eyes watching their exchange. "This guy would have left the car parked around here somewhere. Right on the street, keys still in it and the doors unlocked."

A shadow appeared over the woman's shoulder. Considering her heels, Guthrie put the guy's height at six-eight.

"You bothering my friend?" The voice felt like a bowling ball, the guy's breath even worse. He wore a cut-off tee to display biceps that resembled a blimp. His eyes studied Guthrie more carefully. If Guthrie had worn his Sig Sauer, the conversation never would have started.

"Just looking for a guy." Guthrie studied the dilapidated buildings across the street, where an overturned recycling bin splashed its contents across the curb.

"You see someone leave a black Mercedes here one night a couple of weeks ago? It had a vanity plate, 'TONY F.' The driver would have left the keys in it."

"You shitting me? Nobody's that stupid."

"I think he wanted the car stolen. Maybe you saw a guy get in it and drive off?"

"The meter's running, Jack. You want to talk, take it inside. Two-fifty an hour."

"Talking isn't the same as oral sex, sport." Guthrie tried not to stare up the guy's nostrils. "You see the car?"

"You hard of hearing?"

Guthrie handed both of them his business card. "Ask around. If anyone saw the car, have them call me."

"How much is it worth?"

"I'm willing to discuss that if someone's got something to say. Good enough?"

The man faded back into the shadows and the woman walked away, her hips reminding Guthrie of a pendulum.

Over the next three hours, he held variations of that same conversation twenty-six times. Long before that, everyone knew who he was and what he wanted. Fortunately, he'd ordered more business cards a week earlier. None of the women gave him her own card, but a few mentioned Craigslist.

Cars drifted by and women leaned over the passenger's window to give conditions or directions and showcase their wares. A few got in and the cars pulled away. Guthrie walked across alley openings without looking down them. The gutters were bad enough, overflowing with broken glass, old sandwich wrappers, discarded beer cans and who knew what else. He considered burning his shoes and socks when he got home.

By midnight, he covered three blocks in each direction from where Hot Rod Lincoln "found" the Mercedes. His left thigh ached from all the walking. He'd given out over fifty cards and talked with women whose accents were Spanish,

Polish, southern and "other." He declined two offers to buy him a drink, both from men.

To clear Hot Rod, he had to find the real killer, which meant he had to work twice as hard as Shoobie and Hall with all their resources. All he had going for him was the fact that everyone knew he was not a cop. Reasonable doubt was nice for juries, but when the cops made an arrest, they tended to lock down on it even if the evidence was weak. Weak beat nothing, and a good prosecutor would sell it to make room for something else on the detective's desk. And juries had watched enough CSI to take fingerprints as gospel.

Guthrie had to give Shoobie and Hall another suspect with a motive, opportunity and maybe even bruised knuckles. He wondered where Fortunato had been attacked and died, too. Shoobie hadn't mentioned anything in the car that helped them figure that out, either.

He waited for a beat-up Chevy to rattle across the intersection. The front and rear fenders were both primer, and the muffler could have played in a heavy metal band.

A half block down, he saw the woman in the translucent top and denim skirt. She wobbled on those high heels now, and the top looked smudged. When she got closer, he saw her eyes widen with recognition.

"Hey." Her breath reminded him of the locker room after basketball practice.

"Hey," he said back.

He regained his own car under that same streetlight and walked completely around it twice before he beeped the door open. He looked in the back seat before climbing in, too. After the last few hours, he was something of a local celebrity in the area, and who knew what kind of attention that could attract.

It felt like a long drive home.

8

Tuesday morning found Danny Hammersmith red-eyed and heavy-tailed. He'd told the voice on the phone that he had a plan, which wasn't exactly a lie. He had the glimmer of an idea. If it led somewhere, it would be a plan. If it didn't lead anywhere, it wouldn't be a plan. Or maybe it would be a crappy plan. The morning didn't find Danny ready for semantic and philosophical debates.

He popped two aspirins along with his coffee and headed over to Grosse Pointe with his fingers crossed. He recognized the area when the cracked parking lots became lawns and the telephone poles became trees—without faded posters for lost dogs and local bands tacked on them. The area was so ritzy Danny worried that his Buick violated zoning laws, but no palace guards in fancy uniforms surrounded him.

He parked under a maple tree half a block down from Tony Fortunato's brick house and waited. He had the Free Press, two old copies of Sports Illustrated, and three skin mags from the club. The pages weren't stuck together, which might mean they weren't much good, but they'd help pass the time. He hoped he wouldn't have to pass too much of it.

Two and a half hours later, the dead guy's wife opened her garage door. Danny's travel mug was almost empty. He had to pee like a stallion, but he didn't dare let the woman in the black Mercedes out of his sight for that long.

When she turned into the parking lot of a funeral home, he knew he finally had a few minutes. He watched her pause by the entrance, her mouth moving and her fists clenching as though she was giving herself a pep talk. She stood erect, her shoulders rising for a few seconds, then sagging so her carefully-tailored black pantsuit—Christ, wearing black in this fucking heat—rippled before she opened the door and disappeared inside.

Danny gave her two minutes to be sure she didn't change her mind before he trotted across the street to a gas station. A second look at the gas prices told him the place must have closed years ago, but he felt like a python was dancing below his zipper. Behind the building stood a pile of tires so bald nobody even bothered to steal them. Wonder some of the local kids didn't set them on fire just so they could fill the whole freakin' neighborhood with their stink. He slid behind the pile and unzipped.

Two minutes later and several cups of coffee lighter, he leaned against the corner of the vacant building and studied the Angellini and Frattolo Memorial Funeral Home. Best-looking building in sight, no matter which way you looked. How come these places always looked so good, like historical building with that nice architecture, lots of brick, white woodwork, pillars to last forever? The cobblestone driveway looked like it was built back before Henry Ford started playing with cars, and the flowers along its borders looked so fresh and crisp Danny bet they were plastic. The windows gleamed. Did the stiffs really give a shit about good landscaping and a nice carpet?

Danny told himself he should go back to his car so the broad couldn't sneak out on him, but he figured he had time and he might want to check out those tires again in a few minutes. Undertakers were like every other salesman, they'd try to give you options. A waterproof casket with wrinkle free lining, maybe throw in the extra brass handles, a little funky detailing. All for only five grand. Or with catering and a band, ten—maybe twelve if you want bagpipes.

Why did people spend so much on funerals, did they think the stiff was going to change his will if they just dumped him in a landfill...or behind an abandoned building?

How did the broad pick this undertaker anyway? Maybe it was the first one in the phone book, that Angellini. If there was even an Angellini, the guy's name was probably really Smith or something but he changed it for the listing. Wouldn't put it past them, sneaky, these people. Hey, you got to be a certain kind of guy to soak a family that's in mourning, right?

Danny ambled back to his car and opened all the windows. At least the parking lot for the funeral home had trees all around it. Maybe that was why she picked this place, so she could park her car in the shade.

The black Mercedes looked just like the husband's car, too, right down to the vanity plate: CONNI F. The guy's plate was TONY F.

The woman took so long Danny figured she was signing up for the whole freaking family, matching headstones and caskets. Could you get a family package? Or maybe she was doing the undertaker, drive the price down a little. Was that why they called it a good stiff business? Did they know each other from other funerals? Maybe the guy knew something, or Connie was telling him something.

Like, where was that fucking money?

Danny knew he was dreaming. But the woman had to go somewhere from here, didn't she? Why not to the bank or wherever her husband stashed it.

Or what if she didn't even know about it? What if scrawny Tony was planning to take off one of these days, leave her with the kids and the mortgage, head for Rio or Paris or Antigua? Shit, the guy had less muscle than a celery stalk, but with that kind of money, he could still get broads.

He would've told Danny all about it if he hadn't died. Then Danny wouldn't have to be here following his wife around in the freaking heat.

Danny picked up the last skin mag, hoping it was better than the other two. The ink didn't rub off on his fingers, but that was the best he could say about them.

Connie Fortunato walked out of the building clutching her purse like a parachute she didn't think would open. She dug for her keys and beeped open her car, then sat there for a few minutes. Danny thought she was crying. Christ, did she really love that little weasel? Scrawny little thief. This woman was sort of pretty. A little long in the tooth, maybe a little— what was the word, zaffig, no, but something like that, Danny heard the girls use it at the club sometime—he thought it meant a nice rack. A little broad in the beam, but her ass fit behind the wheel of that Mercedes, you bet.

She pulled out of the driveway and Danny followed her. She wasn't going home, that was the other way. Maybe she was going to meet someone. Maybe she was going to get the money. Maybe...

The Mercedes flashed its blinker and pulled into a mall big enough to call a suburb. Well, maybe that was a good place to meet someone. Danny found a space two rows over and trotted to the end of the aisle in time to see her disappear through the doors fifty yards ahead of him. He sprinted in front of an oncoming junker and flipped off the driver who leaned on her horn, jerked open the door and stepped into the air-conditioned echoes in time to see Connie studying a directory only ten paces ahead of him.

Nobody else was wearing a suit, especially not black, so he hung back a little and watched her weave through the tank tops and tees. She seemed to know where she was going, maybe that was a good thing, too.

She took the escalator to the second level and strode down the right side, the click of her heels lost in the hum of nine million voices, the asshole boys with their piercings, sideways baseball caps and wannabe soul patches, the girls in their sandals and twittering squeals, birds without feathers, and maybe without brains. Nobody gave the woman a second look. Nobody looked at Danny either.

Connie stalked into Liz Claiborne and headed right for the dresses. Danny swerved across the court to a newsstand and bought a copy of People and settled on a bench where he could wait for her to come out again.

When she came out she still clutched that purse. If she bought anything, she left it there to pick up later. Then she walked into Victoria's Secret and Danny almost slapped a high five on the kid coming the other way. *Yes.* The grieving widow wanted hot stuff. Like she was already lining up a date. Or getting ready for a second honeymoon.

His phone pounded against his hip.

"We're still waiting, Daniel."

"I know. I'm working on it. I'm following the broad, the wife. Widow."

The silence on the other end didn't sound impressed.

"No," Danny said. "I may be onto something. She was just at the funeral home."

"Imagine that."

"No, listen. After she left, she went shopping, she's at the mall now, I'm watching her. You'll never guess where she's shopping."

"I shall not even try."

'Shall,' for Christ's sake. What was wrong with 'will?'

"No, no, this is really good. She's in Victoria's Secret. You know, the push-up bras and corsets and shit? What the fuck's a widow doing in a place like that?"

"I would surmise, shopping for naughty nighties."

"But doesn't that tell you something?"

"Of course. She is a widow—thanks to you for that—she has two young children, she is not outrageously old. She would like someone to help her take care of those children. And maybe take care of her, too, while he's at it."

"But so quick?"

"A little patience goes a long way, but perhaps not when you are a woman of a certain age in a particular situation."

"Listen, this is the break we've been waiting for." Danny saw a teen-aged girl frown at him and lowered his voice.

"Oh, I certainly hope so, Daniel."

The phone went dead. Danny stared at it to be sure the guy didn't call back again before tucking it in his pocket. He was reading Hollywood gossip he didn't care shit about when Connie Fortunato walked out of Victoria's Secret.

This time she carried a big red and pink bag.

9

Christine Chapel held the stick over the bathroom sink where the light was better and studied the faint line, blue as Lake Superior. She tilted it like a thermometer and stared again.

"Jersey?" Knocking on her door. "Hey, Jersey, you all right?"

"I don't think so." Christine reached back and flushed, then opened the door, still holding the stick in her other hand. That stick was about to change her life like the wand in those Harry Whatsis books. Laura Lay maneuvered her way into the tiny bathroom, good thing they were used to dressing in close quarters backstage, too.

"So, let's see." Laura's round eyes always reminded Christine of some girl in an old cartoon, or maybe one of those models on game shows, nice dress, lots of leg, turning a platform to reveal a car or a kitchen set or something. She reached for the stick, then stopped herself and held Chrissie's hand up so they could both see.

"Damn, girl. You are most definitely pregnant."

"You sure?" Chrissie wanted to pull up her thong, but there wasn't enough space in the tiny bathroom. "Maybe I should try again later, I've got a whole box of these things, maybe this one's wrong. I could try again tomorrow. Or..."

"Nah, nah, nah, girl." Laura had come over early to lend Chrissie moral support, banging on her door at the crack of noon, big Dunkin' Donuts mugs in both hands. Chrissie answered in her knee-length Tigers Jersey and still prying her eyes open. She let Laura in and went to pee for the first time that day. Hitting the stick while still half asleep, sure, right, more like peeing on her own hands. Had to be a man that invented the friggin' things.

"Don't waste your time. You're knocked up. No question. None. Nada."

"Shit." Chrissie held the stick over her wastebasket. She had to tell her fingers to let go three times before they did. The thing landed in the gauze and mascara-smeared tissues with hardly a sound. She watched her hands turn on the faucet and pick up the bar of soap, washing and washing and rubbing and scrubbing and rinsing. Like it would change anything.

"Shit, shit, shit." She dried her hands and squirted moisturize on them. Laura backed up so they could both fit through the door and into the kitchen, where those big mugs still sat on the table. "I am really fucked, you know that?"

"Well, yeah. I mean, that's how it happens, right?" Laura blinked and Chrissie almost heard tinkling bells. *Don't say tinkle*, she told herself. "Um, you know who the guy is, right?"

Chrissie dug into her purse for her Marlboros. She stuck one between her lips and dug for her lighter.

"Yeah," she said. Two weeks ago, she would've been thrilled, but now things were different. She held the cigarettes up for Laura, who took one and leaned forward for a light. She drew deep into her lungs, swelling her top like she was still on stage, and frowned.

"Uh, I just thought. Maybe you shouldn't smoke now. The baby. You know?" Smoke drifted from her nostrils.

"Shoot, you're right." Chrissie froze with the lighter six inches from her own cigarette. She relaxed her thumb and the flame disappeared. She put the lighter back in her purse. "Um, you want the pack?"

"You sure?" Laura scooped them up before Chrissie could change her mind. "Uh, you don't need the lighter now, either, now that you're quitting, right?"

Chrissie slid it over and picked up the mug at her place. "But I need this coffee."

She forced herself to drink slowly and told herself she couldn't be more than a few weeks, she wouldn't show for months yet. Lots of time.

"You plan this?" Laura blew out a stream of smoke. "I mean, I thought you were on the pill."

"I was." Chrissie dug in the bag for napkins and pastries. "I am."

"It happens sometimes," Laura said. "I knew this girl a couple years back, Danica, something like that. You remember her? Blue eyes, really black hair? I think she dyed her hair, she had a little landing strip, not much, but not like it was really dark, you know? Anyway, she was on the pill—she said, anyway—one day she showed up, told the boss she was taking some time off. He asked her why, she said twins."

That was all Chrissie needed to hear. The cruller shook in her hand.

"Yeah," Laura went on. "I don't know if she married the guy or not. Didn't see her anymore. I don't know if she took care of it or had the kid—kids—or not. But you never know, all this bullshit about the miracles of modern medicine, sometimes stuff doesn't really work, you know?"

"Uh-huh." *Boy, did she know.*

"So, you gonna tell him?"

"Who?"

Laura waved her cigarette. "The guy. The daddy. The one what knocked you up."

The cruller reminded Chrissie of Tony.

"I don't know."

"Whaddaya mean you don't know? Shit, girl, you got to think about the baby, start making some decisions here, some plans."

This from the girl who never showed up with all her own stuff any night anyone could remember. Laura was always borrowing eye-liner or something. Chrissie drew the line at letting her use her work clothes. A hat, yeah, maybe. Or condoms. They all had dozens of those, all over the dressing room, everywhere else, too.

She should've made him wear a condom like she did everyone else. But they were dating and she was on the pill anyway, right? He said it was something more, now he was right about that, too. And now he was gone away, left her all alone.

Chrissie looked in her cupboard, found a bowl with the Detroit Tigers logo on the side and rummaged for corn flakes. She tried to remember how solid the milk was in the fridge. She forgot to go shopping yesterday. Except at the drug store for the test. Should she try again later? What if Laura was blowing smoke out of her ass? Wouldn't be the first time.

"I gotta get more money," she said. "In a few months, I'm not going to be able to work."

"You're gonna have the kid then? You and him?"

Chrissie sniffed the milk carton and didn't gag.

Laura tapped her nails on the table. They looked big as Mandarin orange slices. How did she keep them from breaking?

"Jersey, you don't need more money, you just gotta spend it smarter."

"Laura, I have the kid, I'm not gonna be able to work for awhile." Her mother had four kids besides her, always blew up big as a hippo.

"So, how long you think you got? How far along are you?"

"Can't be more than...maybe six weeks, max."

"Jeez, you mean you were late last month, too? Didn't do nothing about it?" Laura ran those fingernails through her hair. "So you got another couple of months, maybe more before you're gonna show. Just get guys into the VIP room as long as you can."

Chrissie watched the milk splash over the corn flakes.

"Hey," Laura said. "Think about some of the guys you don't like. They'd probably pay more. Maybe you should try to get them in there."

Chrissie felt her stomach surging again.

"Oh, yuck."

The coffee burned her tongue, but it forced her eyes open a little wider. Another cup or two, she could think about this better. The milk was almost ready to turn. She'd better finish as much as she could today.

Laura looked at her watch and picked up her coffee.

"Hey, I gotta run. See you tonight, right?"

"Sure."

"You OK?"

"Fine."

Laura slid through the door, cut-offs so short two pink cupcakes peeked out the bottoms. Chrissie chewed the corn flakes without tasting anything. She dug in her purse for her cigarettes before she remembered they were gone.

Maybe she could get a refund on those damn pills. Did they come with a guarantee?

She went into her bedroom and put her carry-all on the bed. Her make-up kit and four pairs of stilettos on the bottom: turquoise, red, navy, black. Then the Detroit Tigers jersey, number four like a home run, The Red Wings shirt that went clear down to her knees because the store didn't have anything in her size that day. Number 67, not quite her lucky number. Pistons number 35 and Lions 24. Four shows tonight. Bras, thongs, and moisturizer. And condoms. Of course.

Jersey Girl for sure.

When she looked in the mirror, her eyes already looked tired. Tony was gone. She saw in the paper they found his body in his car Down River.

Her car payment was due, not to mention the rent, lights and insurance. Tony'd been helping her out a little. He called it a quit for pro or something like that.

Not anymore. She was on her own.

10

At one pm, Danny counted the take, distributed the tips and watched the bouncers escort the girls to their cars. When the last set of taillights winked out onto 8 Mile Road, he went back inside and changed from the white shirt and clip-on bowtie into black jeans and sneakers and a black tee shirt. He had a pair of latex gloves in his car and worried more about his face. He picked up a Tigers' cap, partly because the navy blue was almost black and mostly because the visor would hide his face if the place had security cameras, which he was pretty sure it would. Besides, in fuckin' Dee-troit, thousands of guys had the same cap.

Following the Fortunato broad was a dead end, and Danny knew he was running out of last chances before he ended up like her husband.

He could change a tire or a light bulb, but the tool kit he kept in his trunk was about as basic as you could get: a pry bar, pliers, and a claw hammer. He slid them into a bag from his last Chink take-out—only a little grease and a lingering smell of soy—and headed out. He had about four hours before the sun came up, and he wouldn't have to be back at work until evening.

He wished he could switch out his Buick for Tony F's Benz, better camouflage where he was going, but you do what you can with what you got. Besides, who in Grosse Pointe was gonna be awake this late, especially on a week night.

Traffic was light as he took the long way down Woodward, past Comerica Park. He knew the Tigers played the White Sox earlier that night because it was on the TV nobody watched with naked girls twenty feet away. Danny wasn't big on baseball, but the Tigers were the only thing even close to good news in Detroit. Years before, he worked a bar where you could get a free beer if you brought in your ticket stub from the stadium on a night the Tigers won. Shit, how long ago was that? Probably clear back before Jim Leyland took over as manager.

Danny passed the PD, ugly old building that seemed to sag in on itself. Miracle it hadn't collapsed and killed a thousand people, but the city had zero dough, no way they could build a new one, and where would you put it anyway? This was a great central location—except for fighting the traffic—and demolishing it would take months and fuck up what was left of downtown in the bargain. The Renaissance Center over to his right was three-quarters empty now, General Motors wasting away like an old man with cancer.

Danny hit all the lights green, no surprise since he'd driven in this town so long he knew its rhythms like his own heartbeat. He knew the people, how they thought, what they thought about, what they thought about it, what they'd pay attention to and what they'd look right past. *Fuckin' Dee-troit.*

The radio leaked some wimpy boy singer and Danny played roulette down the dial without finding anything else worth listening to. His ex-girlfriend took his iPod with her, all his old Motown and R & B stuff, which meant he was stuck with this crap when he drove. He turned off the radio and drove east on Jefferson.

The Lions would have an exhibition game in a week or two. Danny played defensive tackle in high school, so his game was football, even though the locals might be the only team from the original NFL that had never been to the Super Bowl. How do you waste draft choices year after year? Danny tried to remember who besides Barry Sanders was even worth discussing since the eighties, and couldn't come up with a single name.

The street lights showed him the sign up ahead: Grosse Pointe. Almost there.

He drove around the block twice before he spotted the name lumped in with the others on the sign. Fortunato, Montesori & Klein, LLC in a four-story with a bunch of other offices. A parking lot right in front, lots of lights, but no other cars. Danny drifted down to the next block and found a bar, still open. He pulled into the lot with a half-dozen other cars and backed against the brick wall so he faced the exit. Two lights on poles blasted most of the lot, but not his corner.

He took the takeout bag with him, pulled his hat down to his eyebrows and ambled down the street. A few cars went by, but nobody on foot. This was Grosse Pointe, where only the health nuts walked. Probably some local ordinance.

He drifted past the lobby and looked in. Nobody seated at the desk, and he wondered if the building had a guard. Most of the businesses were insurance or realtors or accountants, so maybe not. He crossed the street and watched the plate glass as long as he dared, but nobody appeared.

He re-crossed the street and walked through the lot to the back of the building. A Dumpster squatted next to the alleyway, wide enough for a garbage truck, and lots of light spilling from the parking lot. He wanted more shadow, but the lock on the rear door looked older than his grandmother.

He slipped his hands into the latex gloves and eased the pry bar into the gap between the door and doorframe a few inches above that pathetic lock. He leaned on the end, slowly putting more weight into it until he felt the tip of the bar break through the frame on the other side. He tried to block out the street noise behind him as much as he could and closed his eyes to listen to the inside of the building. He held his breath until he heard his heart beating in his ears, but no sound came from inside. No alarm.

He leaned against the long end of the bar in the other direction and watched the door begin to shiver. He leaned harder and felt the pry bar dig into the wood. With a snap that barely carried across the alley, a grapefruit-sized chunk of the door broke out, just above the lock. Danny reached through the opening and twisted the bolt. He stepped inside and closed the door behind him.

The darkness felt thick enough to wear. He stood motionless, listening again for an alarm. He flashed his Maglight around and didn't see any cameras or wires or funny buttons, so maybe he was all right. He pointed the light toward the floor ahead of him and went through the first door he found. When he opened it, he saw a narrow stairway.

He went up the first flight and found a door with a numeral "1" above it. He should have checked to see what floor he needed, but he didn't want to go back and find a directory now, not in that lobby with the picture windows facing the street. He slid through the door and down the hallway, shining his light on every door as he reached it. None of them was the right one, so he returned to the stairs.

Fortunato, Montesori & Klein LLC was the first door on the third floor. The brass doorknob was shiny and the lock was a double-key deadbolt. Danny stared at it for a full ten seconds, knowing this was a problem. The wood of the frame looked new, too, five times as sturdy as the piece of shit downstairs.

He wondered if he dared to break the glass by the doorknob. People would know for sure he'd broken in, but someone would know that from the back door anyway, so what the hell? Besides, if he got what he came for, it wouldn't matter if anyone knew. Nobody knew who he was and he'd never done a burglary before, so the cops wouldn't find him if he kept the gloves on.

He put the end of the pry bar against the glass next to the door frame and tapped the end with the heel of his hand. The glass broke with a lyrical tinkle and Danny caught the end of it before it fell on the floor. He tapped the glass again and a little more dropped to the carpet inside. He reached through the opening and tried to find the latch.

That was when the beeping started.

Shit.

He swept his hand beyond the door frame and felt a keyboard. When he lowered his face to the opening, he saw blinking. There was an alarm system after all. Probably only for this office, but that was all he cared about. And now that alarm was telling a security system somewhere that he was standing outside.

Fuck this.

He trotted down two flights of stairs and out the alley door. He held his bag of tools tightly against his leg and meandered down the block to his car in the parking lot by the bar. Part of him wanted to hurry, but he knew that was the only way he'd be noticed.

Once in his car, he dropped the bag on the floor next to him and started up. He pulled out and turned right, crossing the first intersection before he saw lights flashing ahead. He kept right at the speed limit and took his first right. The lights passed through his mirror, heading toward the office, no siren at that time of night and almost no traffic. Danny turned left and zigzagged back onto Jefferson, leaving Grosse Pointe behind for Detroit proper.

He turned on the radio and rolled up and down the dial. The White Sox beat Detroit, 4 to 2. Everyone's night was turning to shit.

Plan C, the abso-fucking-lute last chance. And the call went to voicemail. Well, two-thirty am, what do you expect?

"I need a favor," he said. "It's weird and complicated. Call me after noon."

He took a shower and slid into bed at three.

He didn't have to be back at work for fourteen hours.

11

Shoobie watched Barry Montesori and Leonard Klein clean their hands on the baby-wipes provided by the crime scene guys after taking their fingerprints for comparison with the stuff they'd lifted from the office. She was pretty sure whoever triggered the alarm never got the door open, but the lab rats dusted every flat surface they could find because they needed the practice. The whole office had the tint of the old pewter platter Shoobie remembered from family dinners when she was a kid.

"I'm positive, officer." Klein pushed his glasses up his nose for at least the two hundredth time since Shoobie and Hall showed their ID. "Everything on my desk is just where I left it."

"You can be that sure?" Grady cocked an eyebrow, his voice a soft tenor like you'd expect in the best restaurants from the server explaining the wine list.

"I always put things in exactly the same place. All my pens and pencils in the cup, the sticky pad to the left of my computer mouse, the rubber bands in the drawer..."

OK, so Klein had a touch of OCD, maybe not a bad thing for an accountant. Even after they'd called him and Montesori in the middle of the night to tell them someone tried to break in, he wore a conservative tie with a perfect knot. Dark slacks and a blue blazer, and his curly hair combed into submission. Just a hint of gray along the part.

"So whoever it was never really got in." Grady looked out the window at the dark shop windows across the street, desultory traffic still drifting along. The uniforms had already checked whoever they could find outside, and nobody'd seen anything suspicious, whatever that meant.

"No. At least, not into my office."

Barry Montesori nodded agreement. He wore jeans and a polo shirt because he was about fifteen years younger than Klein. But he did have two pens in the shirt pocket.

"I wouldn't expect you gentlemen keep a lot of money in the office, do you?" Grady knelt to study the carpet, a neutral beige, definitely not new.

"None," Klein said. "Well, the receptionist has petty cash, but no more than a hundred dollars or so."

"Most of our customers pay by credit card," Montesori said. "Or even electronic transfer. We encourage people to do that. Cuts down all the paperwork for everyone."

"Sure." Shoobie stared at the keypad again. Someone tried to force the door and the alarm went off. The only way to stop it was by typing in the pass code within thirty seconds, but the monitoring system said nobody even tried.

"Would people necessarily know that?" Grady asked.

"Well, we have the credit card logos on the door," Klein said. "But people are so used to seeing them, that maybe they don't. Really see them, that is."

Shoobie wandered over to look in Montesori's office. It was more casual than Klein's, a poster of Cancun on the wall above the file cabinet, and files lying on top of it. His desk held more file folders and several pens and pencils. They lay all over the blotter, a calendar with several days filled in and most of them with coffee rings decorating them. His ergonomic office chair faced the window. Not a neat freak like Klein. Pictures on his desk showed a woman with dark hair and a girl in a Girl Scout uniform. Shoobie put her at about ten because the uniform showed no curves.

"Any idea why someone would try to break in?"

"No idea." Klein rubbed his hands together like he wanted to dive for his computer and boot up. That gave Shoobie an idea.

"Do you back up your files regularly?"

"Of course," Klein said. "Every client, every day. We can't take any chances."

"Do you keep the files here?"

"Sure." Montesori stifled a yawn and Shoobie fought the urge to do the same. "But we have passwords on the computers and the files, too. And we change them regularly. Even if you boot up the computer, you won't be able to get in."

Klein played with the knot in his tie. "That's correct. And the external hard drives and flash drives all have their own passwords, too. Plus, we use an online storage system that also has a password."

"So even if someone got in, there's no way he could access your files, is that what you're telling me?" Grady's voice still sounded like nothing bothered him, but Shoobie knew something was wrong.

She walked out of the office and down to both ends of the hallway. A realtor, a decorator, an insurance agent, and a social worker. An old water cooler at the far end of the hall from the elevator. Outside, six cars sat in the parking lot: Klein's, Montesori's, one of the Crown Vics that answered the alarm, the crime scene guys, hers and Grady's.

Shoobie walked back down the hall to the stairs opposite the burgled office. The damn yogurt was a little ball in her stomach and her brain felt tangled like a spider web. She'd been in bed an hour, still seething at Brian, who hadn't returned her call when they called her in here. If she couldn't walk it off, she wouldn't sleep for shit when she finally got home again.

She mounted the stairs and pushed through the door to the fourth story. The hallway looked exactly like the third except that the water cooler at the end had a lower level. She examined every door and lock along the way. Nothing. She was afraid of that. She went back down the stairs.

Grady thanked the accountants and stood next to her waiting for the elevator. One of the uniforms stayed behind to guard the door until morning.

"Find anything?" Grady watched Klein and Montesori disappear behind the closing door.

"Not yet." Shoobie watched the lights above the elevator door change. "Walk with me."

They walked down the stairs to the second story, where she examined every door. Then the first story. Nothing.

Grady rolled his shoulders and Shoobie admired the six-pack abs under his shirt. She couldn't see them, but she could tell what he had. Hell, they'd been partners for two years now, all the guys kidding her about having the cute black stud under her. Well, in a city with an 80 percent African population, there were a lot of black cops. She wondered how many female cops were black, too. None of the detectives she knew.

"No other door's been touched," she said. "The guy meant to hit this office."

"Funny," Grady said. His eyebrow arched a little higher. It gave him an impish look, hard to maintain when he was six inches taller than she was, with shoulders twice her width.

"Funny doesn't begin to cover it." Her feet felt swollen. "Tony Fortunato's office."

Grady looked back at the elevator. "You thinking maybe the real motive's in there somewhere?"

"Could be." She just wanted to go home, take off her shoes, and soak her feet. Oh, yeah, and get a few hours' sleep. "Maybe we should pull the computers? Fortunato's anyway?"

"They're gonna love that."

"You think?"

Grady frowned. "You think we ought to find out where Lincoln Fillmore was earlier, too?"

"Can't hurt." Nearly four in the morning, and the air still felt like crotch rot. "I knew Guthrie when we were both in uniform. Good cop."

"If he was that good, how come he's not still on our side?"

Shoobie remembered Guthrie in the hospital, the doctors rebuilding his femur after the shooting, his wife somewhere in the east serving papers on him and not even coming back to visit.

"It's a long story."

Woody was a good cop, so he was probably a decent PI. But you need to pay the bills, so maybe he was taking this even if it was dead at the gate.

But what if it wasn't?

12

Billable Hours Powers burst through Guthrie's door not quite dragging Hot Rod Lincoln behind him. Hot Rod might have been wearing the same denim shirt and jeans from last time, but Powers wore a tie that clashed with every article of apparel worn by everyone else in the room. Guthrie wondered why people who had money to spend on good clothes often did it so badly.

"We—Lincoln, that is—got another visit from the police this morning," Powers said. Hot Rod looked unhappy, but he had apparently learned to let Billable do the talking because he would anyway.

"What did they want?" Guthrie watched Valerie's cinnamon hazelnut coffee still dripping into the carafe before he motioned the men into the office. If Powers got some caffeine into his system, he might attain escape velocity.

"Someone tried to break into Fortunato's accounting office last night." Powers looked out the window at the restaurant across the street, not even open this early in the day.

"Did they take anything?"

Powers adjusted his ugly tie. "They have an alarm system. It scared whoever it was off before he got inside."

Guthrie looked at Hot Rod, whose mouth moved as though he were chewing a huge wad of gum. "They wondered where you were, right?"

Hot Rod wrapped his huge hands around each other. His cuticles were the color of raisins. "I was with Sally. All night. She said so."

"Naturally, they don't believe her." Powers had to get his opinion on record. Guthrie kept his eyes on Hot Rod.

"Sally's your fiancée, right?"

"Yeah, we live together." Hot Rod almost smiled. It made him resemble a bloodhound.

"She's the reason I found that damn' Mercedes in the first place."

Powers cleared his throat. "Let's not get off the subject. The alarm went off about one-forty, and two cruisers arrived within minutes. The officers found the back door of the building jimmied and nobody inside."

"Where's the office?" Guthrie tried to picture Hot Rod breaking into a place. Given the guy's skill with tools, he probably could open locks pretty well if he wanted to.

"In Grosse Pointe. A professional center with about fifteen other offices. Realtors, insurance, dentists, one social worker."

"If there are so many offices, why do the police think the burglar was specifically trying to break into Fortunato's place?"

"The office is on the third floor. And as near as they can tell, no other door was tampered with."

Valerie appeared with three mugs of coffee on a tray and vanished again. Guthrie waited until Powers looked at him again.

"Why do they think a break-in has anything to do with Fortunato's death?"

"I think they're covering their ass. The other accountants say that nothing was missing, not even touched."

"But it's an awfully big coincidence."

"You got it."

Guthrie watched Hot Rod add sweetener to his coffee. Like he had to watch his weight. If he wore yellow, he could impersonate a number two pencil.

"They fronted me at work." Hot Rod's voice barely carried across Guthrie's desk. "I hardly punched in, they were in my face, both of them."

"This is the same two detectives from before? The homicide detectives?"

"Yeah, the black guy and the lady. The Doobie Sister, whatever."

Guthrie reminded himself to spring that one on Shoobie when he saw her again.

Hot Rod glanced at Powers. "I never tried to break into a place in my life. But I wouldn't say nothing. Except I wanted my lawyer."

"They wanted to take him back to headquarters," Powers said. "I told them fuck that, my client's got a job."

"Wouldn't it have been better to talk to the cops somewhere else?"

Powers shook his head. "I didn't want anyone to see Lincoln getting into the back seat of a car with two cops, especially since they wanted to put him in handcuffs."

Hot Rod's throat moved. "Sally had to see it. I didn't want her to, but she was right there..."

"You work together?" Guthrie wondered how he'd missed that. It never came up in their discussion.

"Yeah, she's almost as good a mechanic as I am. That's why they call her 'Mustang Sally.'"

"I'm guessing that's where you met?"

"Couple of years ago. Yeah. She don't need this kind of hassle."

"It will not happen again, Lincoln." Powers seemed to be flexing his muscles, but Guthrie didn't notice any real change.

"I don't think it has to, counselor," he said. "Everyone saw it, and that may be what Shoobie and Hall had in mind. Screw with his mind, maybe shake up his girlfriend."

"That's—"

"Oh, come on, Billable, you know damn well you'd do the same thing if you were prosecuting this case."

Powers glared at his coffee and Guthrie expected to see more steam.

"But this is good," he went on. "It could mean someone else had a reason to kill the man. And that reason is still out there. It helps you establish reasonable doubt and gives me something else to work with."

"More is better." Powers looked like he wanted to bite a chunk out of the mug. If he did, Guthrie would bill him for it.

Guthrie leaned back in his chair. "I talked to some people around where Hot Rod...found...the car. A few of them remember seeing it, but nobody noticed who left it there."

"Shit," Powers said.

"There's a bright side, though," Guthrie pointed out. "Nobody saw who took it away, either. At least nobody I talked to."

"How many people did you talk to?"

"I gave away about fifty business cards. Told the concerned citizens to call me if they remembered anything."

Somehow, he didn't expect to get many calls.

"The break-in was, when, one-thirty?"

"About then."

"Shoobie and her sidekick ought to be through talking with everyone at the office by now."

Powers looked happier. Hot Rod didn't.

"Mr. Powers, why don't you take Hot Rod back to work. I'll talk to the accountants."

He stood and adjusted his tasteful tee shirt and slacks. Anything looked good next to the outrageous necktie Powers wore.

"If I'm lucky, they've wiped the fingerprint powder off everything by now."

13

Guthrie felt immediate kinship for Barry Montesori, whose tie was loose and whose face already showed definite five o'clock shadow before noon. If he went without shaving a couple of days, that beard would become a bandanna and he could go out and hold up stagecoaches.

"No idea," Montesori said. "We went over this with the cops, too. Five or six times."

"I used to be a cop," Guthrie told him. "Sometimes, saying it again helps you remember something else."

Montesori rolled his eyes. "Yeah, well, we got called about two, Len and me, and they said someone tried to break in. We met the cops down here, let them take fingerprints all over the place, ask their questions, take pictures. All a waste of time. I can't see why anyone would want anything we've got here anyway. I'm thinking the guy wanted a different office, a doctor or something, maybe rip off drugs."

"There's a dentist's office on the floor above you," Guthrie told him, "but that's it. A social worker, but they can't prescribe medication."

He watched Montesori move his mouse around on the mouse pad to quell his screen-saver. The sun poured through his window so the glare made Guthrie squint.

"Do you usually have lots of money here, in a safe or something?"

Montesori shook his head. "Like we told the cops, almost nothing. We do most of our work with online transfers or plastic. That way it's already on the computer so we can keep track of our own records more easily."

"Sure." Guthrie watched Montesori's hands, long slim fingers, made for holding a pencil. Megan Traine, his girlfriend, had long slim fingers, too. She'd been a professional pianist for years before becoming a computer wonk with the Detroit PD.

"Do you have any clients whose records might be vulnerable?"

"What does that mean, exactly?"

Guthrie tried to frame his question more specifically, remembering that this was an accountant whose brain probably liked linear and specific patterns. "Oh, maybe government agencies or grants, non-profits. I'm trying to figure out why someone would want to get in here to see your records."

"Beats the hell out of me." Montesori pulled a bottle of water out of a mini-fridge. "The cops wondered if it had anything to do with Tony's death."

"I was wondering the same thing."

"Who the hell knows? But they took his computer, Len and I signed permission and gave them all the passwords that would have been on it when he died. We've already changed all of them since then, but not on his machine."

"How much of a problem was it for you when he died? As a business, I mean?"

"Well, we back up everything, so we could go to his files and load them onto our own computers. Catch up in a hurry. Fortunately, August's a slow time for us, so there wasn't a real crunch. If he'd died in early April, it would've been a nightmare."

"Sure." Guthrie watched Montesori's throat ripple when he drank. "You said the police already took his PC?"

"Yeah. And I think they went over to the house, got that one, too. Connie musta been thrilled to see them show up. She's trying to arrange his funeral—it's tomorrow, by the way, Len and I will close for the day—and now cops coming back and they've got nowhere. Must really suck."

"Murder always sucks," Guthrie told him.

"You never think of it as real until it's someone you actually know. It's like TV or something, you know?"

"Sure."

Guthrie returned to the reception area, where a woman with a perky expression that might have been surgically applied was cleaning the last of the fingerprint powder off her desk. A shiny new door guarded the entrance, a painter carefully copying Montesori's name onto the window.

"How new is your security system?" Guthrie asked the woman.

"We've been with the company about...four years." The girl cocked her head. She had a small stud in her left earlobe and Guthrie saw a mark where she probably wore a nose piercing when she wasn't behind a conservative accounting firm's desk.

"How long has the company been in business?"

"Oh, lots longer than that, but I'm not sure. Mr. Klein is pretty old, you know?"

"Define 'old.'" Guthrie wondered if the girl could count that high.

"Gee, I don't know. Forty, maybe even older?"

Guthrie was thirty-eight.

"That much? Gee, he must be old enough to be your father."

"For sure." The girl looked young enough to bribe with an ice cream cone. "Mr. Klein's in with a client right now." She smiled. "Klein with a client. I just thought of that."

"Funny," Guthrie said.

As soon as he closed that brand-new door behind him, he pulled out his phone and dialed his number one contact.

"IT, Traine." Megan Traine's voice oozed into his ear.

"Hi, it's me."

"Hi, me. I knew it was you, caller ID, remember?"

"So why did you call me 'you' instead of 'me?'"

"The vagaries of the language. What can I do for you? Keeping in mind that we're not really together, which limits our options. And there are other wonky people all around me, so that cuts things down, too."

"That's what I want to talk about." Guthrie could see Megan, probably wearing a bright top and sitting in a lotus at her desk with her feet bare. The first time she played piano for him, she kicked off her shoes. He remembered being in love with her before the song finished.

"Detectives Dube and Hall picked up a laptop and a PC today. They belong to a Tony Fortunato, who was killed about ten days ago. He was an accountant and someone tried to break into the office last night."

"Hmm." Megan held the tone long enough to tune a guitar to it. "And you're interested?"

"Shoobie and Hall—"

"Shoobie?"

"It's an old nickname. I knew her back in the day. She and Hall have a suspect in the killing, but no motive. I'd really like to know if anything on the computer seems to point somewhere."

"Uh-huh."

"I'm working with the lawyer who's defending the guy because I know him, too, and I don't think he killed Fortunato."

He could hear Megan mulling all the questions she probably shouldn't ask.

"So, what you're saying, I should be the one to inspect the computers?"

"If nobody else is doing it already, it would be nice. If someone has them already, maybe you could talk shop with them, work your feminine wiles."

"These are computer geeks, Woody. They're immune to feminine wiles."

"You're just saying you're out of practice since you stole my heart, right?"

Guthrie pushed open the door to the parking lot and the humidity wrapped soggy tentacles around him. "Do you think you can work it into your hectic schedule?"

"For you, anything. Of course, there's going to be payback, tit for tat, as it were."

"I'll cook for you."

"Ooh, baby."

"Thank you."

Guthrie opened his windows and watched waves of heat shimmer from his car.

"How soon do you want it?"

"How much time do you think you'll need?"

"Hard to tell." Megan cleared her throat. "I'm defrosting a salmon loaf tonight, more than a girl who's watching her weight should handle alone."

"You don't need to watch your weight." With her rock star energy level, she could burn off a chocolate cake before bed time. Or, if he were really lucky, in bed before they both went to sleep.

"Thank you again. But why don't you come over and help. I can tell you if I've found anything by then."

"I haven't seen the cats in a few days," he said.

"That's true. And they miss you."

Guthrie heard voices in the background.

"Gotta go," Megan said. "See you around six?"

14

Tobi Loerner looked up from her book to where Chuck and Patty worked on their sand castle. They alternated with yelling at each other about how much higher it had to be or whose turn it was to get another pail of water from the lake. The waves lapped only a hundred feet away and there weren't many kids around, so she could keep an eye on them and still read.

She decided she preferred Garber's essays on Shakespeare's plays over Harold Bloom's. She had three other books with her, too, not to mention her beat-to-shit Oxford paperback of *Hamlet,* rubber bands keeping the pages in order. About one more reading, she'd have to carry it around in a baggy.

"Tobi, hey, Tobi. Tobeeee!"

Patty's shriek could haunt a whole housing complex. They probably heard her back in Ypsilanti.

"Can we go in the water again? Pleeeese?"

"Don't you want to finish building your castle?"

"Chuckie's being a poop. He's ruining it!" Patty tried to stamp her feet, but the wet sand spoiled the effect.

"It looks OK to me." Tobi looked over at Chuck, patting sand into place and pointedly ignoring his sister. "You're both doing a really good job."

Patty's lower lip pushed out so far Tobi expected it to fall off. She closed the book around her highlighter.

"Come on, let's go talk this over."

In spite of being on the edge of tears and arguing all the time—which Tobi thought was part of being ten-and-eleven-year-old sibs anyway—Patty and Chuck Fortunato seemed to be handling their father's death very well. Tobi brought them here to the lake so their mother could make the funeral arrangements now that the police had found the body.

"Chuckie, what's the scoop?" Tobi knew she'd have to call him at least three times. She suspected his shutting out everything was part of his coping mechanism. Sure enough, he turned to her the fourth time she said his name.

"Huh?"

"What's going on? Patty says you won't let her help you with the castle. It's looking really good, but girls can do neat decorating stuff, you know?"

"It's a castle. A fort. For soldiers. Soldiers don't decorate stuff."

"Sure they do."

"Do not."

"Do so." Tobi knelt so her face was level with Chuckie's. He stuck his lower lip out like Patty and it made them look even more like brother and sister. Same eyes, same coloring, same pout.

"You know those medals soldiers wear on their uniforms?" Tobi said.

"Yeah." Chuckie glanced at Patty, who was edging close to the far side of his creation.

"Well, do you know what they call them?" Tobi waited for Chuck to look at her again.

"They call them decorations."

"No."

"Yeah." Tobi opened her eyes wide, what she called her "would I lie to you?" expression.

"Really. Decorations."

"You're making that up." Chuckie's pout returned. Behind him, Patty edged a step closer.

"Nope. Ask your mom when we get home."

Chuckie looked toward Patty and Tobi followed through.

"So, see, girls can help with a castle too because they know about decorations."

Patty stood with her hands behind her back and stuck her tongue out. Chuckie chewed his lip and thought it over.

"Well...all right. But don't do any decorating unless I tell you."

"Patty, is that OK with you?"

Patty heaved a sigh that belonged in opera. "I guess."

"Great." Tobi told herself another crisis was averted. Patty pawed the far wall of a tower.

"Hey," Chuckie said. "What are you doing?"

"I'm putting a window here so the soldiers can see out."

Tobi returned to her books and blanket. She finished Garber on *Hamlet* and unwrapped the rubber bands from the play, sticky notes on all the scenes with Ophelia. She had auditioned for the senior Shakespeare production in May and still hadn't heard if she'd been cast. Classes started in three more weeks. She'd been tempted to audition for some of the summer theaters around the Lower Peninsula, but she needed to save money so the nanny job with the Fortunatos was a better fit. Besides, she adored the kids, who were only brats on their very worst days and never even close to her own brothers, whom she suspected had been spawned by wolves.

Ten days ago, Mr. Fortunato went out after dinner to meet a client and never came back. The police knocked on Connie's door a week later to escort her to the morgue to identify the badly decomposed body. Tobi wondered how she would handle that herself. She could explore that question if she got cast as Ophelia, her father dying mysteriously and all.

The sun moved over far enough to shine under the bill of her cap. She pulled it lower and dug in her beach bag for her phone to check the time. She shifted her books, digging under the moisturizer and sunscreen and her iPod, which she couldn't listen to while reading anyway.

No phone.

WTF?

She looked over at the kids again, Chuckie carefully scraping the corner of a window with what looked like a Popsicle stick to make it smooth. Tobi realized they'd been quiet for nearly fifteen minutes. Too quiet.

She dug through the bag again. Still no phone.

She brushed the sand off her tee shirt and approached the castle. The sand felt like hot coals on the soles of her feet.

Late summer and she still wasn't used to it. But she'd forgotten to cover her sandals from that same sun, so they'd be just as bad.

"OK, who's got my phone?"

"Phone?" Patty's eyes widened in her version of Tobi's own expression. "Did you bring it?"

"I always bring my phone, you know that. In case your mom needs us back at the house, or if one of my friends calls. Or if—"

"Friends," Chuckie said. "You got a boyfriend? What's he like?"

"I don't have a boyfriend right now."

Chuckie nodded like an expert. "That's 'cause you're so ugly, huh?"

"No, I'm not ugly. I'm just not seeing anyone right now."

Too late, Tobi realized she'd taken the bait. This wasn't about her phone anymore, it was about her looks. How do you argue about a girl's looks with an eleven-year-old boy?

"Which one of you has my phone? I want it back. Now."

"I don't have it." Patty shook her head so her braids whipped back and forth.

"Me neither."

"Come on, you two. Lying's not nice. You know better than that."

"Not lying." Patty stuck out her lip again.

"Me neither." Chuckie looked at his sister, then looked back at Tobi with a nasty smile she wanted to slap off his face.

"Search me if you want."

The kid was wearing a pair of swimming trunks and lots of sun block. Tobi knew she couldn't search him here, and he was much too old for her to get away with taking him somewhere. There weren't a lot of people on the beach, but

71

someone would notice. With her luck it would be some woman with a voice you could hear clear back in Detroit.

"I don't want to search you, Chuckie. Just give me back my phone."

"Don't got it. Don't got it, don't got it." Chuckie dashed toward the water and Tobi followed him. Halfway there, she spun to point at Patty.

"You stay right there. Don't you even think of running."

She turned back to Chuckie, who splashed into the lake. The little bugger could swim like a barracuda and he had a hundred-foot lead. Tobi realized that if he was in the water with her phone, it was already too late. She watched him stand in water up to his waist and stick his thumbs in his ears, waggling his fingers at her.

"You..." she knew lots of words to describe recalcitrant males, but most of them were off-limits talking with an eleven-year-old. What would Shakespeare say at a time like this?

She stood with the waves cooling her ankles and told herself Chuckie had to come out of the water sometime. Then she'd tear his ears off and make him eat them.

"Something wrong?"

The voice came right over her shoulder. Tobi whirled and almost stuck her face into a well-tanned chest. When she looked higher, she saw two brown eyes and a nose with a white stripe of zinc oxide. The guy wore a floppy-brimmed white hat and day-glo orange swim trunks. A lifeguard.

"No. I'm...the kid took my phone, and I'm trying to make him give it back."

The lifeguard watched Chuckie waggle his fingers again.

"Your phone waterproof?" the guy's voice felt like a slow, deep massage.

"No. That's why I want it back. Before he ruins it."

"You sure he's got it?" The guy's lips moved in and out like he was sucking on a straw. "If he does, it's already toast. Or soup, whatever. "

He cocked his eyebrow at her and she could smell his suntan lotion. He was two shades darker than a hamburger patty and almost a head taller than she was. Not that she was tall, but he was twice her width, too.

"Well...one of them does."

"Them?" The beefcake looked at Chuckie. "There's only one kid in the water."

"His sister's over there. The princess in the castle."

"Uh-huh." The guy squinted toward Patty, and it made him look older. She guessed he was about her own twenty-one, but all the guys wore buzz cuts or shaved now, so it was harder to tell.

The guy strolled up the beach toward Patty's castle and Tobi checked out his butt.

Nice. Very nice.

She caught herself staring and trotted over the sand after him. The water on her feet made sand stick to them, but it felt cooler now.

"How's it going?" The guy's shadow fell across Patty and she craned her neck to look up at him.

"OK," she said softly.

"You don't have the lady's phone, do you?"

"She's not a lady," Patty announced to the hemisphere at large. "She's just our nanny."

Tobi wondered if the world would open up and swallow her or if she'd have to live through the rest of this.

"Your nanny." The guy nodded slowly. "Got it."

He walked around the castle, his lips doing that straw thing again. "Seriously cool castle."

"Thank you." Patty hesitated and glanced toward the water. "My brother helped."

"I'll bet." The lifeguard turned to Tobi and produced a phone from those sweet orange trunks. "What's your number?"

"Um...excuse me?" Tobi was still looking at his bronzed thighs. The guy was cut like a set of paper dolls.

"Your cell phone number. Let me dial it."

"Oh. Right." Tobi gave him her number and watched him punch it in. A few seconds later, she heard the opening bars of "Take A Chance on Me." It seemed to be coming from the castle.

"Ah ha." The lifeguard circled the moat and Patty drifted away toward their blanket. Tobi approached the sound from the other way. It was coming through the window in the castle, the one Patty dug while Tobi told Chuckie about the decorated soldiers. She looked in and saw her phone lying on the hard packed sand.

"You little..." she caught herself again. She grabbed her phone and shook the few loose grains of sand loose. Then she swiped the screen and answered.

"Thank you."

"Sure." The lifeguard swiped his own phone and put it back in his trunks. "My name's Evan, by the way. What's yours?"

"Tobi. And I really am their nanny."

"Cool. I see you here fairly often."

"That's an awfully old line, isn't it?"

"Yeah, I guess. You live around here? One of the cottages or something?"

"The family has a cottage. It's the one up there with the red door."

The guy looked over her shoulder and Tobi watched Chuckie emerge from the water now that he was no longer the center of attention.

"They're good kids," Tobi said. "They're going through a rough patch right now."

"Aren't we all." The guy watched Chuckie and Tobi realized she wanted him to look at her again.

"No," she said. "Really. Their father died last week."

"Whoa. That's gotta suck."

"It does." Tobi slid her tee shirt up over her head and draped it over her shoulder. Evan's eyes slowly moved from Chuckie to her chest and down to her legs. "He was murdered."

"For real? Wow."

"Yeah." Tobi turned her phone off and moved toward the blanket where Patty tried not to look guilty. Tobi felt Evan's eyes following her. Good.

She flopped down on the blanket and glared at Patty, then back at Evan

"Thank you. Oh, what time is it? I forgot and turned off my phone before I checked."

"Uh, two-forty." Evan watched Chuckie stop by the castle and drizzle a handful of water over a turret. "So, you got everything under control here?"

"I guess. Thanks again."

Tobi wondered how she could make Evan stay around longer. She wasn't used to grown-up conversation anymore, except about death and funerals. She leaned back on her elbows and felt his eyes on her.

"You ought to have sun block," he said.

"There's a tube in my bag." She tried not to bat her eyes and look cartoon seductive. He dug into the bag, frowning at the books and titles before he found the SPF 25 tube at the bottom.

"Here," he said. "Lie back."

"Aren't we going kind of fast here?"

"Not to worry."

She felt coolness across her stomach and jumped. When she understood what he was doing, she lay back again and tried not to laugh. When he was finished, she rose up on her elbows and read the numbers, upside down across her stomach to face her.

"I've got your number in my phone, remember? You called me."

"Yeah." He looked taller than the Renaissance Center. "But you can delete that. With this sun, you're gonna tan around those number in a few minutes. You can't delete them."

"Cute." She let herself smile.

"I try."

She watched him walk away and let the sun work its magic on her stomach. Patty watched Chuckie ignoring them for a few minutes, then rejoined him by the castle. Tobi re-read the Ophelia scenes, occasionally glancing over at the kids. They didn't fight at all, the wonder of the lifeguard helping their nanny apparently creating a bewildered truce.

She checked her phone at three-forty and made sure that Evan's number was in her logs. She shut it off, packed her books back in her bag, and folded the blanket before joining the kids at the castle. She could tell they wouldn't give her the satisfaction of saying they were bored.

"Think we should head back home?" she asked.

"OK." Chuckie shrugged like he didn't care one way or the other. Patty let Tobi help her with her tee shirt and they walked through the sand back toward the cottage. Tobi's

Saturn sat in the driveway under the shade of a maple tree so the interior wasn't like a micro-wave.

She unlocked the doors and opened the windows so the car could air out before Chuckie spoke.

"So, do you got a boyfriend now?"

She crossed her fingers but didn't say anything.

15

Connie Fortunato looked at her watch: three-forty. It felt like midnight or maybe eight in the morning, like time was both flying away and crawling back in her face. Her chest hurt, her stomach burned and her hands shook.

No doubt about it, she needed a drink.

The pinot noir in the fridge was down to only a couple of inches, how the hell did that happen? She opened the liquor cabinet and studied the contents. Scotch, whiskey, bourbon, vodka, tequila, more scotch. Hard stuff took the steering wheel out of her hands too fast, which was why she preferred wine.

But she wasn't driving anywhere else now, not talking with Father Giorgio about Tony's funeral or arguing with her in-laws about the casket or the caterer about the crudités. No, she didn't want a full sit-down dinner for who-knew-how-many people. It was going to be ninety fucking degrees again, the kids would be devastated, the in-laws would be an operatic nightmare—especially her mother-in-law, who still thought her son married beneath him, but hey, she gave the bitch two grandchildren, one of them a son so fuck her—parking on the street would pretty much shut down the neighborhood. And all she needed was a bunch of people turning the house into an oven, spilling food everywhere, talking so loud you could hear them in Ann Arbor.

What she really wanted was to toss a handful of dirt on Tony's grave, cry with the kids for a few hours, drink herself stupid and go to bed.

Not going to happen.

Connie hefted two bottles. Left, wine, right, hard stuff. The hard stuff would hit her faster so she would only need one glass, maybe two. And the caterer was bringing more wine tomorrow.

Scotch, bourbon, vodka, tequila. Tony liked scotch, Glenlivet. The seal was broken, the bottle down a few inches. Drink like her husband. She poured an inch into the glass and went to the kitchen for ice. Maybe a little ginger ale, wasn't that what scotch and soda was? She never paid attention to that stuff. She was only a social drinker, she'd carry a glass of wine around at the business parties Tony and the others held for clients, the stuff she couldn't avoid at the fancy restaurants.

She'd drunk more in the ten days since Tony disappeared than in the twelve years they'd been married. Her feet dragged into the kitchen and her shorts felt tight. Well, yeah, alcohol has sugar in it, doesn't it? After this was over, she had to get rid of those extra pounds and inches. She remembered her mother saying the weight you never gain at twenty-five catches up with you at thirty-five. And it's ten times as hard to get it off.

Connie wasn't quite thirty-five yet, but after the last ten days, she felt fifty.

She dropped two ice cubes into the glass, swirled them around and brought the glass to her lips. It smelled like paint thinner. People actually drank this stuff?

She felt it burn all the way to her stomach and fill her whole body with a warm burst. She remembered that she skipped lunch, too upset talking to that damn' caterer, then all the phone calls. She would have posted Tony's funeral on Facebook, but she didn't want to go near a computer now. Those police detectives came back late in the morning and asked to take Tony's laptop. She said sure, what the hell. If they could get more proof on that man, do it. That probably put her in a bad mood before she called the caterer, too. That officer Do Me, whatever her name was. Blonde with a walk like a gunfighter. Soft voice, you knew she was pretending. If she had to, she'd go for your eyes. Connie knew her type back in high school.

She pushed through the back door and out onto the flagstones around the pool. She should probably change to a bathing suit, but the sun slammed her eyes like a hammer, she wouldn't stay out here very long. She took another sip of the scotch. *Whoa.* Definitely she wouldn't stay out here too long. She'd be so blasted she couldn't crawl back in.

Maybe she should go back and find some crackers or an apple or something. Get something in her stomach. Hard liquor. *You said it, buddy.*

She sank to the chair across the pool. It was like leaning against a frying pan. She stared at the water, so still the surface might be a painting. No breeze at all. Dead as...

The scotch burned her tongue, scorched up her nostrils, and drove down to her stomach.

Her shorts vibrated and it took her a second to realize that meant a call. She dug into her pocket and checked the screen.

Barry.

"Connie, honey, how are you, you holding up all right?"

Connie put her glass on the table next to her chair.

"Barry. I'm...it's been a hard day. The church, the caterer..."

"Yeah, I'm sorry. Listen, I had to call you, this is the first time I could work free, it's been crazy here."

Yeah, it's been crazy here, too.

"The police came back this morning. Someone tried to break into the office last night."

"Last night?" Connie tried to focus on Barry's words. "Why? What did they want?"

"I don't know, we don't think they got in, the alarm probably scared them off. But the police think it might have something to do with Tony. You know, his...death."

"How do they figure?"

"I guess just the timing of it. But they took Tony's PC here, we gave them all his passwords. They were going to come and get his laptop and desktop from your place too, so I thought I'd—"

"They've been here." Connie felt the sun on the back of her neck. "A few hours ago. They took the computers. They looked through his desk, too. I don't know what for."

"Shoot. Well, there's more. A few hours later, a private investigator came by to talk to us, too."

Connie remembered the man she talked to a few days ago. "I talked with a guy a few days ago. I think he's trying to get the guy that killed Tony off."

"Son of a bitch." Barry Montesori exhaled loudly into her ear. "Well, I'm calling because I just thought. Wondered. Do you have a computer of your own, or did you use Tony's?"

"For what?"

"For anything. Email, online stuff. You know."

"Oh. No. I've got a computer too. Mine's in the bedroom. Tony's was in his office. I didn't use his. Why?"

"That's good. I was worried the cops might find messages from you. You know, our emails or...stuff."

Connie's stomach squeezed that little ball of Glenlivet. She took a deep breath and thought what Barry was saying.

"You mean, about...?"

"Yeah. Like when we met, other...details. I mean, if there's a PI trying to spring the guy they think killed Tony, and he or the cops find messages from you and me..."

"No." Connie shook her head and the swimming pool kept moving when she stopped. "No, I never used Tony's computer."

"That's good, Connie. That's real good. 'Cause if they found something about us, that looked like we were...you know..."

"We are, Barry. I need you. It was all over between me and Tony. You know that. You said you understood, that you were there for me."

"Sure, honey, sure. I still am. I was just worried about how it would look. I mean, you know how the police are, they might look at us instead of that car thief. And how would we explain it?"

"Tell them you love me and I love you."

Connie waited for Barry to fill the silence at the other end.

"Barry? You do love me, don't you?"

She reached for the glass again, but it was empty.

"Of course, baby. Of course. But the timing looks bad, do you understand what I'm saying?"

"But we didn't do anything." Connie stared back at the house, the sun burning through her clothes.

"Well, yeah, we did."

"But that's love." Connie hated how she sounded when she whined. "That's not...murder. Killing. No. That's not who we—what we—are. Is it?"

"Of course not, darling. I just wanted to check with you, make sure we're on the same page here."

"We are. I love you." Another five minutes in this sun, Connie thought her hair would begin to sizzle. "I need to see you. I need you."

"I know, I need you, too. Tomorrow."

"At the funeral? I can't wait that long."

"I can't get free tonight, baby. You know that. We'll be at the funeral, then back at your house. Maybe we can talk then."

"Talk then? With nine million other people swarming around. And the kids. Yeah, right."

"No, Connie, no. Listen to me. We'll work it out, we'll find a way. You know I'm here for you. That's what it's all about, right? You and me?"

"You really mean that?"

"Of course I do. Listen, I have to go, baby. I'll see you tomorrow. You be strong."

Barry ended the call and Connie stared at her phone. That private eye had to be the same one she talked to Monday. What if he found out about her and Barry? That would make them look guilty, and they weren't. Not of murder. They just loved each other, what was so wrong about that?

Connie stood up and stared across the pool at the back door and the kitchen.

It looked like an awful long way to drag an empty glass.

16

Megan Traine sat on her leather couch in a full lotus position that drew Guthrie's eyes from her bare feet up her spectacular legs. Her pony tail matched her eyes, slightly darker than Hershey's Kisses.

"You do understand that even if I find something, I can't tell you," she said. "It's part of an ongoing investigation."

Meg was almost exactly a year older than Guthrie, but could pass for ten years younger. Part of that was her rock star energy, a by-product of nearly twenty years as a gigging musician backing everyone who was anyone in the Motor City.

"Well, I figured since I'm working for the defense attorney, you could tell me and call it part of the discovery for the trial."

"Nice try." Meg sipped her ice tea and stretched her legs out to rest her feet on the pile of magazines on the coffee table. The magazines changed constantly, but the battered Oxford Shakespeare had a permanent parking space and the book mark moved regularly. Guthrie suspected she could recite several plays from memory.

They met the previous spring and one thing led to another until she drove her car at a man who held him hostage, his gun tucked under Valerie Karpelinski's chin. Valerie was wearing turquoise stilettos and a matching G-string at the time. She dressed more conservatively now, probably because she was afraid of Megan, who still had her driver's license.

"Nothing I can do to persuade you?"

"No, I'm afraid not. I'm a trained and conscientious professional."

"How about if I take you to dinner?"

"It's my night to cook, remember? And the salad's chilling right now."

Clyde, Meg's huge tuxedo cat, groomed in the bay window. Guthrie watched the cat hold one white paw above its head for an impossible interval.

"Maybe tomorrow night?"

"Tomorrow's Thursday. That's my lessons night. Maybe Friday?"

"OK." He watched her raise her glass again. She was a large petite, but her fingers were half-again as long as his. She started playing piano in grade school, building a reputation as one of the best sight-readers in the Midwest. She still played at least an hour a day and kept that reading sharp by playing symphony scores...upside down.

"Would it make any difference if I threatened to take you upstairs and ravish you?"

"I expect you to do that anyway."

"Handcuffs? Whipped cream?"

"Unless you brought handcuffs, we'll have to borrow Blue's. And I'd blush asking her."

Blue Song Riley owned the other half of the duplex. She and Megan had pooled Meg's divorce settlement to form Blue Traine Enterprises, which owned several apartment buildings.

"Guess I'm out of luck then, aren't I?"

"Well, I wouldn't put it that way. You were planning to stay over, weren't you?"

He followed her to the kitchen, where she checked on the salad, then poured them both more tea and added ice cubes.

"Just so you don't feel too bad, I didn't even get to the laptop today. And if you really think the guy's hiding something, it's probably on that, not the desktop."

"How do you figure?" Guthrie agreed, but he liked to hear things out loud. His former partner said you had to say it often enough so you really heard it.

"Well, the desktop was at his office, right? So if he was out, his partners had to have access. If he was keeping extra stuff on there, they might find it."

"True." Guthrie squeezed lemon into his tea. "If he really was hiding anything."

"Why do you think he was?" Megan opened a can of cat food and Clyde appeared in the doorway instantly.

"Well, it's just somewhere else to go. I knew Lincoln—the guy Shoobie likes for the killing—"

"'Shoobie?'" Meg looked up with the cat food still poised over the cats' dishes.

"We went through the academy together. Her last name's Dube, and we all called her that." Shoobie was the only person besides Megan who knew his real first name was Elwood. Except his ex-wife.

"Uh-huh."

"Hot Rod Lincoln's had a way with cars since he was tall enough to sit behind a steering wheel and reach the pedals. But he's gentle as a breeze. I can't see him killing a guy and stuffing him in the trunk."

Bonnie, Meg's small calico cat, appeared in the kitchen doorway and stopped dead when she saw Guthrie.

"Go ahead, Bonnie," Meg said. "You know him, he's harmless. Get over there and eat before your brother gets it all."

Meg led the way through her dining room and the arch into the living room again. She put her glass on a stack of music and sat at her piano. "So you're saying your boy's not a killer. But what if he got caught in the act?"

"I think he'd run away. And the cops say the victim was killed with one good punch. Hot Rod's tall, but he's built like a rope. He wouldn't have the strength."

"Well..." Meg's fingers picked out a scale and repeated it, up and down. "For now, let's say you're right. Where do you go from there?"

"Well, if it's not Hot Rod, it's someone else. They stuck the body in the trunk and left the car where it would be stolen. Everyone's pretty sure the guy didn't die where the car was found."

"Which was where?"

"Behind the old Grande Ballroom. A couple of kids found the car, called the cops. But the body'd been in there for a few days. In this heat."

"Oh, yuck." Megan changed keys and tried another scale, going in opposite directions with each hand.

"Yeah," Guthrie said. "But if someone else killed the guy, he had to have a motive. And maybe he's afraid there's evidence at the guy's office."

"Maybe." Megan spun around on the piano seat and drew her legs up. "Has anyone tried to break into the man's house since he died?"

"Shoobie didn't mention it."

"Do you think they will?"

"The woman has two kids and a pool in Grosse Pointe. She probably has a good alarm system." Guthrie wondered if Shoobie had someone watching the Fortunato house.

"Our best bet is you find something on the computer. Shoobie and her partner would have gone through the guy's office this morning. They're pretty sharp. They wouldn't have missed anything."

"But if they found something, it might suggest that your client—Hot Rod?—didn't kill the guy." Megan rolled her eyes. "What kind of name is Hot Rod?"

"His name is Lincoln. He used to steal high end cars, so everyone called him Hot Rod Lincoln."

Guthrie finished his tea. "Still won't tell me what you found on the desktop?"

"Zillions of tax forms and ledger sheets from hundreds of people and companies. It would take a forensic accountant a fairly long time to go through them all. I've typed out a list for Dube and Hall, so they'll probably go back to the accountants tomorrow and see how many of them are duplicates."

Guthrie shook his head. "The guy's funeral is tomorrow, so the place will be closed. But if you want to give me the list, I can give it to them when I see them there."

Meg smiled and the whole room lit up. "Nice try, Woody. I emailed it to them already."

"Well, you can't blame a guy for trying."

"I don't." Meg shifted scales again. "After dinner, we can play some duets."

"I didn't bring a guitar with me."

Meg looked over her shoulder and blinked those huge brown eyes.

"Even better."

17

Chrissie locked her car and walked across the crunchy gravel toward the service entrance—nice choice of words—of Cherries Jubilee. She gave her car one last look, knowing the inside would be like an oven when she returned in eight hours. She'd have to open the windows and let out the fireball, almost hot enough to light up that whole parking lot and set her hair on fire. Christ, she hated this heat. But at least it made the guys buy more drinks, and when they got a little buzzed, they got a little generous.

Beyond the building, she could see the sign, three cherries like on a slot machine, with legs growing down to the ground, just in case you missed the point of the name. There were a dozen other clubs on this side of 8 Mile, and they all knew Jersey Girl.

Wednesday night, not a great money night. But tomorrow was Thursday, and then, well, everybody's playing on the weekend.

She checked out the scene from the dressing room. The bar was mostly empty, two girls on the platforms, both new, both green. One was a little plump, Missy something? A voice like Minnie Mouse on helium, but she had nice boobs, they'd look even better if she could lose the tummy. Chrissie felt her own stomach and realized that in a few more months, if she pushed, someone else would push back.

Just for the hell of it, she'd tried another test when she got up six hours ago. The line was fuzzy, but clear enough to see. If she did it again, she knew it would say the same thing. But her aim was better this time. If she kept practicing, she could pee through the eye of a needle. They probably wouldn't let her do that for part of her routine, though.

She sorted through her costumes. Tonight, she'd finish with the Red Wings jersey. Number 38. She'd milk this one for a good long dance. She thought about wearing sneakers, but they'd take too long to unlace, and you don't want to be up there on the platform with long laces flapping. Nothing like falling on your ass to mess up a good routine.

She knew about falling on her ass.

"Hey, Jersey." Megan Whoopie slid over next to her and pulled three wigs out of her bag: silver, flaming red, and purple with gold glitter. They looked slightly less real than Meg's new boobs. "What's new and dirty?"

"Nothing much." Chrissie knew that Megan Whoopie had a kid, but she also had an ex-husband. Megan called it a starter marriage, started after she missed her period.

"God, this heat." Megan put the wigs on Styrofoam stands and started brushing out the silver one. Chrissie's shtick was "the Jersey Girl," Megan Whoopie wore a wig that matched her bra, G-string, and stilettos. It must be working for her, too because the boobs were brand spanking new.

"The only good thing about it is the guys who come in are already a little out of it."

"You said it." Megan reached over the wig head for a brush and her tee shirt shivered with the strain.

If Chrissie took after her mother, she'd only be able to do the VIP for a couple more months. She knew Tony was the father because she made everyone else wear a condom. She shouldn't have made an exception for him, but hey, you get a high roller, you got to keep him happy. That first night, he dropped fifteen hundred on her, became a regular, then he became a boyfriend and they took it outside. His car, that place on the lake... And a boyfriend doesn't give a girl money—not that she'd throw it back in his face—he gives her presents, flowers, perfume, clothes, stuff like that. They were going to go away somewhere, too. He promised.

Megan opened her make-up kit. Chrissie's coffee table had less finish than Megan's eyes.

"Wednesday's Billy Butt's night. He's one of my regulars." Megan pulled out a whole string of condoms.

"Um, let me guess."

"I'm a professional, Jersey, you know that. My number one priority is to keep the customer satisfied. Whatever he wants, I want. Whatever he wants, I got."

Megan flipped up her tee.

"That's how I got these, and they're gonna help me get more. It's like anything else, the more you put in, the more you get back. Next, I can work on a condo, a new car..."

Chrissie didn't hear "husband" on the list.

"I turn the money back into the business. That's something I learned from...What was her name?"

"Who"

"You know. Valkyrie. The business major, the one that talked about us forming a union, shit like that."

Chrissie didn't remember girls as much as she did guys. She didn't do girls. But she remembered a face. Silver hair, blue eyes big as nickels...

"Right, that was her name, Valkyrie?"

Chrissie checked her jerseys for the evening. Start with the Pistons, finish with the Red Wings. The Red Wings were hockey, made her think of ice, cool off in this fucking heat. Hey, lover, want to puck?

"Megan, the doctor who did your boobs. Did you have to get referred by a regular doctor?"

"Why? You thinking of doing it too? Shoot, Jersey, you got some nice girls now, don't mess with them. Me, I had those little bite-sized mounds. Guys don't want a snack, they want the whole meal."

"I was just wondering."

She needed to find someone new to help her with the baby. *You never think about this stuff when you've got lots of time.*

"Keep 'em happy, they come back. Keep 'em really happy, they ask for more. And that's what we're here for."

Megan glanced at the clock.

"You want to go out for a smoke?"

Chrissie almost said "yes" before she remembered she'd quit. Laura'd probably smoked the whole pack by now.

"No, you go ahead."

Megan pushed open the stage door and put a magazine in the crack so it wouldn't close all the way again. There wasn't a handle on the outside.

Chrissie remembered Valkyrie now, the one who wouldn't do the VIP because her body was a temple and she was saving herself. *Yeah, right. Showing your stuff to a hundred guys a night, but you're saving yourself.*

Chrissie checked her phone again. Someday, she'd erase Tony's number from her log. She saw his obituary in the paper Monday, the cops found him in his trunk. Who'd kill a sweet guy like Tony? His funeral was tomorrow, she should go. *No she shouldn't, she wouldn't know anybody and his whole family'd be there. What could she say to anyone? Hi, I'm the dead guy's girlfriend, maybe he told you about me? I just want to see him in the box, see if you're burying him with his wallet?*

Shit, Tony was a Catholic, she remembered him wearing that cross when they did it. She wasn't a Catholic, the only time she was on her knees was at work, none of that genuflecting stuff. She wouldn't have a clue. And didn't they speak Latin? She didn't know from Latin. Latin America, maybe. Like *adios, buenos dias, maricon, puta.*

When would the baby kick for the first time? She hoped it wasn't while she was at work. Christ, only two months, max. How was she going to handle this? First things first. She'd go to the funeral. Maybe seeing people there, people Tony knew, would give her some ideas.

Megan came back, her tee shirt smelling like tobacco smoke, and rummaged in her purse for a breath mint.

18

Guthrie stood at the back of the church because he wanted to watch the crowd reactions. Besides, standing was better for his leg than sitting in the hard pews, especially if they expected him to kneel, too.

The mourners filed past a casket awash with bright flowers. Most of them knelt to pray and crossed themselves when they stood again. Klein was an obvious exception. A few stopped to speak with Connie Fortunato, seated in the front row with the children and the nanny. Many of the women hugged the kids.

Guthrie saw an older couple that shared most of Connie Fortunato's features and decided he was looking at her parents. Another couple where the man had slightly less resemblance followed, and Guthrie decided the men were brothers, which meant the man was an uncle. He looked vaguely familiar.

Shoobie Dube and Grady Hall stood at the opposite rear corner in dark clothing. Guthrie noticed they reacted to the uncle more strongly than he did.

Oh Lord

The priest glared at them over the pews and Guthrie finally took a seat in the last row. Just as he sat, another woman came through the door and stopped at the top of the aisle. She wore black, but her jacket stretched over a low-cut top and her skirt stopped a foot above her knees. A few blonde curls escaped from what looked like a quickly-assembled bun.

The woman hesitated before she took off enormous sunglasses and slid into the aisle across from Guthrie. She didn't genuflect, and he realized she was another non-Catholic. He and the police were the only ones who even noticed her.

The priest began with a prayer and Guthrie followed the service as best he could. Fortunately, nobody sat close enough to notice his missing responses and lack of Latin. The rest of the congregation's fervor made up for it. The blonde woman seemed as lost as he was.

The repeated kneeling and standing and sitting made his rebuilt femur begin to throb and he wondered how much longer the ceremony would last. From the back row, he couldn't see faces, but he thought he recognized Barry Montesori and a woman sitting in the row directly behind the Fortunato family. Klein sat in the same pew.

The congregation rose and joined in a hymn. Guthrie could read the music from the book, but knew better than to inflict his voice on the rest of the congregation. The woman didn't sing, either. Everyone sat and the priest lapsed into Latin again. Guthrie eased his phone from his pocket, set the camera and waited for the service to end.

Finally, the priest raised his hands in benediction and the pallbearers stepped forward. Guthrie recognized Montesori among them. Another man who resembled the dead man enough to be a brother took his place, too. Everyone stood and

Guthrie slid his camera from his pocket. The light spilling through the door meant he wouldn't need a flash.

Across the aisle, the woman couldn't seem to take her eyes off Connie Fortunato and her children. She opened her mouth, then closed it again. The casket approached; Guthrie brought his phone up and took three pictures while the woman watched the family following the pallbearers. When he slid his phone back into his pocket, he saw Shoobie nod slightly from the far corner. She and Hall put their heads together while the mourners leaked from the pews to follow the family.

Guthrie was one of the last out and mumbled sympathetic words while shaking hands with the family. Up close, he saw that the boy had the same face shape as his father and the girl strongly resembled her mother, minus the curves. They both looked like they'd rather be anywhere else, and Guthrie didn't blame them.

The strange woman moved past the family so quickly they might not even have noticed her. Guthrie watched her stride down the church steps in outrageously high stilettos that worked well with the short skirt. Maybe he should follow her to the parking lot and get her license number, too.

The thought was still forming when Shoobie's voice caught him.

"Fancy seeing you here, Woody. I wouldn't have expected hired help to show up."

"We never sleep," he said. Grady Hall looked over her shoulder, his face neutral, then turned back to watch the mourners and family. "You going to the cemetery?"

"Of course." Shoobie looked back at the older men in suits gathered around Connie Fortunato. "Never miss the chance to sling dirt at someone."

"I'm missing something here, aren't I?" Guthrie watched an older woman in a black veil gather Connie Fortunato into a matronly bosom.

"What do you mean?"

"You sound like you know some of these people," Guthrie said. "A couple of them look familiar to me, too, and the only reason I can think of is maybe when I was a cop."

"Flashbacks are a symptom, Woody."

"Yeah. But symptoms mean there's something there." The pallbearers slid the casket into the hearse and cars began lining up behind it. The drivers were all on the far side so Guthrie couldn't tell if the blonde woman was following or not.

"The bereaved widow's family is named Diorio. Her father is Angelo Diorio and her uncle is Carmine Diorio."

Shoobie raised her eyebrows and waited for Guthrie to make the connection.

"The ruling family in Detroit. Was Tony mob?"

"He married into the Mafia. Anything's possible."

"So maybe that's why he was killed and Hot Rod didn't have anything to do with it, is that what you're saying?"

"Nope. Right now, it doesn't mean anything. It's just a fact."

"Everything means something, Shoobie. You know that."

"Yeah, but that doesn't mean it means something for us."

Guthrie struggled with the syntax. "But maybe it does. Maybe another family was making a statement."

"Well, I'm not sure what it was. Carmine runs most of the gambling, drugs, and prostitution in the Lower Peninsula, even if we can't prove it. But that doesn't mean Tony Fortunato was involved. Hell, part of the old Eye-tie culture, keep the women barefoot, pregnant, and ignorant. I'll bet Connie doesn't even know what her uncle does for a living."

Guthrie watched the line of cars extend around the corner and back into the church parking lot. "Listen, did you recognize that woman who came in late? The one sitting in the back row across from me?"

"Nope. But I saw you take her picture. Why?"

Guthrie still couldn't find her. "Well, I don't think she said a word to anyone here, she even slipped past the family on the way out, but she must have known Tony from somewhere."

"Receptionist maybe?"

"No." Grady Hall never took his eyes off the cars. "The receptionist was a brunette, remember?"

"Shoobie, can I ask you for a favor?"

"Sure. Doesn't mean I'll say yes."

"Hot Rod's lawyer told me about the break-in and your taking Fortunato's computers. If you find anything that might clear Hot Rod, can you share?"

"That's a big one, Woody. This is an on-going investigation, remember?"

"But if you find something that says Hot Rod didn't do it, you're back at square one, so we start even, right? And we can work together better if we share information."

"What do you have to share with me, Woody?"

Guthrie knew she hadn't said yes, and probably wouldn't.

"If I can track down who the woman is, I'll tell you."

"What if it doesn't matter?"

"What if there's nothing on the computers?"

The hearse moved away, the family in the two limousines behind it.

Shoobie dug in her pocket for a pair of cheap sunglasses. "No promises."

19

Guthrie didn't want to go to the cemetery, but now that the convoy was pulling away, he knew it was his best chance to talk to the nanny without being noticed. Going back to the house after the interment would be too public.

He turned on the AC and punched up a Reverend Gary Davis CD, old acoustic blues he loved but could never quite play. He didn't start playing guitar until he received a cheap one as a high school graduation present and he never took lessons. He played guitar two or three hours a day while convalescing from his leg surgery seven years before, more than he ever had before in his life. It kept him from going stir crazy, but it didn't make him a star.

His wife had served him with divorce papers only weeks before he and his partner Tim Koerner walked into a restaurant and interrupted a robbery in progress. The leader had a shotgun and recognized Tim, who took a blast in the chest and died instantly, but shielded Guthrie long enough for him to draw his own gun. He got off seven shots and killed all three men, but not before taking another shotgun blast in his left leg. It destroyed his femur, leading to reconstructive surgery that took months. It also led to the Detroit PD offering him a desk job instead of his detective rank because they considered him "disabled."

He turned it down. Shoobie Dube brought a potted plant the day he opened his new office in Ferndale. His divorce was final while he was still in physical therapy and his wife's Christmas card was signed "Sarah and Sam." Guthrie was looking forward to sending a card back this year that he could sign "Chris and Megan." Maybe Valerie would pose as their amazingly mature daughter.

The cars threaded their way between brown stone pillars and up a winding road toward the top of a hill. Marble statuary ruled the horizon and Guthrie wondered if there was a family plot.

The caravan stopped. Guthrie locked his car and eased his way closer to the open grave, where the priest and the family stared at the hole until it looked big enough to swallow Detroit. Connie Fortunato wore a veil that added fifty years to the tableau. Guthrie guessed that she would have preferred slacks to the skirt, too, but the traditional family probably insisted.

The boy held his mother's left hand and his sister's right hand while they stood next to her with blank faces. A young woman with dark hair held the little girl's other hand. She looked exponentially funkier than anyone else in the group and Guthrie knew she must be the nanny. She wore sunglasses that made her look like a security guard, an impression that she strengthened by seeming to survey the crowd. He remembered she was a college student and wondered what she was studying.

He didn't see the blonde woman. He stayed on the outer fringes of the crowd, barely able to hear the priest intoning the graveside ritual. Then Connie Fortunato stepped forward and picked up a handful of dirt to throw into the grave. She turned to her children, who shrank back from the gaping hole that held the box with their father in it. Both grandmothers and the nanny stepped forward and the kids buried their faces in the nearest bosom. The nanny took the little girl in her arms and talked to her for a minute, then looked up at the mother. The woman nodded and the nanny passed the child off to a grandmother who led her away. The little boy followed.

The nanny threw a handful of dirt into the grave and looked after the kids, who were surrounded by grandparents and a whole phalanx of women in black. She seemed to decide they were safe and drifted off by herself, wiping her hands on a tissue.

Guthrie caught up with her leaning against a tree.

"Excuse me, Miss."

The girl started. He saw a smudge across one cheek that made her look even younger, a small child playing outdoors in her good clothes.

"I'm sorry," Guthrie said. "I didn't mean to startle you. But I'm investigating Mr. Fortunato's death, and I'm wondering if you—"

"You're with that lady cop?" The girl looked ready to bolt. "I haven't seen you before."

"Detective Dube and I have known each other for years." Guthrie was careful not to say he was with the police, but equally careful about not denying it. "I'm wondering if you have any ideas about why he might have been killed. Things we haven't heard before."

"Why would I know anything?"

"Well, it's not that you know something, maybe you've just had time to remember details we haven't heard before. Like, do you have any idea where Mr. Fortunato was going the night he...disappeared?"

"No. He went out a lot at night. Meeting clients, sometimes going back to his office. Things like that. He was pretty busy."

"Sure," Guthrie said. "Did he mention that he was meeting someone that night, do you remember?"

The girl shook her head and looked back toward the mourners still filing by the open grave.

"I have to get back. Patty and Chuck..."

"They seem like great kids," Guthrie said.

"They are. And this has really thrown them. Well, we're all still trying to make sense of it. Connie—Ms. Fortunato— she's a mess. I've been taking the kids to the beach every day so they don't keep asking her questions, make her even more upset."

"So she stays around the house then, when you have the children?"

"I guess. She's out a lot at night, her book club, a couple of other things. But during the day, especially before they found Mr. Fortunato..."

"How did he and the kids get along?" Guthrie asked. "Were they close?"

"Oh, he loved them. They worshipped the ground he walked on, too. But he was so busy he wasn't home much. You know."

"Sure." Guthrie saw that the line of mourners was almost at an end. "You said you took the kids to the beach?"

"They've got a cottage near Ypsilanti. I've taken the kids there every day it hasn't rained. We do hot dogs or burgers, play in the water, keep their minds occupied."

"That sounds like a good idea," Guthrie said. "They must like you a lot."

"They're good kids." The girl swallowed. "I really need to get back to them."

"Sure," Guthrie said. "Just a couple more questions, OK? You mentioned that both parents went out a lot. Did you have to watch the kids home alone often?"

"Maybe a couple of nights a week. Ms. Fortunato's clubs are every two weeks, but sometimes Mr. Fortunato was home then. It wasn't always the same night."

"I see." Guthrie handed her his card. "Listen, if you think of anything else, could you give me a call? What's your name by the way? I know you're the nanny, but..."

"Tobi. Tobi Loerner." The girl slid his card into her purse without even looking at it.

"Thank you, Ms. Loerner." Guthrie watched her wipe her face again. "Um, you're spreading a big smudge on your cheek. I guess the dirt you dropped into the grave..."

"Oh." The girl found a mirror and looked. "Shit. Thanks for warning me."

She rummaged around and found another tissue before she returned to the children, walking easily in practical flats, unlike the woman Guthrie still didn't see. He drifted back toward his car while the little girl ran over and threw her arms around Tobi Loerner's waist.

He drove away before anyone even noticed him.

20

Shoobie sagged at her desk and listened to Brian's smarmy voicemail message. He sounded more like a used-car salesman than an advertising executive and she wondered if he'd ever listened to himself.

"Brian, it's Eleanor." She forced herself to keep her voice calm and steady. "Em Stoddard tells me you can't make the next appointment and I'd appreciate it if you'd get back to me—or her—to reschedule so we can move on. Give me a call. Please?"

Using something remotely like his own buzzwords might make him more cooperative. She'd learned to role play from years of interviewing people: witnesses, victims, everything in between. Maybe role-playing was a bad choice of words. Maybe if they'd done more of that in the privacy of their own home...

Stop it, she told herself. *Neither of you is that kinky.*

At least she wasn't. Maybe he was. Did his offer to drink champagne from her stiletto hide a deeper darker need than she'd ever imagined? Well, why the hell wouldn't he tell the social worker? She'd plug up a shoe and dress like a Playmate to get him back. Whips and chains, maybe not so much.

At least she still had some control here. Maybe she could make choices that would bring her husband back. They were separated and neither had filed for divorce yet, so there was still a chance, not like Constancia Fortunato, who buried her husband a few hours ago. Tony Fortunato wasn't coming back to anyone.

And they still couldn't prove that Lincoln Fillmore killed him. She and Grady faced him down at work the previous day and got nowhere.

The body shop reminded Shoobie of her father, who spent most of his spare time in their backyard with the fifty-seven Chevy he'd bought new and kept in nearly mint condition.

This one had newer equipment and the music coming from someone's iPod was different, but the oil and gasoline smells, the rubber tires in the sun, and the hot welding stench all felt like home.

The owner of the garage frowned when he saw them coming again. He waddled over, NASCAR cap pulled down to thick eyebrows.

"Jesus, you guys again." Shoobie didn't bother to correct him. "You want I should give you a regular parking spot in back with the guys who really work here?"

"That's OK." Shoobie held up her ID, just to make it official. "We'd like to talk to Mr. Fillmore again."

"He's busy." Wardell Grimes rolled his eyes. "Christ, you keep coming in, hassle my best guy, how'm I s'posed to get any work done."

"You don't have a problem with him?"

"Shit, the guy knows cars like he's got oil in his veins. And he's never missed a day. I told you all this before, like, how many times?"

Shoobie saw a skinny butt off to her left, the guy's head buried in a car engine with the hood up. It reminded her of the lion tamer sticking his head in a big cat's mouth at the circus. Well, he was working on a jaguar, so there you go. Of course, Hot Rod Lincoln got his nickname because high end cars were all he ever boosted—like Tony Fortunato's Mercedes.

Fillmore seemed to sense their approach and eased himself erect. His expression reminded Shoobie of a gerbil, some innocuous little animal that stayed away from danger.

Even though he looked nothing like her father, Shoobie recognized the same love of what he was doing. It was like he talked to the cars and they talked back. He could probably go all day without talking to a human being, but if you took him away from his cars he'd wither and die.

And she was trying to do just that.

"How are you, Lincoln?"

Fillmore stared at them. "I don't say another word without my lawyer here. That's how he wants it."

"We just want to ask you one question, then we're out of here."

"Not without my lawyer. Uh-uh. Nope."

Fillmore turned around and stuck his head back into the jaguar's innards, basically telling them to kiss his ass.

"Where did you find the Mercedes, Lincoln? We know where you dumped it, but where did you find it when Tony caught you?"

"La, la, la. Boy, this baby really needs a new intake. And I just started looking, who knows what else I'm gonna find. Probably take all day, I'll be so busy, I won't have time to talk to anyone."

"Fillmore, it's a simple question, where was the car?"

"I got orders, detective. I don't say nothing without my lawyer. I don't even got to say that again."

Shoobie felt Grady's eyes looking at her.

"Come on, Lincoln."

Lincoln Fillmore stood again. He was a full head taller than she was and probably didn't weigh much more than she did when she was retaining water. The more she watched him, the less she thought he acted guilty. She'd seen enough guilty people to know most of the tells. Fillmore stuttered a little and hesitated a lot, but he seemed to have a vocabulary of about a hundred words that didn't relate to cars.

"No. You leave me the hell alone or I'm calling my lawyer right now."

He slid a wrench into his pocket and stomped over to the work bench for a rag. He wiped his hands and reached into another pocket for his cell phone.

"Never mind." Shoobie put up her own hands. The thought of Billable Hours Powers screaming at her made her stomach churn. "But you could help yourself if you'd help us."

"Yeah, right. Do I look that stupid?"

Shoobie was tempted to say 'yes,' but thought better of it. She spun on her heel and stalked back toward the street. She told herself that her ass was a lot better than his. She knew enough not to ask Grady for confirmation.

They went to the funeral just because there was a microscopic chance the killer would show up—if it wasn't Fillmore, which was beginning to look more likely—and do something stupid enough for them to notice. That didn't happen, but as soon as they recognized the Diorio family in the front pews, the whole playing field tilted sharply. Shoobie didn't want to say so in front of Guthrie, but that and the break-in were giving her a really bad feeling.

And who was the blonde woman? She didn't show up at the Fortunato home, where Shoobie and Hall watched the whole clan weep and wail and pinch the cheeks of the kids, who resembled two baby deer stuck on I-75 at midnight.

The nanny seemed to have them well in hand, and they seemed less freaked out by her than by the keening aunts and grandparents. The girl looked young and Shoobie remembered she was a college kid. How would these kids be in a few weeks when she went back to school, wherever that was?

They asked four or five people about the woman, and got nothing but blank stares.

Shoobie stared at her monitor and typed another fifty words into the case file. It felt like a full novel. She checked her phone. Nothing. Just like ten minutes ago when she left her last message. She dialed Brian again.

Voicemail. Of course.

"Hi, honey." She tried to keep the sarcasm out of her voice, but she tasted bile in her throat. "This is Eleanor. We need to re-schedule the counseling session with Em." She took a deep breath and felt her chest hurt. "Brian, I love you and I miss you. We can still fix this, but I can't do it alone. Please, Call me when you get time, OK?"

Answer your phone, you son of a bitch.

She should have taken up with Woody Guthrie when he came out of the hospital. Or never left his hospital room. But Brian was funny and could fix anything that could break. Well, maybe not anything. But he loved her and she loved him and the first three years were like Cinderella, tobogganing down a hill in shiny glass slippers.

Where had it started to go wrong? Was it when she made detective and the hours got weird? Sometimes she didn't come home at the end of her shift because she was chasing down a witness or a lead or something, but it got so whenever she got home, he wasn't there either. And if she got in really late and wanted to snuggle, he was fast asleep or too tired. Understanding and a little loving, how much is that to ask for? They were husband and wife, for Christ's sake. And he had regular hours, so he could even learn to cook or order take-out or something, couldn't he? Sure, Detroit wasn't paradise for advertising right now, but there was enough work so they weren't worrying about buying groceries or making the mortgage payment.

What the hell had happened?

She stared at her phone again. Before she could stop herself, she punched in Brian's number again and composed a text, saying everything she'd said in the voice mail. But in a text, he couldn't hear the neediness she hated in her voice. A voicemail and a text in five minutes. Christ, that kind of urgency, her contractions should be three minutes apart.

That was something else that was rapidly disappearing over her shoulder, too. Husband, marriage, the chance for children.

Connie Fortunato had children. But one day she kissed her husband good-bye and never saw him again. Shit like that was why Shoobie joined the police force, to help make it better for people like Connie Fortunato.

Nothing will really fix it, the little voice inside her said.

But I can make sure someone pays for it, the other little voice answered.

Bullshit, the first voice said. *You're losing your own husband.*

Woody Guthrie lost his wife, his partner and his job. He damn near lost his leg. That was why he became a PI.

They were all in the same game because they'd all gotten a shitty hand.

Now they were waiting on the computers. And trying to figure out where to go with that mysterious woman nobody seemed to know. They hadn't even seen her car, never mind her license plate. That seemed to be the way this case was going to go. One step back, two steps farther back.

Shoobie laid her phone next to her keyboard and resumed typing.

21

Usually, being around a bunch of hot and horny girls kicked Chrissie into high gear, but tonight she felt like she was sinking in tar and could barely keep her face above the surface.

Hair spray, zippers, Velcro, voices, and the occasional tinny PA or the thumping bass outside all melded into a heavy shell around her and she went through her prep on autopilot.

Tony was dead, she went to his funeral that morning. And that woman, maybe ten years older than Chrissie, ass getting wide, maybe because she'd had those two kids. Chrissie wondered if that would happen to her after she had this kid. If she had this kid. She caught herself thinking that for the first time.

The old people, too, the women wearing black veils and shrilling like giant birds with trails of mascara running down their faces. The men frowning and nodding at each other, dusty suits, bald heads and bloodhound jowls all over the place. Beyond a certain age, everyone looks the same except for skin color, and the sounds and smells are pretty much the same in any language.

Maybe grief is what makes us all equal.

"Hey, Jersey, you gonna be much longer there?" Paula the Latex Girl raised her plucked eyebrows and Chrissie looked at herself in the mirror. She was starting to put on eyeliner for the third time, and she hadn't even got naked yet, not once.

Tony was dead. And his baby was growing under her G-string. How was she going to dance if she didn't get rid of that kid? Make her car payment? Her rent? How many guys you have to screw just to have life turn around and screw you back? Tony was going to take her away from all that.

"Oh. Right." Chrissie backed away from the mirror and Paula slid into her spot, electric blue wrapping her ass like shrink wrap. It went up to her neck and down to her ankles, shiny black boots over it. In that outfit, Chrissie would sweat to death before the first bill hit the platform.

Tony the Wop Catholic, more family at that church than cars on the freight trains that used to rumble through Chrissie's neighborhood back in Kentucky. Mom-mom and Pop-pop let her look over the back fence, boxcars, tank cars, refrigerated cars for meat and fruit, big flat cars with tractors and bulldozers. More colors than she knew to name. And loud, the wheels rumbling over the rails, the engine thrumming away...

It sounded like the hubbub backstage now. Chrissie blinked slowly to test the new eyelashes. OK, nothing fell off. If it happened five minutes in, great, give her a reason to bend over.

She chose her Lions jersey and forced her mind to the first dance, only minutes away. The kick-off. The first thirty seconds set the tone for the whole evening. Go out there with a smile on your face and a shine on your lips, you come home with a bucket of cash. Go out there sad and dry, you'll eat leftovers tomorrow.

The bass outside sounded like an earthquake. Didn't anybody give a shit about melody anymore? Chrissie closed her eyes to focus and Tony's coffin burst into sight, all those crying old women up and down the aisle in the church. She wanted to say good-bye, maybe even kiss the casket—was that sick, or what?—but all those people she didn't know freaked her out. Too weird.

Tony, Tony, Tony, why'd you go and fucking die? Why'd someone want to do that to you?

"Jersey?"

Tony, Tony...

"Jersey." Blanche shook her, face scrunched up behind those bright red lips, big as a fucking donut. "Jersey, you OK? You're on."

"Shit." Chrissie shook her head and the funeral disappeared. The music pumped away, usually she was up on the platform by now. *Shit, shit, shit.*

She pranced through the curtain and spread her arms as she approached the pole, smiling at everyone like the world was beautiful and she loved them all. She hoped to God they believed it. If this was setting the tone, it was gonna be a long night.

The first dance was all uphill on cinders, the cheapest motherfuckers in Wayne County, all clustered around her platform. She was down to her pumps and panties before the first bill showed up. More followed slowly, but it was a bad sign. She took her time picking them up and flashing her business all around the room before heading back.

She patted herself off with a towel and did eeny-meenie-miney-moe between the Pistons jersey and the Red Wings. The Tigers would be last dance of the night.

"Jersey, you OK?"

Blanche brushed out her hair and gave Jersey a sideways look. She was almost six feet tall and Jersey thought her cleavage was natural.

"Bad day." She never told anyone about Tony because he was married, so now how could she talk about a funeral unless it was family?

"Tell me about it." Blanche spread moisturizer on her ass and thighs, then slowly slid up the bright red stretch pants. Chrissie wondered how she could breathe in the damn things.

"You know it already."

"Yeah. Fucking life, right?"

Blanche plucked a tissue from the box to wipe the excess moisturizer from her fingers before she dug into her purse.

"Here, check these out. What do you think?'

Chrissie stared at a picture of a headlight with a nipple in the center. Below it, "Cadillac Blanche" and an email.

"Uh...business card?"

"You got it." Blanche dug into her purse again. "Two kinds. Here's the other one."

Chrissie assumed that was Blanche's ass, with a gleaming red taillight on her right cheek. She struggled for something to say, but Blanche took up the slack.

"Cadillac Blanche is the best ride in Wayne County. She don't come cheap, but if you treat her right, she comes often."

Chrissie felt her stomach lurch. Was that the baby kicking, already? "Blanche..."

"Call me 'Caddie,' honey. It's my brand."

"Brand?"

"Everyone's got a brand, a trademark? You wear your jerseys. I got my name. In the VIP, I wear stick on decals, I had 'em made, you know, like this taillight or a Caddie hood ornament, stuff like that. So the guys that take the ride remember how they went."

"Um, like..."

"I'm trying to find a way to put frosting on them, or sugar, you know? Something sweet so the guys can lick them off."

Chrissie clenched her stomach muscles and the queasiness went away.

Caddie reached for a tank top. "Goes with the business cards. Guys still see that taillight on my butt, they remember it all. The word gets around, too. Nothing beats word of mouth."

Caddie slid her tongue over her lips. "Especially my mouth, know what I mean?"

Chrissie felt like she'd just walked in on her parents, seeing her mom doing that for the first time.

"Give 'em what they want, right?" Chrissie wasn't really a whore, but she didn't remember the last time she absolutely gave it away, either.

"Sure thing, but you got to make them respect you. You never come cheap."

Officially, the club didn't recognize that anything went on in the VIP room. The girls were free-lancing, so they could set their own rules. Or prices.

"And I don't do dippity-doo without protection."

"But don't they want—?"

"Jersey, listen to me." Caddie put her hands on Chrissie's shoulders and stared into her eyes. "Your body is your business, right? They look, they pay. They use, they pay more. You're out of commission, you don't earn squat. A bruise, a nick, maybe you can cover it up, but clap or worse, you're screwed all the wrong ways. You have to protect your earning power."

My earning power's fucked, Chrissie told herself. *And that's how it happened, too.*

"Jesus," Caddie said. "Listen to me. I sound like What's-her-name. Valkyrie."

"Yeah," Chrissie agreed. "You do."

"Before she left, she told me she was thinking of getting a Viking helmet and shield. Push her brand, too."

Chrissie felt herself fall behind. "I don't get it."

"Valkyrie, right?"

"Isn't that just Polish for Valerie?" Chrissie wanted a cigarette. *No, not with the baby.*

"Valkyrie? No, it's those what-do-you-callems, Norse maidens, carry off the dead soldiers. There's some opera."

Chrissie wished she'd finished high school so she'd know this Trivial Pursuit shit.

Caddie nodded. "She was a business major, remember? She knew about branding and how you make the customers remember you and how you have to protect your ass—your assets, that is."

Valkyrie had the best tush on the circuit. Great smile, too.

"She didn't do the VIP room, though, did she?"

"Nah." Caddie picked up a tube of lipstick. "You remember that riff she always did, like her body was a sacred temple? She didn't have any piercings or tattoos or anything. I figure that was all part of a sales pitch."

"How you figure?"

Caddie put the lipstick down again.

"Hey, think about it. She's not messing with her assets. That's one. But if she's saying her body's so holy, it's like telling guys she's a virgin. Which hasta be bullshit, thank you very much."

Chrissie remembered Valkyrie. Had to be twenty, twenty-one. *And still had her cherry? Not a fucking chance. Not even if she ate off the other side of the plate.*

"I figure she was just letting the demand build. I mean, someone who looks like she did, going in there, tells the guy it's her first time, what do you think she could make him cough up?"

Chrissie closed her eyes and heard cash registers ringing all over the world.

"Whoa."

"Damn straight." Caddie raised her eyebrows. "Jersey, you gotta have a gimmick. Like Valkyrie. Like me. And you've got one. You just gotta build on it a little. Jersey Girl, right?"

"How do you—?"

Caddie stood, her eyes wide enough to read the whole movie screen at once.

"Think about it. You wear the jerseys, get some undies to go with them. Or stick on tattoos or something like I got. You know, the baseball jersey, you wear home plate, tell the guys they'll hit a home run."

Chrissie felt the beginning of understanding. "Or slide into home?"

"Right, right, perfect." Caddie ran a brush through her hair. "And with the hockey, maybe a puck, stick it right over your business. Or have a slit in it. Let the guys score?"

"And a goal post?" Chrissie felt Caddie's excitement carry her along. "And maybe a basket, let them dunk?"

"There you go, girlfriend."

"Wow." Chrissie tried to figure what it would cost up front. Maybe not too much. And one good night, she'd be able to pay for weeks. Which was all she had.

Caddie's eyes narrowed. "You know, you might want to branch out a little, not just Detroit jerseys."

"What do you mean?"

"Well, you could add a few other towns, increase your brand. Like, I'm thinking the baseball team in Minnesota is Minneapolis and St. Paul. They call themselves the Twins."

"Yeah," Chrissie said. "So?"

Caddie took a deep breath. "You wear a Twins' shirt in the VIP, maybe the guy'd want two for one. You know, two girls? Charge even more, like two grand plus extras?"

Chrissie tried to keep her face neutral. Caddie was a switch-hitter?

"Hey, just thinking out loud, you know." Caddie heard the music change. "Whoa, I'm on."

Chrissie watched Caddie disappear through the curtain. Her heart wanted to burst through her chest and her hands shook. She decided she'd wear the Pistons jersey next.

She stood and looked toward the hall and the office where the manager sat, probably watching the shows on the CCTV. Maybe she'd start looking on-line about stick-on bases and pucks, too. After the last few minutes, she didn't want to ask Caddie where she got hers.

She wasn't ready to try the Twins idea, either.

22

Thursday night at Nips Ahoy, everybody thirsting for the weekend, Danny needed three sets of arms to fill all the orders. Bud, you got it. Coors, comin' up. Jack Daniels, absolutely. Decent tippers, too. It kept him from thinking about the next phone call, which would come any time.

Doreen worked the closest platform, guys so thick Danny could only see the top of her head. That meant her routine was almost over, she was on her knees pretending to give someone a little oral service. Maybe get him back into the VIP room now that she had his attention.

Danny wondered how much of a cut Leslie the manager got for private sessions. And how truthful the girls were about what they got. He got a piece of the watered-down champagne, the bouncers got a little to keep them safe, so if Les got something too, the girls were getting screwed more ways than one.

He poured a draft, letting the head build just enough and skimming it off before he slid the glass across to the guy in the Detroit Cobras tee shirt. Poison pounded through the PA system, loud enough so most of the drinkers pointed at what they wanted or held up a bottle. Danny knew the regulars anyway, which helped his tips, too.

Doreen stood, her face flushed, all those capped teeth gleaming at the guy in front of her. Danny wondered how much the guy had in his pants—and in his wallet. Then he wondered what it would be like with Doreen, watered-down ginger ale they called champagne at seventy-five bucks a bottle on the table and her in his lap.

Danny learned long ago about mixing business with pleasure. Women ask questions and they're apt to share the answers. When he was a boxer, his girlfriend let it slip that he didn't see too good out of his left eye anymore and everyone started beating his brains out with straight rights. That's when he gave up boxing. And her.

Now he worked at Nips Ahoy, moving up from a bouncer to head bouncer to bartender to the best bartender they had. But he had too many hours to fill and nobody else to fill them with. He did free-lance stuff to break things up, which was how he ran into Tony Fortunato.

Trisha stepped up on the platform, thigh-high boots the orange of construction cones, matching suspenders and hard hat. Everyone had a gimmick. Danny poured another draft, another Jack, made change and stole a look at the clock. After Trish finished, he'd take a break.

When Trish bent over so he could see her back teeth before she tucked the bills into her hard hat, Danny signaled to

Marty at the other end that he was taking ten. He could smell sweat, second-hand cigarette smoke, and dreams for sale. Just dreams. You never found love in a place like this. Danny knew a few bouncers, a few strippers who'd hooked up, but he couldn't think of a single one that ended up married long enough to mention.

He stepped outside, traffic pushing through the sticky darkness on 8 Mile, humidity turning the lights into fuzzy lollipops. The exhaust dug into his chest, so thick he could hardly see across the boulevard.

His hip vibrated and he pulled out his phone.

"The ideas are not blossoming, are they?" No greeting, no nothing, just that voice.

"I'm working on it."

"I hope your work becomes less subtle. Breaking into the accounting office? Really, Daniel, did you think the man would keep information where his partners could find it?"

"I had to try. I mean, sometimes you look past the obvious. Like that story, you know the one. The something letter."

"Yes, yes, yes. But you have drawn attention to Anthony Fortunato again. The police thought it was a random death, but now they will take it more seriously. That would not help my cause. And that will be bad for you, too."

"Listen, I—"

"No, you listen. You were hired to get information from Anthony Fortunato, but you killed him instead. You are now a liability."

Danny didn't know who this guy was. Someone knew someone who told someone else who gave the guy Danny's name. You can deal with things and people you know, but the shit out there in the dark...that's why kids had nightmares.

"Um, one mistake, not even my fault. How was I to know the guy had a glass jaw?"

"He did not have a glass jaw. He had a bridge, an upper plate. You dislodged it and he choked."

"Well, there you go. Like I'm supposed to know that."

"You were not hired to beat the man, but to question him."

"But I didn't know, so it's not my fault."

"This is not a debate, Daniel."

"OK, listen. The guy—the family hired this nanny for the kids, I don't know if you know her."

"I have heard, yes."

"OK, well, she's not really a teacher, she's a college kid, and she's pretty. I think Tony Fortunato was getting a little on the side, this young stuff, you know. So he might've told her about the money."

"That sounds very tenuous."

Tenuous. Christ.

"Hey, I'm gonna check out the girl. I mean, the guy's wife doesn't seem to know anything, right?"

"On what do you base that surmise?"

Surmise?

"Well, she's not doing anything different. I followed her a couple times, you know?"

"She buried her husband this morning. She's still coming to terms with the loss, never mind rebuilding a life."

"No, but she doesn't even seem to know about the money. If she did—"

"So you believe her husband has been in a relationship with this young girl and she does not even know? With the two children involved, I think that would be very difficult to orchestrate, don't you?"

"Well, let me check it out anyway, OK?"

"I hope you will be more subtle than you were with your bungled burglary."

"Yeah, don't worry."

"I do worry, Daniel. It can take years off your life."

Danny put his phone back in his pocket before the full meaning of those last words sank in. Monica was down to her camouflage undies, her helmet on the stage to catch bills. She had a decent crowd around her. Beyond her, the new redhead in the white gauze was smiling at a guy with buck teeth. Danny knew that smile. First night, the girl was scared three ways past Sunday.

Bud Light, comin' at you. Another Jack? You got it, cowboy.

Ted Nugent's "Cat Scratch Fever" shrieking out of the speakers.

Danny hoped Tony Fortunato'd been banging the nanny. And liked pillow talk.

He didn't have a plan C.

23

Guthrie claimed that he knew only two recipes—coffee and blackened everything else—but he still had to shop for groceries, even with tomorrow as Megan's Friday to cook. Their three months together taught him to pay more attention to amenities such as air freshener and fabric softener. Real guys sleep on rough sheets, but real women mention it.

He unpacked and stowed everything—about two-thirds of it non-edible—before putting on coffee and changing out of jeans to cut-offs. He returned to find enough coffee in the carafe to fill a mug, which he took to his basement and his guitars.

During rehab after the doctors rebuilt his shattered femur, those guitars maintained his sanity. After three hours of physical therapy and two hours on the elliptical trainer he'd bought, he plugged in his Fender Stratocaster and turned his amp up to seven, the loudest it could handle before the speaker rattled. He wanted to sound like Jimi Hendrix had come to visit, but it never happened. He preferred acoustic to electric anyway.

He first heard acoustic blues from a roommate in college and decided to become the next Charley Patton. He sounded more like General Patton.

He put his mug on the battered coffee table and picked up his Gibson Hummingbird, a thirty-year-old acoustic he'd found in a pawn shop while he was still walking a beat. The guitar slid under his ribs like an old love. He focused on his fingers finding the notes and stumbling for a semblance of an even tempo. The guitar seemed to be on his side.

Megan, who had been a session musician for years before they met, told him to stop practicing scales and chords if he wanted to get better.

"Play songs," she said. "Then it has a point. You'll feel like you're really making headway instead of just screwing around with patterns. It's too easy to fall into those same patterns all the time." They'd been together three months now, and she'd never asked him to play for her. Someday maybe he'd feel enough confidence to offer.

His fingers felt loose and he forced himself to sit fairly erect and breathe easily. He let his fingers walk across the frets and his mind wander through the Fortunato case.

Why would anyone try to break into Tony Fortunato's office? The partners said they never kept much money there, and there were other more lucrative businesses in the same building, on lower floors and easier to reach. Whoever the burglar was, he chose that particular office, but not for the money.

What else do people try to steal? Maybe financial records? But why? Montesori and Klein had several businesses for customers, but nobody was a major player on Wall Street. Business wasn't exactly booming in Detroit, and nobody would find anything in the office that would change that. And they backed up all their files.

So maybe whatever the person was after was personal, not financial. Tony Fortunato's office screamed of generic mediocrity. Accountants didn't tend to go all out on the decorating, so no Picasso or Monet hung on the wall—as if Guthrie would recognize one anyway—and Fortunato would have been wearing his watch if it was expensive. He should ask Shoobie about that, but it probably didn't mean anything. A rare plant? Sure.

Guthrie went upstairs to get more coffee, then picked up his guitar again. His fingers tingled, but in a good way.

What about drugs? If Tony Fortunato were a user, it would have shown up in the autopsy and either Shoobie or Billable Hours Powers would have mentioned it. And the guy was light years from the demographic to be a dealer.

Real estate? Fortunato wasn't a realtor, and Connie Fortunato said nothing about property they planned to buy or sell. August wasn't a busy tax time, so the firm certainly wasn't up to their ears in business for the IRS, either. Guthrie pondered that thought for a minute. No, nobody had mentioned that the feds were auditing anyone, and that surely would have come out, too.

Blackmail? What in the world could Tony have been concealing? And if he did have something, he wouldn't have kept it in such an obvious place as his office, would he?

Guthrie went upstairs for even more coffee—caffeine was one of his basic food groups—and stared out his kitchen window. They were still assuming Tony Fortunato was killed for a reason, which meant a motive that would lead to a particular person. Hot Rod stole the car in the Cass Corridor, an area full of hookers—which he hadn't told Shoobie on advice of counsel—and maybe that bore more thinking.

Why was Tony Fortunato trolling the porn district? Again, nobody mentioned any condoms or a large amount of money missing. In fact, his wallet was in his pants when he was found, cash and credit cards intact. The idea that he'd go there to drum up business for his accounting firm was too stupid to consider.

Was he down there to meet someone? Did he see someone or something that he shouldn't?

Guthrie rinsed out his coffee mug. Too many things didn't fit. The only thing he was sure of was that Hot Rod Lincoln didn't kill Fortunato. Everything else was up for grabs.

He sliced a tomato and broke up the remains of a head of lettuce, his hands busy while his mind veered on ahead. Tony had to be down there for a reason. But nobody had seen whoever left the car there—at least nobody Guthrie'd talked to yet. Maybe someone killed Tony miles away and just dumped the car in the Corridor to throw everyone even farther off the scent. If that was the case, it was working.

Guthrie sliced a carrot into poker chips. Then he grated some cheese and found last night's chicken breast in its container. He cut it into cubes and tossed it into his microwave.

He watched the chicken chunks rotate and wondered what else he could do for the evening except play more guitar. After supper, he'd call Meg and make sure they both knew he'd be over there for dinner and whatever developed after that.

Wait a minute. His phone had the pictures he'd taken of the strange woman at the funeral.

He opened his phone and looked. Yes, three pictures, one of a clear profile. He sent them to his PC upstairs and raced through the salad. Then he went upstairs and studied the pictures on the larger monitor.

The woman was trying hard, but there was something a little bit off. The clothes were black, but they were a little too short or too tight and her make-up was a little too heavy. Guthrie prided himself on not judging people any more than he had to, but this woman bore a tacky vibe even in a photograph. The third picture, the full-length shot, showed her feet in four-inch stilettos. Her stance put her weight all on one leg so her hips canted and showed off her rear to anyone behind her, in this case, Guthrie with his camera.

Who was she and why did she come to Tony Fortunato's funeral but avoid both the graveyard and the gathering at the house? Guthrie found himself with an idea, the kind of long shot that kept gamblers coming back.

Tomorrow, he would show the picture to Valerie Karr. Valerie, AKA Valkyrie, ran his calendar better than he ever had now, and showed her business genius every day, but she was only months out of the circuit. Maybe, just maybe she would know the girl who stood like a stripper on a platform.

One chance in a thousand. For all he knew, the woman in the picture was a nun, nurse, or nuclear physicist.

If Tony Fortunato was indeed hiding something, it might not be in his office, but if someone else was looking for it, maybe he could, too. He opened his contacts list and found the man who specialized in finance, not necessarily according to Supreme Court guidelines. Guthrie sent him Tony Fortunato's name, date of birth and address and set no limits on the information.

He told himself that eliminating bad choices was a kind of progress.

Then he went back downstairs to call Megan Traine.

24

Valerie Karr's hair reminded Guthrie of honey. She'd dyed it back to her normal color the day he hired her, replacing the startling silver that made her sister call her "the evil spawn of the Denver Mint." Now she wore it in an elaborate twist above a navy blouse and khaki slacks. They emphasized her blue eyes, which Guthrie thought were contacts until he worked up the courage to ask.

"No." She shook her head and batted the eyes in question, which made her look innocent as Little Bo Peep. "I'm an all-natural girl."

When they met, they'd both been wearing appropriate work attire, which in her case meant a pair of crimson stilettos—period—so her comment moved them into territory he'd noticed but never deeply explored. After that auspicious beginning, linen slacks were a definite step up—or down, depending on your grading system.

"You usually beat me here, Valerie," he commented.

Valerie drew a Tupperware container from her purse and put it in the mini-fridge.

"I know, Mr. G., but I was reading and I lost track of the time."

"At breakfast?"

Valerie lost her scholarship the previous year when an ex-boyfriend told the dean about her extra-curricular dancing after she dumped him. Guthrie knew she'd been reading all the books from the classes she'd missed and suspected all would be forgiven now that she could pay her own way.

"A book? Or the newspaper?"

"One of the business texts, a chapter about Internet promotion. Since it's a book, it's already about six months out of date before it even gets published."

She sat behind her desk and booted up the computer. Her nails were short so they didn't interfere with her typing speed, over a hundred words a minute, which she seldom needed.

"I know—knew—well, I do still know them, don't I?—a few girls who could do everything he was talking about as cutting edge. Including me. But most of the others probably weren't as subtle about graphics."

He was paying her less for a week than she made stripping on a good weekend, and he could tell she was happier about it. This was less risky, and he'd split a reward with her when the man who tried to take her hostage was in custody. That was the main reason she could go back to school.

"Speaking of graphic." He remembered his phone. "I know this is tacky, but can I send you a couple of pictures, see if you recognize the woman?"

She raised her eyebrows. "A former colleague?"

"I'm not sure." He fumbled for tact, never his strength. "I was at a funeral yesterday and a woman showed up that nobody seemed to recognize. There was just something about her that struck me as a little..."

Valerie pointed at her monitor. He hit "send" and she opened the attachments. She studied the first picture with her fingers tapping on the desk. She couldn't even see the woman's face and Guthrie wondered if she was trying to visualize the body naked. Then he wanted to slap himself.

"Nice shoes." Valerie's voice held no trace of irony. "Um, I see why you wondered about her. It's black, but it's not what my family would wear to a funeral, even if we are Catholic. Well, my mother and grandmother."

"You aren't?"

Valerie stared at her keyboard. "I used to go to Sunday mass, but the...exposure...that's a bad choice of words, isn't it? Well, our little episode last spring ticked my grandmother off. She won't let me be seen in the same church. I tried the later mass for awhile, then just sort of..."

Guthrie watched her keep her eyes on the picture. "Sorry."

"Well, the bright side is I'm still alive to be on my grandmother's *gówno* list, isn't it?"

Guthrie watched her flick to the second picture. The woman was turning toward the exit, her hair obscuring her face but her legs even more revealed. Valerie sighed.

"She looks sad, doesn't she?"

"Well, it's a funeral, and she certainly knew the dead man. Otherwise, why show up?"

"No," Valerie pointed at the screen. "See her shoulders? She's got a nice body, but she's slouching a little. She's depressed and worried. I think her whole life is treating her badly."

"When you say life, do you mean *the* life?"

"Maybe. Probably." Valerie seemed to blink back memories and moved to the third picture.

"Oh, that's Jersey Girl."

"Jersey Girl?"

"I don't know her real name—most of us used stage names—but she wears jerseys from all the local teams when she dances."

"You mean...?"

"Lions and Tigers and bare, oh my." Valerie cocked her head. "What other teams are there in Detroit?"

"The hockey team is the Red Wings."

"Hockey, of course." Valerie snapped her fingers. "She wore a mask sometimes. I thought she was trying to be Jason from the movies and couldn't make that fit the rest of it. Duh."

"So she's a stripper." Several strip joints resided within a few blocks of where Hot Rod found Tony Fortunato's car, and more out on 8 Mile Road, where Valerie and Guthrie met.

"She's a decent dancer." Valerie cleared her throat. "Let me rephrase that. Um, she can move. But she was always pretty obvious about what she was there for. It wasn't to get discovered by America's Got Talent. They don't show her talent on prime time."

Guthrie studied the woman's profile again. *Jersey Girl.* "Go on."

"Well, Jersey is the poster child for what everyone thinks of a stripper. She worked the VIP room a lot. Sometimes, she'd go home with a big tipper, too. Lots of the other girls did it, but she was so obvious..."

Valerie closed the pictures. "She kind of creeped me out."

Guthrie tried to follow that thought and it seemed to lead somewhere. "Do you think you could find out where she's working now? If she is working, I mean?"

Valerie licked her lips and he realized he was asking her to revisit a part of her life she was trying to leave behind.

"I could make a few calls. But I'm not one of the inner circle now, remember."

"I know. But she might know something."

"OK." Valerie looked toward the clock. The office was now officially open.

"Thank you, Valerie."

"I haven't done anything yet." Valerie turned toward her purse and found her phone. How many contacts did she still have?

Guthrie barely booted up his own computer when the phone on his desk chirped.

"Mr. G, it's Mr. Powers"

Guthrie felt Powers's energy even through his receiver. "Billable, I may have a lead. You told me Fortunato still had all his personal effects when he was found, right?"

"That's right. Wallet, keys, watch. Even his phone."

"And the cops still have all of them, I assume?"

"They may have returned them to his wife. Why?"

"Well, the cops don't know where Hot Rod...found the car, but I may have found someone who was in that area, or maybe even where Tony was before that, when someone killed him. I'm trying to track her down now."

"'Her?'"

"Yeah, it's complicated and a real long shot, but I'll let you know if it goes anywhere, all right?"

He wondered if Connie Fortunato would let him look at her dead husband's phone. Or if she'd deleted the logs yet.

Maybe she'd already turned the phone in. But maybe he'd be lucky and find Jersey Girl on his contacts list.

Whatever her name was.

25

Guthrie spent the next three hours playing computer games and waiting for a phone call, any phone call. Megan Traine probably wouldn't find anything else on Fortunato's computers, and even if she did, she couldn't tell him too much. Shoobie Dube might share with Powers if it looked relevant to Hot Rod's defense, but maybe not right away.

The financial wizard was more likely, but maybe not much faster. If Tony Fortunato really did have money floating around that someone was looking for, he'd certainly know how to hide it or disguise it. And if his partners didn't know about it, it meant he was careful. Or completely innocent. How can you skim from other people who do your job as well as you do, especially when you share the same server and back-up system?

"Unless he's not using the same back-up." Guthrie heard himself talking out loud and warned himself that was a symptom. He turned away from his chess game—he only played at level two and still lost consistently—and looked out the window and the clouds covering the sun.

Several patrons dared the clouds and ate outside under big black and yellow umbrellas, probably salads and sandwiches at this time a day.

He took Megan there for their first date. He didn't remember what they ate, but they shared a bottle of red wine.

By the time dessert arrived, they both knew the evening was far from over. She wasn't the first woman he'd been with since his wounding and divorce nearly seven years before, but she was the only one that mattered.

He resumed the chess game and told himself he should have brought in a guitar. But that meant Valerie would hear how badly he played. She might tell Megan.

He lost three games of solitaire and opened another game of Chess before Valerie buzzed him. "Mr. G, I've found Jersey Girl."

She cleared her throat and he knew he'd asked her to walk back into the lions' den. She'd never mention it, but she'd make sure he didn't forget it. Some class reunions are more fun than others.

"She's out at Cherries Jubilee on 8 Mile—she's been there for a week. Before that, she was at Lucky's."

"OK, Cherries Jubilee. I'm guessing she's on tonight?"

"Everybody's working for the weekend, Mr. G. Like the song says."

"Do you have her real name?"

"Christine or Caroline something, nobody seems to know for sure. And her last name is up for grabs. Well, nobody ever knew mine either."

Most of the women probably didn't even know Valerie Karr was shortened from Karpelinski.

"Christine or Caroline or something else with a 'C,'" Guthrie repeated. No way he could do an online search with so little to work with.

"Most of us only used our stage names with each other. But she's at Cherries, which is better than it used to be. I think they've got a new manager."

"Anyone I should say hi to for you?" Guthrie asked. "If I go?"

"Maybe Jack Splat if he's around. He was a bouncer with red hair and a red goatee. Really red."

"Big, I assume?"

"Definitely four-wheel drive. But he might actually help you if you ask him politely. My mother always told me to say 'please.'"

"I'll bet it worked, too, didn't it?"

If Tony was seeing someone, especially a woman who was "material," as Valerie described her, he was spending enough money so it would probably show up.

Guthrie had to break his dinner date at Meg's. He didn't think she'd want to accompany him unless the strip clubs had started featuring piano players.

He was considering going out for lunch when his phone chirped the opening bars of "Mystery Train," Meg's ring tone.

"Hey, Woody." Her voice had pretty much that effect. "You hungry?"

"You're killing me."

"Much, much later." She clicked her tongue. "I've found lots of stuff. I'm giving more details to Detective Dube, but let me give you the big picture."

"Does it involve money?"

"Lots. I can't tell how much, but the guy has a slew of different bank accounts, and they're all under different names and with different passwords. I almost wore out our toys here cracking through, and I may not have found everything yet."

"Encrypted, I assume?"

"Tighter than a duck's ass. I can't get at the amounts and I'm not a forensic accountant, but I think he's dipping from somewhere, maybe several somewheres. It's so tangled I haven't been able to follow it. But it looks like he was spreading money around, a little here, a little there, not enough in one place so anyone would pay much attention."

"When did it start? Can you tell that?"

"Um...I think early this year, but that's just a guess. Everything is on his laptop, which has a ton of extra memory. I wouldn't be surprised if there's another hard drive somewhere, too. His office PC doesn't seem to have anything. Well, that's because his partners might have gone on there for something."

Guthrie felt himself starting to sweat. His adrenaline always kicked in when he got a scent.

"And you think we're talking cash?"

"Well, it's easier to hide. You go to stocks or securities or something, you leave a paper trail that stands out like a runway."

"That reminds me," he said. "Valerie tracked down another lead for me, maybe a witness."

"Speaking of runways."

"Um, as a matter of fact." He thought his phone felt cooler in his hand.

"This is going to be good, isn't it?"

"Well, I don't know how good it is, but we've found a woman we might be able to link to Tony Fortunato. Maybe a girlfriend. I'm not sure yet."

Megan's voice became soft, a feather brushing across his cheek. "And your receptionist tracked her down. Why does that fill me with fear and wonder? We're talking about ladies of a certain professional strata, aren't we?"

"Um, well, since you put it that way, yeah. I think the woman is a dancer."

"Stripper, Woody. Women in ballet are dancers. Valerie and her ilk may be very good at what they do, but it's about the clothes coming off. So you think you've found another stripper."

"I'm not a hundred percent positive, but..."

"You need to examine her, don't you? Undercover as it were."

"Um...I'm sorry. I'm going to have to cancel out tonight."

"No. You're going to be late tonight. If it's extremely late, I'll be in bed, but that shouldn't be a problem."

"You're not mad?"

The silence on the other end felt even colder.

"I'm furious. I wanted a nice relaxing dinner at my house, maybe get a good foot massage, talk to the cats, watch a sentimental DVD, then go upstairs and have my man make slow sweet love to me until the wee small hours. But he's blowing me off—let me rephrase that—so he can check out—a woman with conservative tastes in apparel, who will cost a lot more than I will."

"You're worth more," he offered.

"Damn' right." She sighed. "I know, this is what you do. And it's the only reason we even met. Go."

"Sorry."

"You be careful. And don't do anything stupid. Maybe your receptionist can write you a...pass of some kind. Are you taking a gun?"

"A...? No, I wasn't planning on it."

"Why not? You're a private investigator working on a murder. These people might be dangerous."

"I don't know that the woman's really involved. And a bouncer would have a serious issue with my packing heat. He wouldn't let me in."

Megan was silent for a long time.

"You be very careful."

"I will."

"Promise me."

"I promise."

"All right. I'll have a salad tonight and you can have a big meal tomorrow."

"I'm sorry."

"You should be." He heard her sigh again.

"Another evening of piano."

26

Connie didn't remember eating lunch but a plate and glass stood in the dish drainer so she must have eaten something. Tobi had the kids at the beach and Connie was ready to light a candle for her. After yesterday, she needed to be alone, the keening of the relatives still ringing in her ears. And she'd had to stay more or less sober. Nothing worse than a sloppy widow. A sloppy bride, OK, but everyone knew how she was going to finish the night anyway, so what the hell.

She opened the refrigerator and stared at the containers of left-over cold cuts and crudités, enough veggies to feed a family of rabbits for a month. And sandwiches and cheese slices so she wouldn't need groceries until Christmas. Then she realized she wouldn't be wondering what to get Tony for Christmas this year, and she and the kids would be opening their presents without him hovering around taking pictures.

God, what do you give kids who've just lost their father?

She stood before the open door until the refrigerator's motor kicked on. She must have had some of the cold cuts for lunch. And maybe some wine. A bottle of red and a bottle of white both stood open in the door. Merlot and chardonnay, sounded like a couple of female singers. Connie picked the white one and pulled another glass from the cupboard.

Tony's clothes could go to consignment stores. He wore good stuff, especially shoes, so those might be worth something. His camera, she might keep that, it took better pictures than her cell phone, she just had to read the manual, longer than the books she read Cliff's Notes for back in high school. Maybe Barry and the Jew would take his desk and some of his office stuff.

His golf clubs, which he almost never used, or his tennis racket, when was the last time he'd set foot on a tennis court, when they were dating? Tony wasn't much of an athlete, except for jumping into their pool for half an hour over the course of the summer. He liked to lie out there with his iPod and read *Forbes* and financial shit, like being near the pool would keep him buff. At least he had a good tan, but he had that dark complexion anyway. Exercise wasn't his thing, except maybe in the bedroom when he was in the mood, but that wasn't anywhere near as often as it used to be.

It already felt like evening. It was great Tobi got the kids out of the house, but it made the place silent as a mausoleum.

Shit.

Connie stared out the door at the pool. Nobody around, she could go out there and swim, but the sky was getting a little darker. With her luck, she'd be out there two minutes and it would pour.

She drifted into the living room and stared at the entertainment unit. Tony's DVDs and CDs. Maybe she could sell most of those, too. Or give them away. She never quite got the point of a big screen HDTV and a full home entertainment unit. Entertainment was why you went out. You had dinner and saw a show or went dancing—at least Tony liked to dance. Home entertainment, her ass. A movie wasn't a real movie without a bag of popcorn to go with it.

Her cell chirped and she recognized the number.

"Connie, how are you feeling?" Barry Montesori's voice dripped concern.

"I'm just wandering around the place, looking at stuff I gotta get rid of. The place feels big as a shopping mall. And it's so quiet..."

"Maybe put on some music or something?"

"Everything we've got'll remind me of Tony." Connie looked around and tried to remember where she'd left her wine glass.

"I know, it's awful. At least the cops caught the guy."

"Maybe." Connie found her glass on top of the turntable. Tony didn't even have any vinyl, why did he need a fucking turntable?

"What do you mean?"

"I don't know. That detective. And the police still hanging around. I keep asking myself what if they've got the wrong man, the guy that killed my Tony's gonna walk? That's just so..."

"Yeah," Barry sighed. "That would really suck."

Connie needed a refill. "What's going on at your end?"

"Crazy. The cops were here the other day—I told you about that—they took Tony's computer. Len and I are still trying to put together all his clients, figure out who we haven't talked to yet, catch up on everything. What a nightmare. Thank God we back everything up."

Connie opened the refrigerator and poured chardonnay almost to the brim.

"Listen, I'm not going to be able to get free tonight."

"What do you mean?" Connie remembered it was Friday. She and Tony might have gone out to dinner tonight, maybe even take the kids. Tobi had Friday night off, whatever the hell she did. She was old enough, she didn't have a curfew, and she wasn't family anyway. Connie gave her a key and figured if she could answer the bugle Saturday morning, everything was fine. Actually, nothing was fine now.

"Well, Sindee wants to go somewhere, cheer up a little. Yesterday really got to her."

It really got to me, too. Connie didn't say it. *Poor bitch, needing your husband to take you somewhere now. At least you got a husband.*

"The kids are here, maybe we'll watch a DVD or something." Yeah, one of Tony's stupid action things. Or fratboy humor. Thirty-six, he still busted a gut at fart jokes.

"Sure. I was hoping...well, we have a lot to talk over, don't we?"

"Yeah. Maybe tomorrow. Maybe you can tell Sindee you're gonna help me sort through Tony's office stuff, something like that."

"Yeah, maybe. Sindee, she and I..."

Connie felt something freeze up inside. She put her glass down again and gripped her phone with both hands.

"What do you mean, you and Sindee?"

"Nothing. I mean, well, you know..."

"No, Barry. I don't know. I thought you and I...what the hell are you saying?"

"Nothing, we'll talk tomorrow."

"Fuck tomorrow. Talk to me right now. I'm here, I'm alone. Say it."

"Connie, it's not that simple. We've got to look at the big picture, you know."

"Damn right, that's what I thought we've been doing. And when Tony died…"

"But you know how that looks, don't you? If we do something now, the cops'll think…"

"But we didn't. We've both got alibis. Hell, we didn't even know it happened until…"

Connie felt the phone slipping through her fingers and grabbed it tight. "Wait a minute. You didn't know, did you? About Tony? Until those kids found his car?"

"No, no, of course not. Christ, honey, what do you think I'm like?"

For the first time, Connie stopped to think about her answer. Then she didn't say anything.

"Listen, Connie, I'll tell Sindee I'm helping, I'll be over, early afternoon. I'll call you, OK?"

Barry ended the call and Connie stared at her phone until it felt too heavy to hold. She put it down and felt the room tilt a little. She leaned against the counter and breathed deeply until everything settled again.

Barry was getting cold feet. She knew she and Tony were drifting apart, she and Barry finding how much they needed each other, but how to break it to Tony, with that pre-nup. Then he died, it looked like they were out of the woods, but they'd have to be careful, and now Barry was sending out warning signals.

If Tony was dead and Barry didn't leave Sindee, what was she going to do?

Connie drained her glass in two long swallows. Then she went upstairs to change into shopping clothes. She had to get out of this place.

27

The storm held off longer than Tobi expected, but when it came, it kicked the door in without a warrant. Thunder rolled over the clouds and squeezed out raindrops big as quarters, followed by a spectacular bolt of lightning that lit up the entire eastern horizon, jagged steps you could use for a fire escape. The thunder shook the beach and Tobi was surprised the shoreline didn't melt into the lake. Evan the lifeguard blew a blast on his whistle and Tobi turned to the kids.

"Let's go, guys."

"We're not guys," Patty said. "At least, not last time I looked."

Tobi threw a glare at her that bounced off without even leaving a smudge.

"You know what I mean. It's a term of endearment."

Patty rolled her eyes and tossed books, chips and sunscreen into their tote bag. Tobi watched Evan doing the same, except he had binoculars and a big cooler, too, probably about a case of Gatorade or whatever he drank.

"Stay here a sec," she told Patty.

"Why?" Chuck demanded. "It's raining, remember? That's why we're packing up."

"You're going to make some girl a terrific husband," Tobi told him. "You've already got the PIA attitude down."

"What's PIA?"

"Pain in the ass," Patty told him.

"I'm gonna tell Mom you said a bad word."

Patty stuck out her tongue.

Tobi pointed toward the hedge. "Go to the cottage. Maybe this will blow over in a few minutes and we can come back."

She strode over to Evan, who draped a huge shirt over his shoulders. Water dripped off his floppy white hat.

"We've got a cottage over there," she told him. "You want to chill with us until this is over?"

He looked at the sky like he didn't think that would be any time soon and she flashed him her best smile, the one she used for her ingénue auditions, all she needed was pigtails and freckles.

"Sure. Thanks."

His chest was the rich brown of a potato skin. He tucked his cooler under one arm and put hers on top of it. She thought he was going to pick her up and tuck her under his other one, but he waved her on.

Once safely inside, they stared through the kitchen windows at rain so thick they might have been in a car wash. The thunder might have been upstairs.

"Whoa." Evan looked around at the kitchen. "This your family's?"

"The kids' parents." Tobi watched Patty and Chuck abandon the tote bag in the living room and charge up the stairs. "Yesterday was their father's funeral, I told you about that, right?"

"Yeah. That really sucks. They seem to be handling it OK, though."

"It was rough. After the funeral, about two hundred people came back to the house, old, you know, the women with the blue hair, everyone crying and moaning. I mean, I'm not Catholic, and it seemed pretty much over the top. Their mom and I thought we should get them out of the house, away from everything for today."

"Sure." Evan looked around the place. Tobi wondered if it belonged to one of the families before Tony and Connie got married. She didn't think accountants made all that much money, but Tony Fortunato seemed to be doing well. Swimming pool and all back at the house. Come to think of it, some of the old people at the funeral seemed pretty well-off, too, nice cars, good suits. She knew designer labels when she saw them.

"You really think this is going to blow over?" Evan watched rain drumming on the windowpane.

"I'm hoping," Tobi said. Thunder answered.

Patty and Chuck burst back into the room.

"We're hungry."

"You ate half an hour ago," Tobi reminded them.

"I'm always hungry when I'm in the fresh air," Chuck said. "I guess it burns off calories or something."

"Like you need to worry." Tobi thought the kid's metabolism could power a rock festival.

She looked in the refrigerator. A couple of Tupperware containers lurked in the back, probably old enough to vote. A few condiments stood in the door, though, catsup, mustard, a jar of pickle slices that didn't look too fuzzy. And a full pack of hot dog buns. She checked the freezer and found hot dogs, too, six of them, still in their sealed plastic.

"Let me toss these in the microwave to thaw for a few minutes."

"Yeah!" Chuck stuck his head under her arm. "Hey, there's pop, too. Ginger ale and Bud."

"That's not pop, dummy." Patty slapped Chuck's arm. "That's beer."

"I was being funny."

"Not."

Tobi looked back at Evan.

"Would you like a hot dog or two? And maybe a beer?"

He looked at the window where the rain continued as if it had all the time in the world.

"Sure, thanks. I don't think this is going to let up for awhile." He looked around the room and found the clock on the microwave. "Most people'd be leaving in another couple of hours anyway."

"Sure." Tobi tore open the hot dogs and put them into the microwave. "What do you think, maybe a minute?"

Evan pulled out the bag and hefted it. "They look like they been there awhile. Maybe two minutes on medium? Then we can check again."

"OK."

They listened to the whir and watched the numbers count down. Tobi tried to figure out what to do with her hands. Crossing her forearms always made it look like she was trying to draw attention to her breasts, which she didn't think were that great anyway. Every time she was on stage, she had the same problem. That and fidgeting with her right foot. Three different directors mentioned that. She knew it meant she wasn't really focused on what she was supposed to be doing.

"You're the kids' nanny?"

"Oh. Just for the summer. I go back to school in another three weeks."

"Wayne State, right?" His wet shirt stuck to his chest and made him resemble a superhero, The Incredible Hulk.

"Right. And you're at...Eastern?"

"You got it. And you're in theater? I thought most of the actors worked in the summer. You know, musicals and stuff."

Tobi felt her face heat up. "There weren't any roles around that looked that interesting, so I didn't audition. But I'm hoping I'm in the senior production of *Hamlet* this year. I'm still hoping to hear about how I did on the audition, any day now. I've been doing lots of research."

"*Hamlet*?" Evan shook his head. "I could never get Shakespeare. We had to read Macbeth in high school, it might as well have been Chinese."

"No, it's really not that bad. You just have to forget that it's poetry and look at the story."

He shrugged. "But it's that old English stuff. I don't get it."

"Actually it's modern English." She watched his eyes start to glaze over. "But Shakespeare does take some getting used to."

The microwave beeped and she stuck a fork in one of the hot dogs. "What do you think?"

He studied them for a minute. "They seem OK. Maybe warm the buns up in the oven, too?"

"That sounds good." She turned the oven to warm while he looked toward the arch to the rest of the place. "You want me to show you around?"

"Sure." He let her lead him toward the living room. "You stay here overnight?"

"I guess you could, there are beds upstairs, but there's not a lot to do here, the TV's older than I am, they don't have cable or Internet."

"Uh-huh." She could feel his eyes flicking around at the old paint and few pictures on the walls, the door frames that were settling a little so the doors scraped on the floor. Most rooms just had a throw rug in the middle of the floor, the doors all dragged on them.

"See?" She pointed to the TV, an old portable with rabbit-ears. It sat on built-in bookcases to the right of the old stone fireplace.

"Yeah." He leaned down and she checked out his butt. Outstanding. "The fireplace is cool, though, big stones. Someone knew what he was doing with this. How old is the place?"

"Beats the hell out of me." She pointed to the railing up the stairs. "The woodwork there's nice, too."

He leaned in and nodded. "Are the beds antique or anything?"

"You wish." She led him upstairs. The two rooms were small. She looked at the larger one and realized the bed looked mussed. The sheets probably needed washing anyway. If it was made up, the moisture off the lake would make them a little funky, even with the windows closed.

He looked at the hatch in the ceiling near the chimney. "Too bad there's not a fireplace up here, too. Be nice and cozy on a day like this. Or night."

She tried to imagine it, a warm fire and snuggling under a quilt. It felt a little unreal, like a set in one of her plays, cozy until you stepped into the wings and saw all the cables and ties behind the flats.

They went back down stairs where the kids found an old game of Monopoly. It looked like half the game pieces were missing. Tobi spread the hot dogs on a plate and put them into the microwave. The rain was coming down even harder.

Evan separated the buns and laid them on the grill in the oven.

"You said something about an audition?"

"Oh, for *Hamlet*."

"Yeah. How does that work? I mean, what do you have to do?"

"Learn a couple of speeches and act them out, show them what you'd be like. But they wouldn't let me do anything from *Hamlet*, I had to pick another play. So I did Viola from *Twelfth Night*."

He shook his head. "I don't know that one."

"Oh, it's fun. About shipwrecked twins, a boy and a girl. They both think the other one is dead, and the girl pretends to be a guy so nobody will, you know, mess with her. They get mistaken for each other a few times, and another woman falls in love with the girl because she really believes she is a man."

"People were that dumb then?"

"No, it's a comedy. Shakespeare has girls pretending to be guys in a lot of the plays. And since men were playing all the roles, it makes it even funnier, a guy pretending to be a girl pretending to be a guy."

He shook his head. "Crazy."

"But fun." She felt herself wanting to make him understand. "Hey, you want me to show you my monologue, the one I did to get the part?"

He shrugged. "Sure. But I won't understand it."

"Yeah, you will, it's easy. See, this is Viola, the girl dressed as a guy, and the woman who falls in love with her sends her servant to return a ring to him. Well, her. But Viola didn't really give her a ring. It's Olivia—the real woman—her way of telling Viola she wants to see her—him again."

Evan shook his head. "I'm lost already."

"No," Tobi said. "It makes sense when you see it all. Watch."

She shook out her hands and bounced on the balls of her feet a few times. She took a deep breath and let it out, feeling the cool air all the way down to her diaphragm. Then she knelt to pick up the invisible ring from under the kitchen table and stood again. She looked at Evan and let her eyes go wide.

"I left no ring with her. What means this lady?
Fortune forbid my outside have not charmed her!
She made good view of me; indeed, so much
That sure methought her eyes had lost her tongue,
For she did speak in starts distractedly."

She rolled her eyes toward the ceiling and told herself not to be too broad. Evan wasn't used to Shakespeare, but that didn't mean he was an idiot. She looked off toward her right and nodded slowly while she let herself realize the truth and move her into the middle of the speech.

"Disguise, I see thou art a wickedness
Wherein the pregnant enemy does much."

She felt herself pumping out energy as she tried to make him live the scene along with her.

"How will this fadge? My master loves her dearly..."

She strolled to her right, then returned even more slowly, feeling Evan's eyes on her while she led up to the finish.

"O time, though must untangle this, not I.
It is too hard a knot for me t'untie."

She caught herself before thanking the auditors and walking briskly off-stage.

"Notice how the last two lines rhyme? That's Shakespeare's way of telling the audience it's the end of the scene."

"They'd actually notice that?" He crossed his arms across that massive chest.

"Oh, yeah. Most of the people couldn't read, but that meant they were really good listeners. You know how little kids seem to have amazing memories? That's because they have to get it when they hear it. The people in Shakespeare's time were like that."

"OK." He frowned for a minute. "Uh, she's figuring out what she's gonna do next, right? 'Cause she didn't expect the other woman—what's her name, Olivia?—to fall for her."

"You got it. See, it's not that hard. And Shakespeare gives an actor lots of clues about how to play the lines."

"How do you mean?"

"See how the rhythm changes in the middle? That line about 'she loves me sure' has four strong beats in a row, that's where I realize what's going on. The early part is kind of regular while I'm figuring it out, then the rest is me figuring out what I'm going to do about it."

He uncrossed his arms and looked down at her. "What was that one word you said, like fudge?"

"Fadge? That's like turn out or succeed. She's asking what's going to happen now, and at the end she realizes she's just going to have to go with it and find out."

"Wow." He shook his head again. His chin reminded her of statues of the Greek gods.

"You got to know all that to act Shakespeare?"

"Oh, you do it in everyday speech too, but if you go through the plays and do it, it makes them a lot easier to understand. I try to do it while I'm learning a speech because it helps me."

"That seems like a lot of work just to be in a play. Do you get a lot of money for this?"

"Well, not in school, no, they don't pay. In theater, once you're equity—union—you make some, but nowhere near as much as you do in films."

"So why do it, if it doesn't pay much?"

She heard that from her family, too. "I don't know how to say it. It's just...you get up in front of those people, and you're telling them a banging story, bringing them along with you. It's like...I don't know. It's so great, like nothing else I've ever found. You know, like they're with you and you're with them..."

"Sounds sort of like really good sex."

She glanced toward the living room where the kids were making airplanes out of the Monopoly money and sailing them around the room.

"I never thought about it that way. I guess you're right."

He nodded. "It was cool, though. I think I understood what you were saying, too, except that part about her eyes losing her tongue."

"Yeah, she was looking at me so hard she couldn't speak. And she seemed distracted when she talked after that. It's how I figure out she's fallen in love with me. It's pretty easy when you get into it. The whole play kind of builds on the first few minutes. It's a lot of fun."

"And *Hamlet*. That's fun too?"

"Oh, God, it would be. If I get the part."

"Who's the girl in *Hamlet*? Or is it another girl pretending to be a guy?"

"No. Ophelia's Hamlet's girlfriend early in the play, but he dumps her and she goes insane. She finally drowns herself."

"Whoa, downer."

"Yeah, but she has this amazing speech when she's crazy, all about flowers and her dead father."

She realized she was losing him again.

"Let's check the hot dogs."

She watched him open the oven door and wink at her.

"And your buns, too."

28

Danny gave Connie Fortunato about thirty yards before he got out of his own car to follow her. She walked like she had a major bug up her ass so he didn't dare let her have more space. At the rate she was swishing those shorts, if he lost sight of her, she'd lap him twice before he figured out which way she'd gone. As soon as she passed through the revolving doors, he sped up.

Three strides in and he had to swerve around a group of teen-aged girls squealing over a display window. Connie Fortunato walked straight to the escalator and he stayed close enough to watch her ass glide up to the second level, purse on her hip that looked weighed down with credit cards. She seemed to know where she was going, and he hoped she was meeting someone, not just buying shit. She marched down the level, passing Liz Claiborne, Verizon, Ruby Tuesday, Diamond Jubilee, Abercrombie & Fitch, and Victoria's Secret. When she swerved into Nordstrom's, Danny sank to a bench inside to catch his breath and watch her move into the shoe department. He wished he'd brought a newspaper, but he looked enough like a bored husband so nobody would notice him.

He turned away and found her reflection in a display case. She was wearing a bright red blouse and white shorts, so the red was easy to track. And those shorts fitted her like a tattoo. He wondered if she had one, then decided the pants were so tight he'd be able to see it through them.

A sales clerk came over and gushed like she was offering up her first born and her fingernails for the chance to help. She nodded a couple of times and hustled off somewhere, returning with four boxes. *Shoes. Women and shoes.* Danny figured it had to be genetic. Women needed more shoes than he had tee shirts, but at least he wore them all pretty often. Women, some shoes, they only wore them once. He wondered if Connie'd ever wear the shoes she wore to her husband's funeral again. Maybe if she buried a second husband.

She walked around in one pair, stopped by a mirror to examine how her heels looked—like anyone really gave a rat's ass about a woman's heels—and strode back to her chair to switch to another pair. The clerk smiled like she was drinking piss and put the first pair back into the tissue paper.

Danny's phone vibrated and he pulled it out. *Number blocked. Naturally.*

"Yeah?"

"Where are you?"

"I'm following the woman. OK with you?"

"Are you learning anything?"

"Yeah. The day after you bury your hubby, you buy shoes. At Nordstrom's."

"I see. How is your investigation with the nanny faring?"

Faring. Danny wondered if the guy said "excellenting" and "gooding," too.

"I'm working on it, all right? Why, you got a better idea?"

"As a matter of fact. Do you remember where you picked Anthony up?"

"Anthony? Oh, Tony. Yeah, why?"

"You understand why you found him there, don't you? Where I predicted you would."

"Uh...yeah."

"No, you don't. Just say so, Daniel. There's no shame in asking intelligent questions."

"All right, yeah, it was on 8 Mile. And I dumped the car on Cass when I was...through."

"Very good. Do you know why Anthony was out in that section of 8 Mile?"

Danny thought about it. Nothing out there but a few fast food places, most of which had never seen days good enough to call "better," some discount stores, skanky motels and strip joints like where he tended bar.

Connie Fortunato stood by the mirror and pointed at the shoes she was trying on. The clerk nodded hard enough to get whiplash.

"Think about it, Daniel."

"OK, it was out on the Boulevard. Near...wait a minute. You're telling me...?"

"Exactly. Anthony had a girlfriend."

"A dancer?"

"Very good."

"So why the hell didn't you tell me before? I coulda been talking to her instead of dicking around with the wife. And the freakin' nanny."

"It's good to cover all your bases, Daniel. And I don't know the woman's name, but I know it has something to do with sports."

"Sports?"

Danny tried to shuffle everything in his head. He was following the dead guy's wife and trying to check out the nanny—half the wife's age—and now he's hearing about a third broad?

Connie Fortunato whipped out a credit card and the clerk slid the shoe box into a plastic bag big enough to hold a compact car. Danny figured the idea was if you give people a really big bag, they'll keep buying stuff to fill it up.

"What do you mean, sports? Like baseball or football or something? You know how many teams there are in Detroit? Just pro teams, never mind all the freakin' colleges around here. U of M, Eastern, Wayne, Michigan State, U of D..."

"The clock is running, Daniel. And that is not a sports metaphor."

Connie took the bag and marched toward the mall entrance again.

Danny stood to follow her.

"I gotta go."

"Keep me informed." The voice disappeared into crackling and Danny slid his phone back into his pocket.

A girlfriend. Tony was porking someone else, his wife didn't even seem to know it. Or did she? Maybe they had a deal of some kind, something kinky. What if the girlfriend and the wife...No. Don't even think of going there. Tony Fortunato looked like a little math geek, but he must've had a helluva pencil. The wife was getting a little soft in the caboose, but she was still hot. Maybe that's why she was getting new shoes, get back into the hunt.

Danny looked up, directly into the eyes of a guy about his own size. The guy wore dark slacks and a blue polo shirt, a Tigers cap on his head. Danny wouldn't have even noticed him except that the instant they made eye contact, the other guy flicked his eyes off to the right.

Oh, shit.

Danny watched the guy for a few seconds more, then glanced toward the escalator in time to see Connie's red blouse at the top. He hustled after her, keeping one eye on the guy in the Tigers cap.

Connie stopped at the top step and Danny leaned over the parapet and looked down at the people below, baseball caps and straw hats and a few low-cut blouses. Once in a while someone with sunglasses pushed up on their head so the dark lenses seemed to stare at him.

Out of the corner of his eye, he saw Tigers Cap amble over toward him, keeping the same distance he himself kept from the woman.

Connie pulled out her phone and talked for a couple of minutes. Danny wondered who she'd be talking to at this time, a day after the funeral. More than that, he wondered who the guy was who was following him.

Now he knew just how fast that clock was ticking.

Connie stuffed her phone back into that huge purse and stepped onto the moving stairs. Danny moved to follow and some woman with a baby carriage cut in front of him so suddenly that he almost ran over her. He stepped around her and saw the top of Connie's head vanish below the floor line.

A pair of grannies shambled in front of him, where the hell did they come from. He cut around them and reached the top of the escalator, Connie already stepping off the bottom, those little white shorts almost glowing. Danny stepped on the stairs.

By the time he reached the bottom, Connie was out of sight again. *Jesus H. Christ.* What if she was still meeting someone? He looked both ways, saw a red blouse and headed after it. Where did all the people come from, they hadn't been here half an hour ago. He sped up and got close enough to see the red wasn't Connie, it was some girl in a tee shirt the same friggin' red. *Shit, if he lost her...Christ, what else could go wrong?*

He decided to wait near the door, pick her up again on the way out. He stopped at a Barnes and Noble and bought a

Sports Illustrated, never letting the revolving doors out of his sight, then sank onto another bench.

The big guy he'd seen upstairs pulled out a newspaper and leaned against a pillar. He didn't seem to care if Danny saw him or not.

Danny was only a page into an article on Miguel Cabrera when Connie materialized with another shopping bag. She stopped by the door and reached into her purse and pulled out a folding umbrella. She pushed through the door and he saw the thing blossom above her.

Shit, it was raining now, too?

He looked through the glass. Sure enough, rain coming down heavy enough to give Noah a hard-on. He watched Connie Fortunato walk down the aisle under that umbrella and get into her car, that same fucking Mercedes like her dead husband. His own car was a good ten cars beyond hers, and he was pretty sure he'd left all his windows cracked.

Son of a bitch.

29

Guthrie parked his car between two ATVs and approached the entrance of Cherries Jubilee with the sun drilling between his shoulder blades. He figured if he showed up early, there wouldn't be much of a crowd yet so he could talk to Jersey Girl—whatever her real name was—more easily. Besides, he'd rather spend his time with Megan. Her idea of "something special" for dessert would leave anything he found here in the dust.

The bouncer had three inches on Guthrie and probably twice his width; the sun turned his scalp a reddish orange as though his head was on fire. He took Guthrie's ten dollars and called it a "cover charge" without the slightest hint of irony and stamped the back of his left hand with a red logo that might have been a cluster of cherries.

Inside, the place smelled of cigarettes, sweat, beer, and "other," all fighting for dominance. All three platforms seemed to be in the pink of condition, but none of the women seemed to have shed a sports jersey. Guthrie meandered to the bar and ordered a Bud while he studied the layout of the room. The sound booth lay to his right and cameras faced each other from two corners. Hot pink letters over an arch to his right said "full nude." Another had a shiny curtain but no label.

When the bartender slid his glass over, Guthrie slid him a twenty and nodded toward the sign.

"Does Jersey Girl dance here or in there?"

The bartender took the twenty and returned two fives. "In there."

Guthrie didn't leave a tip. If these prices were typical, he had to be frugal. Valerie suggested he bring seven hundred in tens and twenties, but now he wondered if that would be enough.

He seemed to be one of the smaller men in the place, but probably in better shape than all except the bouncers. One of the requirements seemed to be either a beer gut or pattern baldness.

The beer tasted weak. At ten bucks for a glass of watered beer, how much did you clear in a good weekend? And how much did the women make? Guthrie remembered his last two times in a strip club. They both involved Valerie, and both times he'd had a gun.

He didn't have it tonight, though. Now he wore a Tigers tee shirt and cap above jeans with sneakers. He had a flannel out in the car where it always stayed along with three hats and three pairs of sunglasses. He kept them in case he had to follow someone alone and change appearance to keep them from noticing. He had his Sig Sauer locked under his front seat, too, but it wouldn't do him much good there.

He slid his glass onto the bar and the bartender raised eyebrows like burnt French fries.

"If you're here for Jersey Girl, there's no alcohol in the fully nude section. That's the law."

"Can't blame a guy for trying."

"Nope. We got Coke, ginger ale, Sprite..."

"Never mind."

Guthrie wondered if the PA system had a treble setting. The bass and drums could pass for an artillery barrage, but he couldn't begin to guess what the song was. Boomp whump boomp whump whump boomp boomp whump didn't narrow it down much.

In the "Fully Nude" area, the platforms were slightly higher and they had lights at the four corners aiming upward so you could enjoy the show more fully. Guthrie wondered if gynecologists trained here.

Two women swirled their hips on the platforms, both vaguely in rhythm to that artillery beat. One was African American and the other looked Latina. The black woman seemed proud of her enhanced breasts. It seemed to work for her, too. Bills almost covered the platform. She spun to grab her ankles and look through her legs at a guy who had to weigh three hundred pounds. He grinned and tucked a bill into her strappy sandal.

The music stopped a minute later and a tinny voice blared from the PA.

"Juicy, let's give it up for Juicy. Thank you very much. And now, for gentlemen of taste, will you please welcome our own Motor City minx, The Jersey Girl."

Guthrie recognized the woman he'd seen at Tony Fortunato's funeral as soon as the light hit her face. Same chin, same hungry eyes. With nothing between her stiletto heels and the bottom of her Red Wings jersey, her legs seemed ten feet long, but Guthrie remembered she was only medium height. She was only a medium good dancer, too.

None of the guys around her platform seemed to mind, though. By the time she'd shed the hot pants, the jersey and her bra to show the sequin in her piercing, Guthrie estimated she had fifty dollars on the floor. He watched until she seemed ready to finish and swept the room until he spotted another bouncer lounging under a camera by a hallway with an "Employees Only" sign, probably the dressing rooms. His hair and goatee belonged on a fire truck.

"Sup?" the guy said. Verbal skills weren't big in the strip joints.

"Jack Splat, right?"

The guy nodded.

"Valkyrie told me to say hello."

"No shit."

"Can you tell Jersey I want a private dance when she's finished?"

"You shy?" The guy looked down at Guthrie. In winter, maybe he moonlighted as a ski slope.

"I can't talk loud enough for her to hear me over the music." Guthrie held up a twenty and the guy took it. They watched the woman lower herself so her crotch was at the same level as a bald guy's face. She spread her knees a little wider. He reached in with a bill and she looked like she was laughing. The guy reached a little farther and she stood abruptly.

The bouncer was there in four strides and grabbed the guy before anyone else even saw him approach. He plucked the bill from the guy's hand and tossed it on the platform before striding toward the exit arch with his prey kicking his legs helplessly. When he returned, he swung by the platform and leaned close to the stripper. She saw Guthrie and gave him a smile that made him sorry that his gun was out in the car. She said something to the bouncer, who returned to Guthrie.

"VIP room in ten minutes." He pointed toward the arch with the curtain across it.

"Our ladies expect you to buy them some refreshment. Out at the bar. Tell them it's for Jersey."

Guthrie returned and bought a bottle he knew was probably ginger ale and watered down more than his beer. When he returned to the curtain, the bouncer was waiting for him.

"Room rental's two-fifty."

"What if I just want to talk?"

"You're still using the room. Anything else is between you and the lady."

Guthrie counted out twelve twenties and a ten and slid into a room that featured dark as the main theme, a few platforms and couches that might have been found along a curb, and two cubicles big enough to hold a futon.

Jersey girl appeared a few minutes later. She wore a Detroit Lions jersey, number sixty-nine, and white biker shorts. Up close, Guthrie could smell a heavy dose of a perfume he couldn't name over the sweat from her recent dance.

"Hi, honey." Her voice reminded him of Jessica Rabbit with less class. "Oh, good, you've brought me a present. A lady gets thirsty out there, you know?"

"Sure." Guthrie watched her pour two plastic glasses and they both pretended to sip. "I wanted to talk to you."

"Talk. That's a good start. I like what you're saying, we can do more than talk. But let's prime the pump."

Guthrie held up a twenty. She frowned and he held up another one. She smiled and poured more liquid into his glass.

"Why don't we sit down, honey."

He sat next to her on one of the battered couches and watched her slide her shoe off and run her foot up his shin.

"What do you want to talk about? I love a man who knows how to use his mouth."

"I'm hoping you can use yours, too."

"Oh, I can, baby, I can. But that's going to cost you another two hundred. For starters."

"I figured." In the dim light, the girl's features looked almost soft. Her eyes glittered and he wondered if she'd fueled up before coming out here. "We've got a mutual friend. Well, had, that is."

"Mutual friend?" She screwed up her face. "You mean like on Facebook?"

"Something like that." He only had about two hundred dollars left. He held another twenty in front of him and the girl didn't even look at it. He added another. "Tony Fortunato."

"Tony." She reached for the bills before the name registered and her hand froze. "What do—? Where do you know Tony from?"

"Work," Guthrie said. "He told me about you."

"No. Uh-uh. No fucking way. Tony and me...who the fuck are you?"

"I'm a friend of his," he said. "I'm wondering what you know about that last night."

"Nothing. I don't know shit. Who the fuck...?"

"He was supposed to meet you, wasn't he? That night. But someone took him away before you met him."

The girl stood, her head swiveling violently back and forth.

"No. No no no. I don't know you. Get the fuck out of here."

"I'm OK, Jersey. Valkyrie will vouch for me. You know Valkyrie, right? Dancer with silver hair."

"Valkyrie? No, she's gone. She split. That guy tried to...No, I don't know you. Get out of here."

"Listen, it's OK." Guthrie saw the girl look toward the curtain. "I'm willing to pay, but I want to know about Tony."

"Jack!" The girl's voice made Guthrie's ears ring. Before the echo subsided, the bouncer from outside appeared. He should have been wearing a football jersey, too, but he could accommodate three digits.

"You bothering the lady?" His fists looked bigger than Guthrie's head.

"I just wanted to talk," he said. "Ask a few questions, no big deal."

"She doesn't think so. Come on, asshole, let's move it out."

"Hey, I've still got half a bottle left, and lots of time."

"There's no clock. C'mon, move it."

The guy telegraphed his punch. Guthrie sidestepped and felt the breeze when a wrecking ball missed his chin by a fraction of an inch. He ducked back to the table and grabbed the bottle of fake champagne. When the guy approached, he feinted left. When the guy turned that way, Guthrie swung the bottle and caught him solidly above his left ear. The bottle shattered and splashed all three of them.

The guy didn't even blink.

Guthrie had just enough time to realize he was in trouble before the second bouncer burst through the curtain. He turned toward the new threat and the first bouncer grabbed him from behind, arms bigger than Guthrie's thigh clamping around his chest.

Guthrie relaxed and let his head sag forward. When he felt the bouncer lean forward to compensate, he slammed his head back into the man's face. He heard a muffled grunt but the vise tightened and Guthrie felt his breath whoosh out of his mouth. His ribs felt like they were collapsing.

The second bouncer put his face in front of his.

"Enough, OK?"

Guthrie waited until the room started to hum. Through blurry eyes, he saw Jersey Girl vanish through the curtained arch. He nodded.

Cold air rushed into his chest and made him feel light-headed. The bouncer behind him dropped his arms and stepped into sight again. He dug into a box on one of the cheesy tables for tissues and held them to his mouth.

"Fucker."

"What's the problem, guy?" That was the second bouncer, smaller than the first one, like an SUV is smaller than a tank.

"I was talking to the girl, and she went nuts." Guthrie's voice came out between a wheeze and a croak.

"What, you want to do something sick? We take care of our ladies here."

"Nothing like that." Guthrie pointed to his pocket. When the guy nodded, he fished for his ID. "I was trying to ask her about a guy she might know. Get some information. She must've thought I was someone else. I'm one of the good guys."

"Doesn't look like that to me." Jack Splat stuffed the bloody tissue in his pocket and took a clean one.

"The guy I was asking about died a couple of weeks ago," Guthrie said. "Jersey Girl might be able to help me find who killed him."

"Uh-huh." The second bouncer leaned close to his face. "You remember where you parked your car, or do we have to escort you?"

"Listen, if the girl's that scared, maybe she's in danger."

"We'll take care of her, bud. Thanks for your concern."

The bouncers flanked him and clamped fingers on his biceps, lifting him off the floor. He still had to look up at both of them.

They passed through the curtain and back into the fully nude section. Two more women were dancing, and nobody in their audience even turned to watch Guthrie's quick trip to the front entrance.

The bouncer with the bloody lip deposited him outside.

"If you see Valkyrie, say hi for me."

30

Guthrie's townhouse lay between Cherries Jubilee and Megan Traine's duplex, so he stopped off for a quick shower and change of clothes before heading up Woodward and into Royal Oak.

By the time he pulled into Meg's driveway and parked in the turnaround near the garage, his ribs only hurt if he took a deep breath.

Meg's Toyota with the bumper sticker "Keyboard Players Love Big Organs" sat in the garage bay on the right. Blue Song Riley, the chiropractor who owned the other half of the building, drove a Mercedes with the vanity plate "HANDS." That bay was empty.

Meg held the back door and he stepped into the kitchen, trying to look casual and innocent, a challenge when you've already told your girlfriend you're stopping off at a strip club. She looked him up and down twice before speaking.

"It's a little late for dinner, but I'm afraid to ask if you ate something."

He shook his head, which turned out to be a bad idea. "I'm good."

"Well, that's a matter of opinion." She wore a crimson tee and cut-offs that revealed legs that rivaled Jersey Girl's. Those legs and her energy level made her seem much taller than five-four.

"Did you find what you were looking for?" She frowned. "That's another bad choice of words, isn't it?"

"Not necessarily." He rubbed the back of his head. "Do you have any beer? In a can?"

"A can? What, you're becoming a connoisseur at your advanced age?"

"I'm younger than you are." He opened her refrigerator and found a six pack of Guinness Draft.

"So I'm a cougar. You never complained before." Meg's eyes studied his. "Are you OK? You look a little funny."

"Yeah, I'm fine." He put the can against the back of his head where the bouncer's jaw had nailed him. "Bumped my head awhile ago."

"Let me see."

"It's nothing. Really."

"Come here."

She led him through the dining room to her couch. Clyde looked up from grooming in the bay window. Meg sat Guthrie on the couch and moved next to him on her knees.

"What happened?" Her long fingers moved through his hair. He remembered that she'd started nursing school but dropped out after her freshman year when piano gigs started coming thick and fast.

"Nothing, really. I just...Ouch."

"Nothing my cute little ass. Let me see." She tilted his head toward the lamp and turned it to the highest setting. "Oh-oh..."

"What?" He asked.

"You're getting a bald spot."

"No way." He sat up straighter.

"No, you're not. But you've got a little nick there. You hit a sharp corner or something?"

"A guy was holding me from behind and I threw my head back to hit him. Maybe he bit me."

"People skills, Woody. Haven't we talked about that before?"

"I'm working on it." He sighed and felt his ribs complain.

Meg moved away and cocked an eyebrow. "Something else?"

"I'm just a little worse for wear, no big deal."

"Well, you're not *that* much younger than I am, it catches up with you."

"I figure if I can convalesce here..."

"Good plan." She wiggled two fingers in front of his face. "I don't think you've got a concussion, but I'd better not let you fall asleep for a few hours, just to be sure."

"How do you plan to do that?"

"Finish your beer, but don't chug it. Then I'll show you. What happened tonight?"

She stretched out on the couch with her bare feet in his lap. She listened with her whole body, something he didn't understand at first, partly because he did it too. It helped explain why she was the best session keyboard player in Detroit until she retired. She read the music, heard it, and felt it while she played.

He gave her the high points of his evening. While he talked, he realized that she might have been playing piano until he arrived. Some of her legendary status in the studios came from playing barefoot because she claimed she could feel the pedals better.

She waited until he stopped talking and put the half-empty beer can against his head again.

"Has anyone pointed out that there seems to be an unfortunate connection between you and strip clubs? Someone roughed you up tonight, a couple of months ago, you and Valerie got taken hostage..."

"They wouldn't even give me a receipt, damn them."

"Well, jeez." She rolled her eyes. "How much worse could it get?"

"I guess it's part of that people skills thing you keep talking about."

She laced her long fingers over her knees.

"The woman you tried to talk to, does she have anything to do with the guy I'm doing the computer check on?"

Guthrie remembered the girl's face when he mentioned Tony Fortunato. "I saw her at his funeral yesterday morning, but it didn't look like anyone knew who she was. So I took her picture and showed Valerie."

"Valerie." Meg shook her head. "I worry about her, being around you all the time."

"She's going back to college in the fall," Guthrie reminded her. "She'll come in a couple of days a week after she has her class schedule worked out."

Meg nodded. "I still have trouble with that. A perfect 'C' cup and a degree in marketing."

"She calls it 'branding.'"

"Yup. I'm sure." Meg watched him sip again. "Listen, I can't give you any specifics unless the detective on the case approves it, but I'm finding lots of interesting files on the laptop. Complicated passwords, encryption up the ass. The guy had bank accounts all over the greater metropolitan area under a whole slew of names. We've got one of the forensic accountants going through everything right now, but it's going to take him a while to match up the real tax stuff on the desktop. It's all detail and it's slow going, but it looks like the guy was skimming from somewhere."

"What if he's been fudging the figures he's putting in?"

"That could get ugly. We'd have to pull in the computers from the other accountants and see if we could match them. It could take weeks and still not turn up anything."

Guthrie put his empty beer can on a magazine on the coffee table. The *Oxford Complete Shakespeare* had fresh duct tape on the binding.

"So if the guy's been embezzling..."

"Maybe," Meg said. "If there really is a lot of money. What I found gives that impression, but we don't know for sure."

Guthrie stood and the room didn't wobble. He went over to Clyde and scratched the cat's back.

"If the guy really was skimming, maybe whoever killed him did it by accident."

"How did he die?" Meg moved her feet to the coffee table.

"Someone punched him in the mouth. He had a bridge, some false teeth, and he apparently swallowed them and choked."

"Are you serious?"

"Yeah, Shoobie thought it was pretty weird, too."

"Is she pretty?"

"Not like you." Guthrie moved by the piano. Sure enough, the music on the stand was Dvorak, a symphony score, upside down. "But the girl at the funeral was a stripper, and..."

He turned to Meg.

"Those bank accounts or whatever they are. Did you find any large cash withdrawals, like the guy might be spending money on presents for a girlfriend?"

Meg looked at the ceiling. "Now that you mention it...there were a couple. One was about eight thousand dollars. Sometime in the spring. April, maybe?"

Guthrie tapped enough piano keys to remember that he didn't play. "OK. Something that big, you'd use a credit card or a check most of the time, so you'd have a record, right?"

"I would. So you're thinking that might be something the guy didn't want traced?"

"Maybe." He moved back to the couch again. "I've sent Tony's info to a specialist, but if he was using these fake names, my guy might not find anything."

"Well, he buried them really deep," Meg said. "But there's something else detective Dube mentioned to me this morning. Maybe you know already since you were at the funeral. Did you recognize anyone else there, besides the girl you couldn't talk to tonight?"

"Yeah." He put her feet back in his lap so he could play with them. "Tony married into the Diorio family. His wife's uncle pretty much runs Detroit." He tried to go somewhere with that. "The Diorios run the strip clubs and prostitution around here. What if Tony met the girl through cooking the books? If she's involved, no wonder she freaked when I asked her about him."

"You don't look like a hitter, Woody. No offense, but you look less Italian than Clyde over there."

"But now I've got something I might be able to work with."

He kneaded Meg's foot and she purred softly.

"Tomorrow, I'll talk to Connie Fortunato again and find out if hubby made a big purchase a few months ago."

"Maybe they redid their bathroom or something."

"But maybe not. It won't hurt to be sure."

He trailed his fingernail up to her knee. Goose bumps sprang out all the way up her bare shin.

"Do I sound rational? Like there's no concussion?"

"Actually, no weirder than usual." Meg swung her legs off his lap and stood up. "But you can't be too careful. I still think I should keep you awake for awhile, just to be sure."

She pulled him to his feet.

"Come upstairs."

31

After breakfast and a hot shower at Meg's the next morning, Guthrie's ribs felt much better. So did everything else. He stopped off at his condo long enough to check his email and call Connie Fortunato. The Saturday morning TV fare was still cartoons but her voice already had a slight blurriness that told Guthrie she was self-medicating.

His specialist had no answer about Tony Fortunato's finances yet. Now that Meg and Shoobie had the other names and accounts, he wondered if he'd get anything worth the money. He'd charge it to Billable Hours anyway to make up for Jersey Girl's fees.

He dumped the spam from his other accounts and was on the road to Grosse Pointe by ten-thirty, visions of Megan Traine floating through his head.

The morning sun pouring through her window under the shade turned her body into a warm caramel sculpture. Bonnie the calico lay in the bedroom door and Clyde lay on Meg's cedar chest at the foot of the bed, his pea green eyes watching Guthrie realize that Mom was already awake.

Meg knew that he was, too, and moved on top of him to celebrate the new day. When they were finished, she lay on Guthrie's chest.

"You didn't really have dinner last night, did you?" Her face was still pink and shiny with sweat. When she shifted, he could see the pink extended down her entire torso, which he knew by now was a very good sign.

"A beer before I got here, I think."

"Tell me you had a Busch and I'm tossing your sorry ass in the street."

"Hard to tell, it was so watered down." He slid his hand across her back and cupped her rear.

She wiggled against him. "How's your head?"

"After the last few minutes, you have to ask?"

She kissed her way down to his navel. "Let me shower first, then I'll start breakfast. You need to keep your strength up."

She bent over to pet the cat, a view Guthrie never got tired of admiring, then disappeared toward the bathroom. He made the bed and took his own shower before joining her in the kitchen.

"Ham and spinach omelet OK?" The oven mitt on her hand clashed with her black silk robe. She never wore anything under it, so the red dragon on her back seemed to smile.

"You're spoiling me beyond all hope, you know that, don't you?"

"I figure if I can satisfy all your appetites, you'll be back."

Connie Fortunato answered his knock so quickly she must have been watching for him out the window. Her hair needed a brush and her eyes needed focus, but the buttons on her blouse were fastened correctly.

"You again," she greeted him.

He followed her into the same living room and watched her drift around the space as if she were browsing a tag sale.

"Ms. Fortunato, we may have a lead in your husband's killing, but it brings up a bunch of new questions."

"Like what?" She seemed incomplete without a glass in her hands.

"Well, did you have a major expenditure in the last few months, something out of the ordinary? Several thousand dollars, maybe in the spring?"

Connie's lips moved.

"Maybe major work on your cars? Or the house? Re-modeling, a new roof? Anything like that?"

"Uh...no."

If Connie's uncle was really the local crime boss, she probably didn't have to worry about money. Unless the guy didn't like Tony, which brought up a whole different scenario.

Guthrie tried to come up with more hints.

"Maybe a trip somewhere? A vacation?"

Connie seemed to wake up.

"We got luggage. Tony was talking we should go away, but we hadn't decided where yet. Maybe somewhere warmer, Christmas vacation, so the kids didn't miss school."

"You have the luggage, do you?"

"Mine's up in my closet. Tony's is probably in his."

Guthrie tried to guess how much luggage eight thousand dollars could buy. "Would you mind showing me?"

He followed the woman upstairs to a bedroom with a comforter thrown over a queen-sized bed that was clearly unmade. Connie opened a door and flicked on a light.

"Here." She slid a large suitcase out from behind a rack of dresses.

"There's two smaller ones inside it," she said. "And a trunk with a hanger bag, too. That's up in the attic."

Guthrie could smell the leather. When he ran his hands over the suitcase, it felt alive, soft and rich enough to moo. There was definitely money here, but no eight grand.

"Does your husband's luggage match this?"

"Well, same style. His is darker, real dark brown."

"Does he have a separate closet?"

Connie opened a door to an adjoining room, which Tony seemed to have used as a combination home office and dressing room. His desk had a large bare spot where the computer usually sat and the monitor looked lonely.

The closet held several tailored suits and a half-dozen pairs of shoes, but no luggage.

Connie leaned in and looked behind the suits, but the closet was much smaller than hers and there was no room to conceal anything that large.

"Huh," she said. "Maybe the attic."

"Never mind for now, then," Guthrie said. "Can you think of anything else you and your husband bought last spring that you wouldn't ordinarily buy?"

Connie bit her lip and Guthrie saw that she needed more help.

"Furniture, maybe? A new TV set, like that home entertainment unit you have down in the living room?"

"Uh-uh, nothing like that."

"New kitchen appliances? Maybe a barbecue pit, new pool equipment?"

He felt himself running out of ideas.

"Maybe a motorcycle? Did Tony like riding? Or golf clubs?"

Connie shook her head slowly.

"How about something for your children? Surgery? Classes? Anything?"

"Uh, we tried to get them interested in music, but they could care less. All they can play is their iPods, and they like it that way."

"When you say 'music,' do you mean playing an instrument?"

"We were hoping they'd—one of them, either one—try piano. I did when I was young, and I sucked. Tony liked to dance, but he didn't play anything. And neither of us can carry a tune, except maybe if we had a couple of drinks."

Connie stared out the window as though looking for the barbecue pit or the motorcycle Guthrie had suggested.

"I can't think of much of anything. Oh, except that guitar."

"Excuse me?"

She nodded. "I forgot about it 'cause he never played it. He bought a guitar a few months ago. It's down in the basement."

"I play guitar," Guthrie said. "Would you mind if I checked it out?"

"What the hell." Connie shrugged.

The finished basement had a ping pong table with a smooth layer of dust and some ancient furniture that looked too fragile to support Guthrie's weight. The far side sported a washer and dryer and a few old boxes. A door next to them led to what he assumed was a hatchway to the backyard.

In the corner next to an armchair with badly worn fabric stood a shiny black guitar case. Guthrie recognized the Gibson logo from across the room. A feeble coffee table held a few music books.

"You say your husband just bought this guitar?" he asked.

"Yeah. Maybe after tax season. April's always their busiest time, lots of business, you know."

"Sure." Guthrie picked up the guitar case. Heavy. He laid it across the arms of the chair and opened it.

A sunburst Les Paul electric guitar stared back at him. Guthrie didn't think he had any fetishes—and if he did, he certainly wouldn't tell Megan—but looking at that guitar made him swallow. The body glowed with the colors of autumn leaves, from almost black to rich burnt amber. The volume and tone control knobs were gold like the pick guard, and the fingerboard had trapezoids in what might have been mother-of-pearl to mark the various frets.

He lifted the guitar from the case, noticing the weight. Les Pauls were twice as heavy as his Fender. This one still had that new wood smell and the luster of a polished coffee table. The strings still glittered, and so did the tuning pegs. Guthrie opened the compartment in the case, but it was empty. He turned the guitar over and looked at the back. No scratches from a belt buckle, either. He could take the instrument to a music store and put it on display as brand-new.

"How often did Tony play?"

"I never heard him. Maybe he only did it when I was at one of my meetings."

Guthrie put the guitar back in the case and leafed through the music. Two books on learning to play guitar, both with CDs still in the plastic pockets inside the cover. Neither had been opened. The third book was a collection of classic rock songs, and the binding showed no wear. Guthrie held the book gently by the covers and jiggled it, but it didn't fall open to a particular page.

He looked around the room again. "No amplifier?"

"What?"

"This is an electric guitar. I'm wondering where he has the amplifier."

"Uh, I don't think he got one."

There was nothing in the guitar case, no cable to plug into an amp. No guitar strap. Not even any picks. Guthrie didn't know the exact model of this Gibson, but he knew the high-end versions could easily go five grand, maybe even more.

Vintage Les Paul guitars drew hundreds of thousands of dollars from collectors.

"Do you know where Tony bought this?"

"I don't know the store, but it was around here."

Guthrie felt his energy level rising. "If he kept the sales slip, where would it be?"

32

The Fortunatos' pool had three rafts, all the same blue with bright yellow undersides. Tobi couldn't tell them apart and she was pretty sure the kids couldn't either, but they both wanted the same one. If it wasn't the raft, it would be a ball or a chair. She wondered if it would be even worse if they were the same sex, or—dear God in heaven—twins.

Connie—Ms. Fortunato—was inside talking to that detective again, and Tobi knew that would slow down her drinking for awhile. Maybe she'd even find something else to do, watch a movie with the kids or something tonight. They were still upset about their dad—which struck her as both healthy and normal—and they needed their mother to help them through it.

Tobi adjusted her sunglasses and saw a blurry blob appear on her right lens. *Shoot, sun block.* The stuff spread smoothly, but you couldn't get it completely off your hands. This was the waterproof kind, not that she went in the water much. Chlorine would destroy her hair, who knows what it would do to the color, too?

She puffed on her glasses and wiped them on her towel, which only spread the film across the whole lens so she couldn't see anything at all. Reading with one eye was too crazy. She walked over to the edge of the pool.

"Tobi, hey, Tobi, you coming in? You wanna play Marco Polo or something?" Chuck's shrill scream could etch glass. He woke up slowly, but then he was on overdrive for about twelve hours. Patty was quieter, thank God, or Tobi would understand why Connie—Ms. Fortunato liked her wine.

"I'm just cleaning my glasses, Chuck."

"Oh, come on. We're bored."

"Why don't you do a few laps, build up your muscles?" Both kids could swim like sharks.

"Boring. Come on in. Pleeeaase?"

Tobi swished her glasses in the water and walked back to her chaise longue to wipe them again. The tiles were warm under her bare feet. It was going to be another hot one, and the rain yesterday translated into more humidity, like looking through waxed paper. Tobi felt Chuck's eyes on her back. Well, if he were a few years older, they'd be on her ass. She had a couple of thongs, but she never wore them in front of the kids.

"Not Marco Polo," Patty wailed. "I wanna swim. Do laps. How about we dive?"

"Don't want to," Chuck said. Tobi should have known him before she worked on her Viola monologue. The kid was only eleven, but he was already an alpha to the max.

"Chuckie, sometimes you have to compromise, you know."

"It's her turn to compromise," he complained. "I did it last time."

"Did not."

"Did so. You wanted mushrooms on the pizza and I hate mushrooms."

"So we had mushrooms on half and peppers on half. That's not a compromise."

"Yeah it is."

Not even noon and Tobi felt a headache coming on.

"Tell you what," she said. "Why don't I toss the ball, you see who can get to it first."

"Yeah!" Chuck punched the air with a fist. Patty rolled her eyes.

"Come on, Patty," Tobi said. "Just for a few minutes, OK? Then I need to read some more."

"What you reading?" Chuckie leaned over the edge of the pool. His skin glistened with beads of water.

"Shakespeare."

"You always read Shakespeare," Patty said. "You oughtta read something else. Something good."

"Shakespeare's good." Tobi tried not to sound defensive. She picked up the yellow Nerf ball and moved to the deep end.

"Boring. He talks funny, too." Patty moved to the far side of the pool so she could push off when Tobi threw the ball.

"That's poetry," Tobi said. Why did she always pick arguments she couldn't possibly win? She wound up and threw the ball, which floated near the middle of the pool. Chuck kicked off the edge while it was still in the air and beat his sister to it by a good six feet.

"No fair," she shrieked. "That was closer to you. No fair."

"Was not." Chuck waved the ball over his head. "I swim better than you do 'cause you're a girl and girls don't swim good."

"Uh-uh. Tobi, tell him girls swim good."

"Girls swim as well as guys do, Chuck. Here, toss it back and I'll throw it again." Tobi told herself to throw it closer to Patty this time. Chuck's voice was less piercing when he yelled.

She watched the ball arch toward Patty. Chuck was tracking it before it hit the water, but she was close enough to get there first. He tried to grab it from her but she shoved his face into the water and he came up sputtering.

"No fair, no fair, no fair. I woulda had that but you cheated."

"Did not. I had it."

"But you dunked me."

Tobi wondered if Connie had enough wine to share.

She tossed the ball until Chuck's minimal attention span ran out, then returned to her Oxford paperback of *Hamlet*. She'd already highlighted the Arden, Penguin, and Signet (which cleaned up some of the cruder lines in the footnotes) and Folger. Another few days and she'd have both Ophelia and Gertrude's parts memorized. *Hamlet* was Shakespeare's longest play—she remembered Kenneth Branagh's uncut film lasting four hours—and knew they'd probably end up cutting the hell out of it for a performance.

She rubbed more moisturizer on her stomach and arms and wished she'd brought a hat out with her.

"Guys? I'm running in for a hat. I'll be right back, OK?"

Patty waved and she scurried through the kitchen. She heard voices from the basement, Ms. F and that detective, and continued to her room near the attic. She found a floppy hat she'd had so long she didn't remember where it came from and checked her phone on the table. After what happened at the beach, she didn't keep it where the kids could get their little paws on it.

A text message. Two, both Evan's number—still on her stomach—and an email from "Wayne.edu." She opened it.

Thanks to everyone who auditioned for the autumn production project. We apologize for the delay in getting back to you, but you gave us difficult choices and the logistics became something of a burden. We have made our final selections. Please remember that if you have not been selected it is not a reflection on your performance. In some cases, other factors came to bear and we hope you will still choose to participate in the production in some other capacity.

Tobi knew the routine. It came down to they liked someone. She skimmed the rest of the message until she found the part that mattered.

Unfortunately, even though you gave a strong and intriguing performance, we have decided that the roles you expressed interest in will help fulfill our vision of the Hamlet project more fully if we go in a different direction. Thinking outside the box is the way to keep any play, but especially a foundation of the theatrical canon, fresh and vital.

We wish you luck and success in your future endeavors.

They wished her luck, but didn't cast her. She wondered who they did cast. Probably that chubby bitch Elaine whatever for Gertrude. She bordered on matronly anyway, even if she had the enunciation of a cheese grater. Maybe "a different direction" was code for color-blind casting. Shit, what if they'd cast a minority *Hamlet*? She'd thought about Horatio as black or Latino, or maybe Rosencrantz or Guildenstern, but what if...? Christ, that might mean a black Ophelia, too. That girl with the dreads who thought everyone's first name was "yo."

Tobi closed the message and considered throwing her phone at the wall above her bed. Then she remembered the texts from Evan.

Hey wn 2 hang out 2nite? I no band playng in Mad Hites. Let me no OK?

The last one was only forty minutes ago.

Tobi's thumbs moved across her keyboard faster than a spider on crack. Then she looked at her closet and tried to decide what to wear.

Out the window, she saw that detective's car pull out of the driveway and disappear.

33

Guthrie knew a dozen music stores in and around Detroit that sold guitars, and four of them were in Grosse Pointe so he decided to start there. He started his car and turned on the AC, then dialed Valerie's number.

"Good morning, Mr. G."

"Hi, Valerie. Did I wake you?"

"Oh, no, I've done three loads of laundry and read about fifty pages."

"Oh. I...it's one of those rhetorical greetings."

"I know. I'm a smart Polish blonde, remember? I'm even going to collitch in the fall."

He pictured her trying to look dumb. It was easier if you didn't look at her face.

"Um, I know this is a nuisance, but can you try to find me Jersey Girl's real name? If you could get an address too, it would be great, but I'll take whatever you can give me."

Valerie cleared her throat. "Um, I'm betting Ms. Traine would like you to rephrase that."

"Ouch. I guess 'I'll take whatever I can get' isn't much better, is it?"

"Not really. It could take awhile, Mr. G. what should I say if people ask?"

Guthrie remembered Jersey Girl's face the previous night. "I think she knows more than we thought. If she really does know something, she could be in danger. Or dangerous."

"Um." He could almost see Valerie biting her lip. "I'm not going to promise anything."

"Thank you, Valerie. I appreciate it."

Somehow, talking to Valerie always brought out his good manners. In spite of her past history, she looked like she belonged on a cereal box, Corn Flakes or something equally wholesome.

"Mr. Guthrie, if Jersey's in trouble, how can you help?"

"I can't do a thing until I know her name." He suddenly thought of another way to go. "Oh, something else you can ask about. If I'm right about Jersey Girl, maybe some of your colleagues know the dead man, too. Could you ask them if the name Anthony or Tony Fortunato rings a bell?"

"Um, Mr. Guthrie, my contacts are dancers. If they engage in anything more tactile, it's on their own time, so they might not want to discuss it."

"I know, Valerie, but everyone knows you're discreet, right?"

"Well...maybe. May I throw your name on the table? My associates like a man who stands up for women in our position. Hm, maybe I should re-phrase that, shouldn't I?"

"I wouldn't presume. Thanks, Valerie."

Tony Fortunato bought an expensive guitar and pricy luggage. The luggage suggested he was planning to go somewhere, maybe with Connie, or maybe not. The fact that Connie couldn't find that luggage might mean he had other company in mind, possibly Jersey Girl. Or, if he really was stealing, safety deposit boxes weren't big enough to hold a lot of cash, but a couple of suitcases would be.

Life would be a lot easier if Valerie could track down Jersey Girl.

Guthrie spent the next three hours visiting music stores. Three of them carried guitars from more manufacturers than he'd ever heard of, in price ranges from a small child's allowance to something that probably involved a federal grant. But none of them sold a Les Paul to Anthony or Tony Fortunato.

At three-thirty, Guthrie reached Pro Musica, which carried everything from pianos to kazoos, with a massive showroom and a nearly-full parking lot. They also gave lessons, so Saturday was a busy day.

Several pre-teens wandered around the store, most with a parent in tow and several carrying guitar cases. Guthrie didn't start playing guitar until his late teens when he figured out that it was a good way to impress girls. On the other hand, he knew that Megan was under ten when she started the lessons that would lead her to a very nice living for decades.

He found a salesman who didn't appear much thicker than a guitar neck. The ID tag on a lanyard called him "Rudi," and his perm made him look like a wannabe late-sixties rocker. His fingers looked even longer than Megan Traine's.

Guthrie showed his ID. "I'm trying to find where a man bought a guitar, probably about three months ago. I don't know if he bought it here, but can you check?"

"No sales slip, huh?" The guy's voice floated along like a slow solo. "Course not, or you'd know when he bought it, right?"

"Right." Guthrie pulled out his notebook. "It's a sunburst Les Paul, and it looks like a high end model. Here's the serial number."

Rudi slid behind the counter and Guthrie examined a display of effects pedals. Wah-wah pedals, compressors, fuzz tones, chorus pedals and phasers all sounded vaguely familiar, but he wasn't even sure what some of the others were supposed to do. Maybe that explained the prices. If he bought enough of them, he might actually sound fairly good. He would also be broke.

A kid who looked too young to get through the day without a nap was tearing up speed-metal riffs ten feet away. He had a guitar plugged into a Marshall amplifier the size of Guthrie's bureau, cranked up full, the equivalent of sitting on the runway at Detroit Metro Airport and having a 747 take off over your head.

Rudi looked up and caught the kid's eye. He held his thumb and forefinger close together and the kid turned down. A hair. Rudi sighed and tapped a few keys on his computer. Guthrie knew that music stores were high-end everything except computers.

He wandered over to look at acoustic guitars. Gibsons, Taylors, Martins, Takamines, all several times what he paid for his Gibson years ago. He picked up a Takamine and played a few chords that he could barely hear over the kid who was still making love to every seismograph in the Midwest.

Rudi bent over his screen, then waved Guthrie back to him.

"Yeah, we sold it. May tenth. You need the guy's name?"

"Fortunato, isn't it?"

"Yeah. Lives here in Grosse Pointe."

"Right," Guthrie said. "That's the guy. What's the bite?"

Rudi read it off the screen. "Gibson Les Paul '59 reissue, hard shell case, three instruction books..."

"No amplifier?"

"Nope. I guess he already had one he liked. He may have tried the guitar in something like what he already had. You play?"

"I'm a Strat man," Guthrie told him. "And an old deluxe reverb, probably older than you are."

"Probably great sound, then." Rudi checked the invoice again. "Hm. This is a little bit out there."

"What is?"

"Well, the guy didn't get any kind of extra warranty. Usually, someone buys a guitar this expensive, they want to take care of it."

"How much would that cost?" Guthrie asked.

"You kidding? He's just dropped six grand on this bad boy, he's gonna be all pissy about another three hundred bucks for five years on parts and labor?"

"Good point." The shredding demon put down the guitar and the store sounded unnaturally quiet. "Anything else stand out about the sale?"

Rudi studied his monitor. "The guy paid cash."

Guthrie nodded. "How often does that happen? A big purchase like that?"

"Not very. We get a few checks, but people who write a check can't take the merchandise with them until it clears. Most of our big sales—say a hundred bucks and up—are credit cards. But this guy apparently came in with the green. Sixty-two hundred bucks. Man, bet he had a lump in his pants to make women on the street look twice."

"I'll bet." Guthrie watched the kid stalking another amp, even bigger than the Marshall. "Can you do me a favor and print out a copy of that invoice? I don't know if I'll need it, but it'll save me second trip."

He watched Rudi weave between other clerks to the printer, which looked even older than the computers. The paper had perforated edges and carbon copies.

Rudi returned and glared at the kid.

Guthrie thought of one last question. "Do you know if the guy came back after that day for anything else?"

"No idea." Rudi looked at the invoice again. "The guy who made the sale isn't here anymore, so if he did, we might not've known him."

"OK. Thanks anyway."

"Hey, we're having a back to school sale next week, if you're looking for something for your kid."

Guthrie never came into a store like this with a credit card so he didn't walk out with a Les Paul like Tony Fortunato had.

34

They'd rinsed the dishes and filled Meg's dishwasher and now they sat on the couch, both fully clothed but barefoot, an important first step.

"You always say you can't cook," Meg said. "But that salad was great, especially for a night like this."

"I figured fruit would work either as an appetizer or a palate cleanser." He'd picked it up at a supermarket on the way home from his guitar hunt, but why mention that. "It was great with the sherbet."

"Always keep sherbet around in the summer. My mom said that." Meg stretched her legs and rested them in Guthrie's lap. "Along with condoms and fresh batteries."

Meg lowered her lashes slowly, a move she might have learned from one of the cats.

"I added that part myself."

"I was wondering." He cleared his throat and sipped his coffee. It was still above eighty outside, with the humidity of a weightlifter's armpit, but both he and Meg had a serious caffeine dependency.

"What is it you love most about me?" Meg watched Clyde grooming in the bay window, his usual hangout. "My eternal beauty, my infinite wisdom, or my limitless talent?"

"I was going to say your humility," Guthrie said. "And your sense of humor."

"I left those off so you didn't feel paralyzed from having too many choices."

Actually, what he cherished most of all was her practical streak, which might have come from years in the studio having to work with the epic egos swirling around her. That and her love life—only slightly less cursed than his own—had shown her early that shit happens, but it doesn't have to kill you. Many of her scars were inside and he was still finding some of them, unlike the six-inch gash on his left thigh where doctors had rebuilt his femur.

"Maybe your killer cheekbones," he said. "Or maybe your forgiving nature."

"I never forget though." She wiggled her toes and he began to massage her left foot. "I learned that from the cats."

"I know. It's why I fear you, too."

"And here we were talking about *my* intelligence."

He stroked her arch and watched the sun sink behind the houses across the street. The family pictures on the mantel glowed gold and the rest of the room took on a soft dreamy aura. Meg's legs became heavier and he thought she was dozing off until she sat up and brushed her hair behind her ear.

"You should bring your guitar over sometime," she said.

"Why?" Meg played with the biggest names in Detroit in her prime, and occasionally backed touring stars in local venues. He knew he couldn't play at her level.

"Because I can't fit my piano in the Toyota when I spend the night at your place."

"I suck though."

"No you don't. You just don't get to play with anyone else very often."

"I'm doing everything I can to fix that."

"It's going to work tonight, too." Meg lay back down. "Don't let me fall asleep."

"I won't." He moved his hands up to her ankles. "Tony Fortunato bought a six-thousand dollar guitar last spring, and his wife says she never heard him play it."

"Maybe she should give it to you," Meg said. "Encourage you to bring it over here and jam."

"Fat chance. It's a Les Paul. They weigh more than you do."

She let his hands work up to her knees. "Seriously? The guy bought a Les Paul and doesn't play it?"

Guthrie slid his fingernails down her shins and she shivered. "I looked at it this afternoon, and he doesn't have an amplifier or a cable to plug it into one. In fact, he doesn't even have a strap for it. Or picks."

Meg sat up again.

"When did he buy it?"

"About three months ago."

"Long enough so it definitely wasn't a present for anyone, was it?"

"Nope. And neither of the kids seems to have any interest in music."

"How old are they?"

"Ten, eleven. Older than you were when you started piano."

"Weird." Meg slid her feet to the floor and stood. He watched her stroll over to her piano and stretch her fingers. He knew she'd probably played at least an hour that afternoon, but she did some of her best thinking at the keys.

She sank to the bench and he felt her energy spike. This was her home base. She raised the lid over the keys and played a scale up the length of the keyboard, then a different one descending.

"What do you—we—actually know?" she asked.

"The wife says he bought the guitar and some luggage. She showed me hers—very nice—but his wasn't in his closet. It might have been in the attic, I didn't bother to check."

"And the guitar." Meg's left hand found a slow bass line that might have been Beethoven's "Moonlight Sonata."

"Yeah," he said. "I talked to a guy at the music store. Tony bought the guitar and a couple of instruction books at the same time, but he's never been back. Paid cash, too. The books have CDs with them. In plastic inside the cover? I've got a couple of books like that, too. But the CDs haven't even been opened, either. The plastic's still sealed."

Meg added a right-hand melody to the bass line.

"Guess he didn't want to become a guitar hero, did he? Was he going through his mid-life crisis? His kids are ten or eleven, so he was in his thirties, right?"

"I guess. The wife is mid-thirties."

"What's she like?"

Guthrie listened to the plump notes floating in the air. "Pretty, big-boned, I guess you'd call it. A little taller than you are."

"Italian, of course. Her uncle is a heavy-hitter."

"Yeah. Which gets us nowhere."

"You're right." Meg shifted keys. A few months ago, Guthrie wouldn't have noticed.

"So why does a guy buy a very expensive guitar and not do anything with it?"

"Maybe he was going to play and changed his mind." Guthrie shook his head. "No, that's stupid. He'd return it and get his money back."

"Probably." Meg shifted rhythm and kept playing.

"So why do you buy a guitar you're not going to play? He's not using it as a door stop, and he hasn't taken it out anywhere. I was thinking maybe he'd meet someone somewhere, you know, like a date, I'll be the guy carrying the guitar."

Meg stopped playing. "That's kind of a stretch, don't you think?"

"Yeah," he agreed.

"Nothing else he bought?"

"Not that his wife mentioned."

"If you can't find the luggage, maybe he gave it to someone else."

"Hmm." Guthrie stood and began pacing. The sun sank behind the houses across the street, turning them into looming silhouettes. "The woman at the funeral is a dancer, and I was thinking maybe Tony was having a little fling with her. The way she freaked when I tried to talk to her last night makes me think so even more."

"So talk to her again."

"I've got Valerie trying to find out her real name," he said. "If she's still at that same club for awhile, I'll have to try her at home or somewhere else. The bouncers won't let me back in, and she sure won't talk to me there."

He stopped pacing.

"Could Tony have given her the luggage? Maybe they were planning a trip together?"

Meg thought about it before she shook her head.

"Doesn't sound right. Why buy luggage for his wife then?"

"Good point." He stopped behind Meg. "That woman's the closest thing I've got to a lead, except for the guitar, which makes no sense at all."

"So until you find her—if you do—where else can you go with this?"

Meg played a quick figure with her right hand, gradually moving it down the keyboard. After she reached a vocal range, she let her left hand join in.

"I don't know. It would probably help if I knew the names on Tony's laptop."

"No way I can give them to you unless your cop friend decides to let me. And that's not going to happen until at least the day after tomorrow."

"Yeah."

"So," she said. "It's still all *cherchez la femme.*"

"Some things never change, do they?"

He glanced toward the stairs and saw the shy calico peeking through the banister.

35

Shoobie and Grady Hall spent one of those Saturdays. Real people shopped or spent Quality Time with their kids— little league or camping or whatever—or cooking or maybe even—should she dare think it?—making love. But she sat at her desk listening to some crap that made her think that Muzak—if that was somebody's real name—should have been strangled in an elevator before he was old enough to walk. Why couldn't places even use decent music when they put you on hold? Maybe it was so you'd hang up and they wouldn't have to deal with you. What healthy person would even think of a New Age arrangement of Ted Nugent's "Cat Scratch Fever?"

Two desks away, Grady didn't seem to be having any better luck than she was.

"No, I don't have a warrant. I'm not asking for any sensitive information. If you tell me yes or no, I can get a warrant if it becomes necessary, but I was hoping..."

She had never stopped to think how many banks there were in Detroit until the IT chick found those files on the laptop. Nine different names, most of them variations on Anthony Fortunato, and twenty-four different accounts, but the numbers stood alone without telling which banks they belonged with. So she and Grady were checking them out.

Megan Traine. Shoobie wondered why an IT kid would actually offer to check out the laptop. She figured it must be some kid, new and almost obscenely eager, but then Max and Lowe told her the woman was Woody Guthrie's girlfriend. Shoobie's opinion of Woody slipped a little when she thought he was seeing some computer nerd, probably with the social skills of a screwdriver.

Then she took the damn laptop down to IT. The brunette who greeted her had the cool to address the major stockholders, a face that belonged on a magazine cover and the voice to match. Even in jeans and a tee shirt, she made Shoobie understand that Woody Guthrie was one lucky son of a bitch.

Grady hung up and puffed out his cheeks.

"Any luck?"

"Two names. But they wouldn't tell me how many accounts or how much was in them."

Shoobie nodded. "I got one guy to admit the holder—that was Antonio Fortune—had a CD, but he wouldn't tell me how much was in it."

There were nearly 500 banks in Greater Detroit. It took them forty minutes to figure out how many separate banks they really were—fifty-one—and split those so they could get into the main computers. Since most of the banks weren't telling them jack shit, it didn't matter. What with all the arguing and waiting on hold, Shoobie was less than half-way through her half of the list.

Grady rubbed his eyes. "How much do you think we're looking at? Money, I mean?"

"God, who knows?" Even with a cushion, the ancient chair made Shoobie's butt hurt. "If he's got twenty-some accounts, maybe he's figuring to keep less than ten grand in each so the banks don't have to report big transactions to the feds."

"Which would still mean a quarter of a million." Grady blinked toward the windows, so streaky you couldn't see the pollution on the other side.

"Yeah," Shoobie agreed. "And if the guy has been stealing, he could have been doing it for years. And that means it could be a lot more than that."

"Fuck me," Grady said.

Shoobie bit her tongue.

"Sure gives us a better motive than Fillmore getting caught with his hands on the keys, doesn't it?"

"We've still got his prints on the mirror, though." Shoobie knew that was blowing smoke out her ass, but it was the only concrete lead they had so far. Everything else was "maybe" or "what-if?"

Was Tony's uncle-in-law—was there even such a title?—Carmine Diorio involved in this? Was Tony's death supposed to be a message of some kind? They spotted the two gorillas keeping a low profile at the funeral, but neither seemed on high alert, and Carmine came across as just a sad relative, not expecting any trouble. Was Tony stealing from a rival? That meant they would have to go through all that friggin' accounting firm's records and see who their clients were and if any of them were fronts for family business. *Fucking swell.*

Shoobie dialed the next bank and punched her way through a menu that must have been designed by someone with ADHD. All she wanted was a human voice. When it finally came, she missed the friggin' music.

"I'll be glad to get a warrant, Mr. Kellerman." The bug crawled a little farther up her ass and she felt the rasp in her voice. "But I'm sure you can see your way to helping us out in a murder investigation without making us do that."

"Well, Detective, I don't know you." The guy sounded like he'd probably worked his way through college selling used cars. Or his sister's used underwear.

"And I'm not asking for any information that would be a breach of confidentiality, am I? All I want to know is does your bank have accounts for people with any of these names."

Stop it, she told herself. *The asshole is just doing his job. Like I'm trying to do mine.*

She wondered what would happen if she told the Health Department this bank had rats in the vault.

Still nineteen different banks to call in ten minutes.

"You remember that woman we saw at the funeral?"

Grady rolled his eyes toward her. He was apparently on hold again.

"The one in black, with the fuck-me stilettos?"

"Begging my pardon." Shoobie's shoulder holster was rubbing under her breast. "Yeah, the one who didn't talk to anyone."

"Yeah. I don't think she went back to the house. At least I didn't see her there, did you?"

"No." Shoobie tried to visualize the woman again, blonde hair pulled back in a bun that called attention to her eyes with too much liner. She glanced around every time the priest called on the congregation to pray, or rise or kneel, like she didn't know what was going on. Shoobie was raised Catholic. She didn't get to church much anymore, but the service choreography was still deeply ingrained. The strange woman wasn't Catholic, which meant she wasn't part of either family.

She sure as hell didn't look like a client, either.

Lincoln Fillmore had been stealing vehicles since they'd taken the training wheels off his first bicycle, but nothing in his record said he'd ever killed a fly. They fingered him for Tony because his prints were on the mirror, but that was looking like more and more of a long shot.

But he'd been driving the car and Tony Fortunato was in it, probably already in the trunk. He picked up that Mercedes somewhere and dumped it behind the Grande, but thanks to his friggin' lawyer, he wouldn't tell them where he found it or when he dumped it. All they knew was Fortunato was missing for five days before those kids smelled him.

Shoobie listened to the Muzak again and watched the sweep hand on the wall clock move straight up. The message switched and told her the bank was closed. The office hours were...

She hung up.

"You got any special plans for tonight, Grady?"

"Nah." The kid shook his head. "Probably just watch a movie. My wife's got about ten she wants to see."

Shoobie wondered if it was worth getting drunk that night. She had nowhere else she had to be, no husband to eat dinner with, no kids to feed, no pets to walk. She didn't have a date to look pretty for, or even a hobby.

On the way home, she stopped at a grocery store and pushed the cart up and down the aisles, weaving in and out among the wives and mothers with lists in their hands and purpose in their eyes, some with kids in tow or in the baby seat in the carriage. She picked out a head of lettuce, two boxes of cereal, a few oranges, two rolls of toilet paper, a quart of 1% milk, and a package of chicken legs. Then she retraced her steps and found shampoo and conditioner. And double-fudge chocolate ice cream. Even dragging her feet and doubling back over and over, it only took her an hour.

She drove the scenic route to the house in Oak Park and watched the garage door inch its way up. Four-fifteen. The rest of the day and evening stretched ahead of her like a desert with cactuses and buzzards and hot, sharp sand. No road, and nowhere to go anyway.

She put away the groceries and decided to put the perfect end to her perfect day by calling Brian again. The sonofabitch had to answer sometime. If he didn't, she'd find him at work and put him up against a wall in front of his co-workers. She wanted to fix this. The empty house was becoming a constant ache in her chest. They could make it work. She knew they could.

She listened to the ringing, already composing the message in her head if the asshole didn't answer.

"Um, hi?"

The voice sounded about eighteen, both age and IQ. Shoobie heard roaring in her ears and her stomach dropped as though the elevator was plunging to the basement from twenty stories up. Her hand clenched around her phone.

She took a deep breath and forced herself to speak slowly. "May I speak to Brian Trask, please?"

"Who's calling?" The voice sounded suspicious, more than Shoobie would have given her credit for. Her cop mind kicked into overdrive and she felt her palms become slippery around the phone.

She's there at four-thirty, sure as shit she's there a lot. Brian doing the mattress tango with a kid half his age. Was the little bitch even legal? Did her kisses taste like bubblegum?

Shoobie let her voice drop into the "freeze, motherfucker" cop register.

"His wife."

The silence on the other end was long enough to file her nails.

"Oh. Um, he's in the shower." The voice rose even though it wasn't a question. "And then he's taking me—uh, can I take a message?"

I doubt it. You sound too dumb to take his fucking temperature. Shoobie didn't doubt for a second that he was taking hers, though. And she felt her eyes burning when she imagined how he did it.

Her husband was blowing off the counseling session because he was sleeping with a kid half her age. He wasn't going to come back. Ever. It was really over. She struggled to keep her voice calm and devoid of tears.

"No, never mind. I'll...try again later."

She didn't throw her phone across the room, she placed it gently on her bureau. Then she lurched into the bathroom and threw up. She rinsed out her mouth three times and studied her face in the mirror. She didn't look that old, did she? She narrowed her eyes and leaned in closer. Were those wrinkles around her eyes new?

The evening looked even longer. She could shower and cook dinner, then put on make-up and drive downtown to a bar and get sloppy drunk. Or find some guy and bring him home. Except she felt so old now, an old dry ugly crone. Her husband left her because she was so old and ugly.

She needed to call someone. Who? Grady didn't need to know. He was probably going somewhere with his wife tonight, anyway, why screw up his evening?

Woody Guthrie. No, why inflict herself on him, either? He probably had a date with that girl from IT, what's her name?

Shoobie shook her head and started undressing. Nothing had changed except that now she knew for sure what she'd been denying all along. Screw it. She'd find something on television or read a good book. Maybe she'd polish off that whole container of ice cream and go to bed early. Maybe she'd cry herself to sleep.

Tomorrow was Sunday. Maybe she should go to church and pray for a miracle. Like a good lead.

Or her cradle-robbing asshole of a husband getting hit by a garbage truck.

36

"Jersey, you ready?" Tina stood at the peephole in the door. "Sally Jean's down to her pumps and waving her ass in Flannel Boy's face."

Flannel Boy. Nobody knew his real name, but if you let him get a good look—maybe more—he was good for at least twenty a dance. How much did the guy have, he dropped a few hundred every night he came in, which was like three nights a week. He didn't look that old, or that young, or that much of anything, but he had money.

"Hot to trot, give 'em all I got." Chrissie adjusted her bra and slid her catcher's mask into place. The guys all loved that. She was keeping the hockey mask for last dance. Jason with a rack.

Chrissie took Tina's place by the stage door and saw Sally Jean picking up bills around the stage and showing that pasted on smile to everyone. Great smile. If she turned it sideways and stuck it between her legs, she'd make a mint, and not one to suck on. Well, maybe.

Chrissie pushed through the door and squinted in the dark. The rubes were in shadow, someone said that made the girls look better, but the guys weren't choosy. You see naked, you don't mind a few freckles. Chrissie swished her hips between the tables, two of them with girls giving lap dances and suggestions for more in the VIP room, a couple of guys watching like they wanted some too, a couple of others pretending they weren't looking. *Yeah, like that's gonna fool anyone.*

Chrissie stepped onto the platform and Loverboy came up, her third round song, "Standing in the Strike Zone." Loud, hard, the singer with that high voice like his pants were too tight. That's what she was there for. But she didn't want a no-hitter, not tonight.

She stood with her arms raised, give everyone time to check out the mask, see the Tigers jersey, long legs disappearing under it. Those legs, her best parts, looked like they went clear up to her scalp, imagine these wrapping around you, honey, how much you think they worth?

She bent over and gave Flannel Boy a look, everything still covered, but get his attention right away. Standing in the strike zone, come on, lover, you ready for a home run? Maybe slide into home?

Maybe she should have tried to hook up with Flannel Boy instead of Tony. But Tony asked and nobody else did.

"Hey, Baby, over here."

Kid looked too young to be up this late, but Chrissie saw bills in his hand and gave him a smile that hurt her cheeks. She inched the jersey up a little, reached under it. He dropped the bill between her heels and she crouched down to get it, let him think he was getting a look between her legs, but not yet, boy. Not yet. She flicked the money to the center of the platform and spun away. There were four or five other guys on stools and two of them were smiling, either they liked her or they were already buzzed. Either way worked.

She dropped her mask behind her and shook her shoulders a little. She heard a couple of "yeahs" in the shadows. The light pooled around her platform like a big hot mouth, guys surrounding her like sharks. Or maybe sheep, after all, she was the one in charge.

"Nice, honey." The guy in the yellow tee shirt with a cigarette pack rolled in the sleeve, real old-school. But he dropped a bill.

She reached under her jersey, unfastened her shorts, let them slide down her legs.

Loverboy pounded into her brain. When people asked her about dancing, she couldn't explain it, but she could smell the beer or whatever the guys had in front of them, the sweat, both theirs and her own as the evening wore on, the cigarette smoke on their clothes. On a good night, she was wet enough she could smell herself, too. If Flannel Boy was still here in three hours, she'd give him a little whiff, maybe he'd drop some more big bills.

Red light in her eyes. Blue now. Green. Yellow. Red again. She couldn't see more than arm's length beyond the platform, just enough to see hands holding out money. Show me what you got, baby. Show me what you got first, sailor. You want some of this, give me some of that. Loverboy squealed about turnin' up the heat.

She slowly inched the jersey up over her head and held it up, the number right-side-up either way, spinning it in front of everyone's face, running it between her legs like a towel, drying off her business. They all hooted, loved it. Loved her.

She dropped it near the guy in the white polo shirt, glowing blue in the strobe, and he slid a bill across the platform. The light reflected off his glasses, he looked dweeby like Tony.

Tony, little guy, but he knew how to hum her tune. Make her sing. And now he was gone. And she was carrying his baby. Shit, shit, shit.

The singer's falsetto pounded in her gut.

Yes, please. Thank you. Smile pretty at the mark, light flashing on her belly button ring. A little higher up, honey, you like these?

She kicked her jersey toward the guy in the yellow shirt and he grabbed at it, a bill in his hands. Crouched again and slid her panties down her thighs and over her stilettos.

Three minutes later, Christine Chapel left the stage wearing her blue stilettos, everything else wrapped up in jersey number 69. Sweat trickled down her back, between her cheeks and she knew the last minute of her act she was so shiny the lights turned her into a Christmas tree. Give 'em what they want...almost. Always leave them wanting a little more.

That costs extra, darlin'.

If she was like her mom, she'd start to show in another two months, tops. And who's gonna hire a stripper with a baby bump?

She still smelled the cigarette smoke on the mens' clothes, made her want one, too, just slip out the stage door for a minute. Then she remembered she'd quit. Smoking would be bad for the baby.

Last dance. And nobody's taking her home.

Chrissie sagged in front of the mirror and tried not to cry. Everyone else was packing up and heading out. Some had boyfriends and a couple of others were hooking up with bouncers even as she sat and watched. A few probably had pets.

The face in the mirror looked tired enough to sleep until noon...Monday. Did she have anything edible in the fridge? At least she didn't have a pet or a kid...yet. She didn't have a husband or a boyfriend now either, but she had bills up the ass and a detective asking questions. He didn't show up again tonight, though, so maybe that was a good sign.

Or maybe he was outside, waiting to follow her and get her alone, when Rocky and Jack Splat weren't around to toss him out.

Did Tony's wife know about her? Did the cops think she had something to do with Tony's getting himself killed?

The waiting was making her nuts. It was bad enough needing the money for those bills Tony wasn't helping her with now, and if she was going to have a baby, it would get worse, especially when she couldn't dance anymore. Christ, quitting smoking was bad enough, but this shit on top of it...

Tonight she got three different guys back into the VIP room, should've been some kind of record, should've solved her money problems for the whole freakin' month. And one guy's got like nothing in his pockets, enough for the bottle of "champagne," and five dollars left over. She wouldn't even flip a guy off for five bucks. She watched Jack Splat carry him out, legs riding an invisible bicycle all the way through the curtain.

She did her next dance, guy at the end of the platform smiling up at her, she gave him a real good look, he slid a twenty toward her.

"Like what you're seeing, sweety? Want to see more?"

He nodded like a freakin' woodpecker. So she got him into the same friggin' room, smells like last week's fish in a locker room, but she's looking to score big, rubs the guy up, gets him all hot, asks if he wants more. He's reaching in his pants, sure for bills, this is gonna be her quota for the night...and he looks up and wipes his hand.

Two more hours before she's got another live one, and by then she's half-dead herself, the music turning her brains to snot, she's got to pee, she's hungry, her feet hurt, her nipples hurt from taking her bras off and putting new ones on, her eyes feel like pincushions, this guy shows up. It's late, she doesn't get him in there soon, they're gonna close. And Milt the Stilt won't let them do overtime because they gotta clear everyone out and count the money, make sure the doors are locked, all that shit.

The clock's ticking, she's got a guy who's hot to trot, and two other girls are back there, taking long enough to service all of Selfridge Air Force Base. She does a lap dance for the guy, taking her time, drawing money out of him like oil out of Oklahoma. A hundred bucks and she's down to her piercings, still glancing at the curtain, Jack Splat looking back at her, his head moving a quarter inch.

The clock is still ticking, they'll be closing soon. The PA announces "last call for alcohol," not that they can serve the hard stuff on the naked side, but hard stuff's what she's looking for and it ain't getting any better.

"Sweetheart, it looks like the VIP's going to close soon."

"Shit, you wanna come outside?'

"You mean in the fresh air?"

"No, baby, you wanna come to my car?"

Yeah, right, do him in the car. They've got enough lights out there to have a Taylor Swift concert, Eminem for the opening act. Fuck me. Well, yeah.

"Your car?" How big is it?"

"It's an SUV, we can go in back."

"Well..." She's really thinking about it, then he pulls the deal-breaker out of his ass.

"But we gotta be quick, you know, just blow me, something. I gotta be home before my girlfriend."

Fuck me sliding down the banister.

So she gives him a really quick handjob under the table—if Jack noticed, he didn't say anything. If he tells Milt, she's screwed the wrong way, they've got the VIP room just for that.

So here she was, wiping off the make-up, only a few hundred bucks ahead. Her car payment is due tomorrow—

Sunday, so she's got 'till Monday, but they don't open Sunday—and she's over four hundred short. She hoped Candy and Angelita made a shitload while they kept her out. She should go ask them for a percentage.

Any day now, she knew she'd start getting morning sickness. Her mother puked her brains out every morning for months. She hoped the apple didn't land too close to the tree on that one, but the way her luck was going...

She slid a tee shirt over her head and turned off the lighted mirror. She looked around the room, nobody else in sight. There wasn't even much noise outside.

"Anyone else here?" She didn't hear an answer, so she hoisted her bag over her shoulder and turned the light out when she went through the door.

The fluorescents turned the main room into someone's big cheap basement, black and white tile, four platforms the size of kids' sandboxes, she could see the tape holding the seat cushions together. Sandy at the bar was counting the money, Geraldo seconding it. Milt the Stilt stood watching, the night deposit bag already in his hand, the deposit ticket ready to go.

One-fucking-forty. Chrissie felt old enough to be in a museum.

Jack Splat leaned against the exit arch.

"You OK? No trouble tonight, right?"

"No." She realized that detective might really be out there, waiting. By now, most of the cars were gone, if he was waiting, he might have already figured out which one was hers.

"You see that detective guy tonight? The one from last night?"

"Uh-uh. Don't worry, he won't be back anytime soon." Jack looked Chrissie up and down, his eyes like the tongue on a Great Dane and she felt like he'd slobbered all over her shirt.

"You want me to walk you to your car?"

She did, actually, but then he'd want to get in with her, and then follow her home. And then he'd open her door, turn on her bedroom light, help her undress, and...

"No, thanks, I'm good." She felt her courage oozing away. "But maybe keep an eye out until I drive away?"

"You got it, babe."

She felt his eyes on her ass, all the way to her car, the bag over her shoulder so heavy she should put wheels on it, get one of those luggage things like you saw people hauling through the airport. Christ, she could hardly walk.

She unlocked her car, checked the back seat, rolled down her windows and waited for the heat to drift out. The sun went down six hours ago, the car still hot enough you could grow weed in it.

She had a couple of joints home. Maybe she'd have one before she went to bed. She needed to unwind.

She pulled out of the parking lot and turned right down 8 Mile. Even at two a.m. there were enough cars so she paid attention to see if someone was following her. Shit, she should have let Jack come home with her. In a few months, she could tell him the kid was his.

She turned right on Woodward, back into the city. To her left, the nicer burbs, but she only had a shit apartment. She deserved better, needed more. She put her hand on her stomach. Nothing moving. Yet.

And before she knew it, she turned east on McNichols, followed it a few miles and turned right—south—to aim at Grosse Pointe and Tony's house. She crossed the town line at two-forty and tried to read the street signs. She'd never seen his house, never been there, but she knew about where it was.

She zigzagged through strange streets for the next forty-five minutes before she found it. It wasn't anything like what she expected, just an old brick house, two story with an attic and a basement. Fenced-in backyard. Somehow, she figured he'd have more. This place looked out of old TV shows.

No lights on anywhere. She saw a garage with the doors closed and an old beater in the driveway, she drove by slowly enough so her headlights showed the hood ornament. She recognized a Saturn. Tony drove a Mercedes, who the hell had a Saturn? They must have had hired help, a maid or something.

Or maybe Tony was old enough to have a kid driving. No, she saw his family at the funeral. No way either of those kids could drive. Tony was driving a Mercedes, though, the Saturn sure as shit didn't belong to his wife. Someone else was there.

Chrissie realized it didn't matter anyway. Three a.m., what was she going to do, ring the doorbell, wait for the wife to answer, say "Your husband owes me." She'd be lucky the woman didn't call the cops.

Which reminded her of that detective again. At least he didn't seem to be following her, be thankful for small favors.

What was she doing here, almost dawn? She had no plan, no money, and not much else.

Christine Chapel's throat tightened up and she felt like she was going to cry.

It wasn't fucking fair. None of it.

She had to come up with a plan, a better one. Soon.

She drove around the block and headed down to Jefferson. In another half hour, she'd be home.

At least she didn't have to get up for church. And she had one last pregnancy test left.

37

Danny's coffee tasted more metallic than usual and he wondered when he'd last cleaned the pot. The *Free Press* scattered all over the table reflected the way his mind was working that morning, too. The guy he saw at the mall hadn't shown up at work last night, but Danny kept looking over his shoulder anyway. He picked up his phone and dialed, wondering how many shots he had left before the gun was empty.

The phone on the other end rang three times. At four, Danny knew it would go to voicemail. If that happened, he'd drive over and find the asshole in person. Then he realized maybe he wasn't answering because he found something.

Yeah, nine-thirty on a Sunday morning. If he got anywhere, it was last night while Danny was pouring drinks and watching every loser in Wayne County playing doctor with the dancers. He'd asked around about a broad who had to do with sports, and a couple of guys thought they knew who he was talking about, promised they'd ask around, too. It felt like that old kids' game, listen how the story changes as it goes around the circle. Danny didn't want the story to change anymore. He just wanted it to end.

"Yeah." Sounded like the guy still had his face pushed into the pillow.

"It's me. What you got?"

Grunting came through the phone, like the guy was trying to sit up.

"If he was getting any on the side, it wasn't this girl. I think she likes the kids enough she wouldn't do anything behind their mother's back."

"What if the guy made it worth her while?"

He heard a cough at the other end. "Christ, I need coffee. I was out late."

"So was I. Suck it up." Danny knew he'd be more effective in person, where he could pick the guy up by his throat, push him against a wall. They didn't call him "Danny the Hammer" because he loved ballet.

"OK, the girl. I'm not sure she even talked to the guy much, she was with the kids most of the time the guy was at work, and I don't think they ever went anywhere together without the kids and the wife."

"But did he talk to her? Maybe tell her something?"

"I don't see it. My read is that she likes the kids a lot and thinks the wife's OK, but the guy was hardly on her radar."

"Shit."

"But..." Danny could hear a brain straining through ignition on the other end. Water running in the background. "Christ, my eyes feel like burning matches."

"Yeah, yeah, my heart bleeds for you. 'But' what?"

"They've got a beach house, cottage on the lake. You know about that?"

"Uh-uh. Why?"

"Well, they probably stay there once in a while, there's a kitchen with stuff in the fridge, a couple of bedrooms. Small."

"Yeah, I got you."

"OK, one of the beds has been used lately. Maybe the guy did have a girlfriend, but not the college chick."

Danny felt it coming together. *The stripper. Sure, that's why he found the Mercedes outside one of the clubs. Tony Fortunato was banging a stripper. Now he really had to find out the broad's name.*

"You're sure about this?"

"Yeah, pretty much. So...what now?"

"You just gave me another idea, I'll check it out. But keep going just to be sure, OK?"

"'Kay." Danny heard another grunt on the other end. "Catch you later."

Danny poured the last of his own coffee and picked up the sports section. The Tigers lost a close one. The Lions were barely in training camp and they already looked bad. Who the hell cared about golf? The coffee still reminded him of copper wire, but now he had something better to chew on.

Tony Fortunato was banging a stripper. Those broads wouldn't even blow their nose for free, so he had to be dropping a lot of dough. That meant maybe he was spending time in the VIP, or someone was showing up with new clothes or presents. Which meant someone else might notice.

Danny knew half the bouncers and bartenders in Detroit. And they knew a lot of the girls. All he had to do was get the ball rolling.

He picked up his phone and called Junior, the head bouncer at Leggedy Splitz. If Danny didn't know someone, Junior probably did.

"Junior, I got a guy who's looking for a girl, a dancer. He doesn't know her real name, but she dances under some name has to do with sports."

"Sports? You mean like baseball or something?"

"Yeah. I don't know exactly what it means, maybe Tiger or something. But I want to find the broad for him. He wants it bad enough there might be some bills coming back. She might be showing up with presents or new clothes, too, like she's got a new boyfriend, one with some bucks."

They both called two friends, and they called two friends. In an hour, Danny knew that at least fifty guys and dolls were asking each other the same questions.

He plugged in his phone and dug through his cupboard for a bottle of vinegar to pour into his coffee maker. When the whole kitchen smelled like he was dying Easter eggs, he sorted his laundry into light and dark and headed for the basement. Most of it was tee shirts and jeans and underwear, so he wouldn't have to worry about ironing. He stuck quarters into two machines and returned to the kitchen to pour out the hot vinegar.

He was running the second pot of water through the machine when his phone buzzed. Jack Splat from Cherries Jubilee. They had a stripper called Jersey Girl.

"Jersey Girl?" Danny wondered if the guy was sober. "How is that sports?"

"It's her whattayacallit. Costume. She wears jerseys from all the teams in Detroit. You know, the Tigers, the Lions. She wears them over her other shit."

"You sure this is the girl?"

"How do I know, you asked, remember? But this girl, she seems to need money all of a sudden, and I don't think it's going up her nose."

"Uh-huh." Danny had to put his stuff in the dryers in another ten minutes.

"Yeah." Jack Splat cleared his throat. "And something else. Two nights ago. Friday? Yeah, Friday."

"Yeah." Danny scratched under his rib cage. "Two nights ago was Friday. So?"

"A guy came in, he gave this broad some trouble. Asking her lotsa questions, I don't know what about, but it really spooked her, you know? Scared the living beejesus out of her. We had to kick him out."

"You know who he was?"

"Some PI. I don't know his name."

Danny felt the room get quiet like before they announced a big name dancer and the spotlight was waiting to burst up to full again.

"You know why he was talking to her?"

"I guess he thought she knew someone. Or about someone. She was so freaked, I thought she was gonna piss herself. I was kinda surprised she showed up again last night, but there she was. I guess she needs the bread. Like I said, I don't know why."

"You know who the PI thought she knew?"

"I didn't hear all of it, she was too fucked up to tell me much but I think it was some Eye-Tie name. Joey. Or maybe Tony?"

Danny felt better than since he'd stuffed the dead motherfucker into the trunk of his Mercedes. "Jersey Girl. You know her real name? Or a phone number maybe?"

"Uh-uh. But she's here every night for another week."

38

With his clothes on, Evan Roenicke looked even bigger than he did in trunks and a tank top, his white shirt big enough to show movies on and turning his lifeguard tan into a rich brown that reminded Tobi of pizza crust.

"So, how are the kids doing?" He held the door for her, but she was pretty sure it was so he could check out her butt when she climbed into the high seat of his Murano.

"They're getting there." Butt or no butt, she gave him props for asking about Chuck and Patty. "Some friends invited them over to play video games this afternoon. That's probably good for them, get out of the house."

"Yeah." He closed the door and walked around the hood to his own door. "I mean, something like that, they probably have nightmares."

"Actually, I don't think so." Tobi knew she wouldn't ask them and plant the idea. "They're getting along better than usual, though. I guess they figure they've got to stick together."

"Makes sense." Evan backed out of the driveway. "I've got some burgers and beer in the back. I figure we can swim a while, get a little sun, whatever, then eat at your cottage. Unless you want to do something else."

"No, it sounds great."

He glanced over at her. "You don't look too upset about not being in that play. Yesterday, you were pretty pissed."

"I guess I have to get used to rejection. And it means I've got to get better for next time."

She heard the words coming out of her mouth and wondered who said them. A week ago, she would have been burning incense and finding hair and fingernail clippings from the girl who beat her out. The only thing different was Evan. Maybe he was a good influence. Maybe he'd even end up more than a summer distraction. Well, Wayne State and Eastern Michigan were only a few miles apart, not like a coast-to-coast thing where you'd need frequent flyer miles to keep things simmering.

She leaned back in the seat and his hand brushed hers.

"Tough morning?"

"Oh, God."

By the time Connie pulled back into the driveway after church, Tobi felt twice her age. Everyone in the free world came up to hug Chuck and Patty, talking in those fake voices that always sounded like a perv with candy. If the kids didn't have brain damage after inhaling that old woman powder scent a hundred times, it would be a miracle.

Tobi wasn't Catholic and her field trip Thursday hadn't made her want to convert. This morning was twice as scary because it was supposed to be about Jesus, not them, but Connie milked it like a lounge singer. Tobi braced to shield the kids with her own body if a thunderbolt came through the roof, but it never happened.

Connie kept up a steady commentary on the drive back, too, about how everyone was so nice and generous at church but nobody was calling to help them with anything, like she needed help. The liquor cabinet was so full the living room floor needed shoring up, the refrigerator still had enough leftovers to keep them fed until the kids went back to school, and she—Tobi—was taking care of the kids half the time. Not that she minded, they were great kids, but, Jesus, Connie, give it a rest.

She spent most of the ride back thinking that Hebrew was a better language for cursing than Latin. Hebrew, you could get guttural. Her own grandmother could wish someone eternal happiness, wealth and many children for all of her days and it sounded like she was calling down floods, locusts, and ten years of menstrual cramps.

Driving to St. Paul's in a Mercedes with a CONNI F license plate might be a shade tacky, too, but the other choice was Tobi's Saturn, and the back seat had a permanent weed smell. The kids never recognized it, but Connie might have been hip enough to figure out that it wasn't oregano. It wasn't even Tobi's weed. She bought the car pre-perfumed. It inspired her to name it "Doobie Gillis."

Connie pulled into the driveway without even breaking off a sentence. Chuck and Patty looked almost as wilted as Tobi felt. Patty handed her mother the garage remote, and as soon as they were in the garage, both kids bolted. Tobi pushed the seat forward and slid out, stretching her legs. She wasn't that tall—it occurred to her for the first time that maybe they'd turned her down for *Hamlet* because she was only five-five—but the Mercedes had a back seat designed for any two of the seven dwarves.

"Christ," Connie said. "Now we've got to figure out how to get through the rest of the day. I hate Sundays."

"They all suck right now, don't they?" Tobi was about to offer to take the kids somewhere when they heard the phone ring.

"Mom! Mom!" Chuck burst through the still-open door. "Artie and Joanna want to know if we can go over there and play video games."

Tobi crossed her fingers behind her back and Connie pretended to think about it.

"When would you be back?"

"Later. Before supper. Please, Mom?"

"Oh...I suppose. But you be sure to thank Ms. Anselmo. And don't be a nuisance."

They were off to change out of their church clothes before the last word was out of their mother's mouth. Tobi felt the first twinge of envy.

"Well." Connie turned toward her. Up close, Tobi could see the tension easing in her neck. "I guess that means you're free for the afternoon, doesn't it?"

"I guess." Tobi escaped to her room and shed her church clothes. The humidity turned her hair into a Brillo pad. She heard her phone, the theme from *Jaws* that she'd set for Evan Roenicke.

"Hey, whachu doing?" His voice smooth as peanut butter. "You OK after last night?"

"Sure." She'd managed to get him out on the dance floor every time he offered to buy her another beer. She wasn't a great dancer, but she was even less a drinker. He'd still slammed down at least eight Buds and never missed a beat.

She waited in her room until his SUV slid into the driveway. She was out the door before Connie could even take her lips off her glass.

The next thing she knew, Evan was pulling into the driveway at the cottage. She reached behind her for her stuff. "We can change in the cottage, easier than going down to the cabanas."

"Sounds good."

An hour later, she was lying on the towel and re-reading Cohen's *Acting in Shakespeare*, Evan's fingers spreading moisturizer under her bra strap. His hands were bigger than her head, but he treated her gently as a kitten. She hated to admit it, but the warmth she felt didn't all stem from the sun. She pushed back against his hands and willed them to move down. She should have worn her thong. But then he might get the wrong idea. But *was* it the wrong idea?

"Do my legs?" She had to clear her throat. He started at her ankles and by the time he reached her thighs—stopping discreetly about half-way up—she was afraid he could see her squirming.

He took his time and she forced her breath to stay even.

"Let's go back to the cottage." She felt her voice shaking in her chest and wasn't sure she could stand up without his help. They strolled through the back door and the next thing she knew it was like she was watching herself lead him upstairs into the larger bedroom with that queen-sized bed. She pulled his massive white polo shirt over his head, his arms bigger than her own legs, and pulled him down to taste his lips. When they touched hers, she heard humming in her ears.

She leaned into his chest and felt his arms slide around her shoulders. She pulled back and struggled to find her voice.

"Untie me?" She felt those huge gentle fingers fiddle with the bow holding her top up. He tossed it aside and she sank to the bed to look up at him, big enough to straddle her like a colossus, his eyes softening while he looked down at her. He lay next to her and one hand gently cupped her breast. She heard herself whisper "yes," and closed her eyes.

His tongue probed her lips and she opened her mouth a little to let him in. His hand moved to her nipple.

"Evan." She wanted him inside but didn't have the breath to say the words.

"Tobi."

His hand moved from her breast to her stomach, his phone number finally filling in. She felt so hot she was afraid she'd burst into flame right there in the bed, burn away to nothing before they could even make love.

His hand slid lower and her breath caught in her throat.

"Yes," she whispered again.

His hand moved even lower, one finger sliding under her bikini bottom, and he kissed her again, gently, not like some horndog just wanting to get his rocks off. He seemed to understand how much this meant to both of them, real love, the start of something magical. His fingers moved lower, touching her and she arched against them.

"Evan..."

She rolled her shoulders and raised her hips so he could slide the bottom off, then moved against him. He kissed her again and she rolled over to press against him, even tighter.

Something dug into her hip.

"Oh."

"What?" His eyes jerked up to her face. "Don't worry, I've got protection. I wouldn't..."

"No, it's not that." She tried to sit up, her breasts in his face. "I just...wait a minute."

She ooched her butt away from him and groped under the bed spread. The bed hadn't been made, she remembered that from last time, the spread just pulled over the rumpled sheets, and now she swept her hand under those sheets. Her fingers found something hard and cold.

She held it up, a blue stone the size of a dime, it had to be glass, she didn't recognize it as precious, and a gem that size would cost a mint anyway. A gold setting, and dangly chain thingies, about an inch long. She'd never seen Connie wear anything even remotely like it, it looked expensive and fake at the same time. And tacky as ketchup on a prime rib.

She held it up for Evan to see, too.

"An earring."

39

Guthrie missed the patience gene in his DNA. He'd always hated Christmas Eve and the night before his birthday. He was impatient the night before his wedding, too, even though he and Sarah had unwrapped most of the surprises long before that. And his senior prom.

He still couldn't understand why Tony Fortunato would buy a six-thousand-dollar guitar he never played. Jersey Girl was still out there somewhere, too, but unless Valerie came up with a real name, Guthrie wouldn't be able to find her until Tuesday night, and he knew his chances of getting to talk to her at Cherries Jubilee were between slim and none.

He dumped his overnight bag on his own bed, visions of Meg in her dragon robe still fresh in his mind. His bruised ribs felt almost normal and the nick on his scalp itched. He filled his coffee maker with high test. When he was restless, he drank even more coffee than usual, a habit Meg pointed out probably didn't help things much, but she turned to coffee and music too.

While the coffee brewed, he went upstairs and booted up his computer. His consultant had found nothing significant with Anthony Fortunato's finances, both his income and expenses typical for a man in his position. Guthrie noticed that the cash for the luggage and guitar was missing, though. What else did Tony have hidden? With so much business conducted online, cash had become the new cloak of invisibility.

He deleted his spam and checked his phone—again. No messages from Valerie or anyone else. He played a game of chess on his computer and lost in 21 moves, bad even for him.

Meg was probably outside working in the garden she shared with Blue Song Riley. They might even be comparing notes on their evenings. Blue Song viewed dating as a journey, not necessarily with a destination, and had probably broken more hearts since Guthrie had met her three months before than he had in his entire lifetime. Her Mercedes with the license plate HANDS should have been known throughout the Metropolitan Detroit area.

Guthrie told himself he had to do something before he went crazy. He picked up his phone. When the voicemail kicked in, he had his message ready.

"Mr. Klein, this is Chris Guthrie, the detective who spoke to you a few days ago. I've thought of a couple of questions you might be able to help me with, so—"

"Hello?" Klein either screened his calls or couldn't get to the phone. Maybe the number was a land line.

"Mr. Klein, sorry to interrupt you on a Sunday."

"That's quite all right, Mr. Guthrie. Sundays for me are not such a big deal."

"Right. Sir, I'm still investigating your partner's death and I've learned a few things that you might be able to shed some light on."

"Such as...?"

"Well, I saw a woman at Tony's funeral, but she didn't speak with anyone and nobody seemed to know her, either. Maybe you saw her, a woman with blonde hair and a very short skirt? She sat near the back of the church."

"Ahh, no, I don't think I remember her. What was her name?"

"That's the problem, sir. Nobody seems to know, and I'm trying to find her. I think she might be able to tell me a few things. In fact, I'm wondering if she and Tony had a...relationship."

"A relationship? You mean like a girlfriend? Anthony was having an affair?"

"I'm wondering about that, yes. Would you happen to know?"

"I'm...astounded, Mr. Guthrie. Anthony always seemed to dote on his family. Such adorable children—you must have met them, yes?"

"I have, and I agree. But this woman..."

"I don't remember her. Did she go to the cemetery? Or back to the house?"

"No. I don't think so." Guthrie hadn't seen the woman's car, but if Klein didn't know Jersey Girl, he probably didn't know her car, either.

"Now that I think of it, though, those other officers, the young lady and her partner, seem to think that Anthony was embezzling from our company. Or our clients. Barry and I will be bringing in some other accountants to start a complete audit tomorrow morning. If Anthony was stealing, perhaps a woman was the reason why."

"That's what I was thinking too, sir. Do you have any idea how much he might have actually taken?"

"Not yet. And we aren't certain he really took anything, but the police say he may have established several accounts under different names, which looks very bad."

"It might explain why he was killed, too. Someone knew about it and wanted to get at the money."

Klein sighed. "Barry and I were talking about that, too. It's so hard to believe, you work with someone, you think you know them, and then something like this...It's such a shock. And now we may have to find a way to make reparations. If

Anthony stole a great deal, we could be in serious trouble with clients."

"Yes sir." Guthrie felt Klein's agitation rising on the other end. The guy felt almost as wired as he did himself.

"Sir, if you hear anything, I'd appreciate it if you'd let me know."

"Of course."

Guthrie hung up and wondered what he could do next.

A picture of a Les Paul guitar floated across his monitor, looking a lot like the one Tony bought. Then a Stratocaster, a sunburst like Guthrie's own. Buddy Holly used one like it. Then John Lennon's Epiphone Casino. A Gibson acoustic like Robert Johnson played...

Guthrie went to the basement. If his neighbors weren't already awake by noon, that was their problem. He plugged his Stratocaster into his old amplifier and turned the volume up to seven.

After thirty years, Meg knew her chords and theory backwards and inside out. She told him that if he had to think about a note, chord, or scale, he didn't know it well enough. As a result, he thought of music differently now.

He opened a book of classic rock and started playing the songs in keys other than what was printed. He played with his reverb foot control, trying to find a sound he liked for each. Since he sang less often than his feathers molted, he never really paid attention to a song's key before except to transpose it into something with easier chords to play, but Meg had shown him that it would help his still pathetic reading skills.

He stumbled his way through the solo from a Judas Priest song, not because he loved the song, but because it forced him to read notes farther up the neck than usual. In the upper registers, a Stratocaster with the tone switches full up threw out a treble that could crack glass, probably designed so the guitar could be heard over horns in the days when amplifiers were still in their infancy.

"You Got Another Thing Coming," not "think." Maybe Brits weren't familiar with the cliché, an American usage.

Just as that idea flashed through his mind, he bent a string a little too far and heard the "pop" through his speaker. The string came loose and he heard the whole guitar go out of tune. The strings were attached to a bridge that had springs on it so he could get a tremolo/vibrating effect, and that meant if a string broke, the springs took up the extra tension.

He turned off his amplifier and dug through the junk on the table for new strings. He pawed through the ashtray that held picks, capos, and a tuner until he found his string winder and a Phillips screwdriver. Changing strings meant taking off a plate on the back of the guitar and threading the strings through that spring-loaded neck. It was a pain in the ass, which was why he changed strings about as often as he bought a new car.

He loosened all six screws and put them into that ashtray so they wouldn't roll away. The guitar had a small cutout, about four inches square and an inch deep, enough room for the springs to stretch and the bridge to rotate. Guthrie pulled out the short end of the broken string and laid it on the coffee table.

He was unwinding the string from the tuning peg before it occurred to him that the strings fed through a space about the size of a deck of cards. Not all guitars had a tremolo handle, so they didn't have that space for the moving bridge.

Guthrie closed his eyes and tried to remember what the back of Tony Fortunato's Les Paul looked like. The guitar didn't have a tremolo, but he remembered seeing a square plastic panel on the back of the body. He didn't know Gibson electrics as well as Fenders, but he thought that plate lay directly beneath the tone and volume controls.

Sure, if there was a problem with the pick-ups, you'd go in through the body to fix it.

Les Pauls had two volume control knobs and two tone controls because there were two pick-ups to give different sounds. And the guitar was nearly twice as heavy as Guthrie's strat.

How big was the opening under that plate?

Guthrie threaded the new string into place and tightened it until it was almost in tune. It would stretch a few times before it was really tuned, but he didn't bother to wait. He picked up his coffee mug—now cold—and hustled back upstairs to call Connie Fortunato.

40

Connie opened the door and Guthrie didn't see a glass anywhere in the living room. Maybe she'd left it outside by the swimming pool, but then he realized she wore shorts and a tank top instead of a bathing suit.

"You keep showing up here, neighbors are going to think you're making a play for the rich widow." She had a piece of lettuce stuck between her upper teeth, but that meant she was eating instead of drinking.

"Sorry, but I'm already spoken for." Guthrie studied the woman's eyes, which reacted normally. "And I have simple tastes."

"Me too. Good thing, 'cause if Tony left us anything, we don't have a clue where it is."

"Did he leave a will?" Guthrie remembered that the Fortunatos were both under forty, so they might not have gotten around to that yet.

"Yeah, it's being probated, but there's not a lot to talk about." Connie swept her arm around the living room. "He had life insurance, but it'll probably take care of the mortgage, period. I may have to sell the house, like that's going to work now, the market going to shit."

"Did he leave everything to you?"

The woman nodded. "Such as it is." She sank to the couch in the living room and Guthrie felt the AC chill the back of his neck.

"Ms. Fortunato, I thought of something a little while ago. It's a long shot, but may I look at the guitar again?"

"The guitar? The toy Tony never played with?"

"Right. I checked yesterday, and he bought what sounds like the same guitar a few months ago, but I'd like to look at it more closely, check the serial numbers, see if he's had it modified in any way."

"Why the heck would he do that?" Guthrie watched her try to follow him. "He didn't even play the damn' thing. I still don't understand why he bought it."

"Neither of your kids has any interest in music, right?" Guthrie glanced around. "Where are they, by the way, outside?"

"They went over to a friend's house. The mother—bless her heart—offered to take them for awhile, maybe get their minds off..."

"Sure." Guthrie took a deep breath. "Look, I don't want to get your hopes up, but may I examine that guitar again?"

"Yeah, OK." Connie stood and Guthrie followed her down the basement stairs again, where she pointed to the guitar case leaning in the corner near those same unopened music books.

Yes, a re-issued 1959 Les Paul with the original Patent Applied For humbucking pick-ups and the trapezoid fret markers in the rosewood neck. The plastic plate between the tuning pegs sported Les Paul's signature. Even though the guitar was much heavier than the Stratocaster he played only two hours earlier, he could tell that it was beautifully balanced.

He turned it over and stared at the serial number stamped into the back of the machine head above the tuning pegs.

"What, you think maybe this guitar's stolen?" Connie forced herself to look interested.

"I don't know." Guthrie stared at the pristine finish on the back of the instrument, slowly moving his eyes down the neck to where it met the body, then down to that plastic plate behind the control knobs. Four tiny Phillips screws. He tilted the guitar so the light fell obliquely across those screws. One of them looked slightly uneven.

Bingo.

"Ms. Fortunato, when did you and your husband write your wills?"

"When Chuckie was born. Tony wanted to be sure he'd be taken care of."

"Did you modify it when your daughter was born?"

"No, we had the lawyer write it so I'd get everything but we had him put it so all the kids would be taken care of after that. We didn't know how many, but..."

She swallowed. "We didn't figure..."

"Of course not." Guthrie told himself to stop listening to that little voice in his ear, telling him he was slime.

"Did you make any changes to your will recently?"

"Uh, I didn't. I don't think Tony did, either. He would've told me, right?"

"Maybe." Guthrie felt the Swiss Army knife in his pocket. "I'm just wondering if your husband mentioned this guitar."

"I don't know. It wouldn't be in the copy we've got upstairs."

"Are you sure?"

"Um..."

He waited until Connie disappeared up the stairs again, then opened the Phillip's screwdriver on his knife and loosened the screws enough to lift off the plastic plate. Sure enough, he found a hollowed-out rectangle with a few soldered wires leading into control knobs. He tipped the guitar to spill four tiny envelopes into his palm and stuffed them into his pocket.

By the time Connie Fortunato reappeared, he had replaced the plastic and was moving chords up the neck. The fingerboard was amazingly easy to play on. He understood why so many musicians swore by Gibsons.

"It's not there," she said. "Not in my copy. I just called my lawyer, but it's Sunday and nobody's in."

"It's probably not worth bothering him anyway." Guthrie put the guitar back in the case. "This is the same serial number they had on the sales record at the store. If a guitar worth this much was stolen, they'd have a record of it and spot it right away."

"So the guitar's no big deal."

He heard voices upstairs. Connie led the way back to the kitchen, where they found Tobi Loerner looking shiny and tan with a young man who towered over her and only slightly less-so over Guthrie. He had shoulders wide enough to support headlights.

"Oh, um, Connie—Ms. Fortunato, Mr...Guthrie, is it? This is Evan, he's a lifeguard out by the cottage. We met last week."

"Cottage?" Guthrie shook hands with the man. Sure, he had the shoulders of a swimmer, and a tan two shades darker than the sunburst finish on the guitar downstairs.

"Oh, yeah," Connie said. "We've got a cottage over on Belleville Lake."

"Really." Guthrie saw the nanny and the hunk exchange glances as if they knew it intimately.

"It's nice," Tobi said. "I take the kids there a lot, they swim and play, I get a lot of reading done."

"What do you read?"

She rolled her eyes. "I'm a theater major at Wayne. I'm reading a lot of Shakespeare right now. Mostly *Hamlet*, some of the other plays with good female roles."

Guthrie suspected Megan could tutor the girl.

"Well, good luck with that." He turned back to Connie Fortunato. "Thanks for letting me come by again. I'll call you if anything turns up."

He nodded to the couple and left.

Two blocks away from the house, he pulled to the curb and fished in his pocket. Four small white envelopes lay in his hand. They looked just like the one that held the key to his own safety deposit box.

41

Connie waited until Tobi kissed the beefcake goodbye and went upstairs before she grabbed her phone. Barry Montesori's voicemail kicked in and she swore during the message.

"Call me back as soon as you get this, it's important."

The kids would be home any time, and Connie hoped to God they'd been fed. Chuckie whined about the sandwiches, and she had to admit that after three days, she was getting sick of them too, even if she didn't have to make them herself.

She was pouring her first pinot noir of the day when her phone vibrated in her pocket.

"Hello?" She should have kept the ringer on so she could tell if it was Barry or not.

"Connie, love, what's up?"

"Listen, Barry. That private detective came back again this afternoon. I'm not sure what he's looking for, but he was asking a shitload of questions."

"Like what?"

"Like about Tony's will and stuff. He was here yesterday asking if Tony bought anything big in the last few months."

"Um. The will? What's he trying to do, make you look like a suspect? That's crazy, you've got an alibi for the night he was killed, right?"

"For the night he didn't come home, yeah. But the cops don't know exactly when he was killed."

"Close enough, honey." The sonofabitch was calling her "honey" again. But he wasn't going to divorce his wife now. *Asshole.*

"Yeah, right. The will leaves everything to me. Not that there's much to leave, but it gives me a motive, doesn't it?"

"Well..." Barry sounded like he was rolling something around in his mouth. "Actually, the police talked to Lenny and me the other day. They've been looking at Tony's computers. Well, you know about that, right?"

"Uh-huh." Connie saw a car pull into the driveway. *Shit, the kids were home. Why couldn't they wait a few more minutes?*

"They think Tony was stealing from some accounts. They aren't sure who or where yet, but Len and I are going to have to do a full audit. The cops seem to think we're going to find a lot of shortages."

"Well, that detective, he asked about Tony buying stuff, I told him we got luggage last spring. And you know what? I can't find Tony's. It wasn't in his closet—we looked. Three suitcases, a garment bag, and a trunk. I thought they might be in the attic, but all I found was the trunk. Where the hell is the other stuff?"

Barry said something muffled, his hand over the phone. Probably talking to his bitch wife. The one he wasn't sure he wanted to leave.

"And today that detective came back, he wanted to look at Tony's guitar."

"Guitar? I didn't know Tony played guitar."

"He doesn't, but he bought a guitar a few months ago, a really nice one. The detective knows something about guitars, I guess, he was checking it out this afternoon. I don't know what's going on, but I think he thinks that guitar means something. He even wanted me to check and see if it's mentioned in Tony's will."

"What the fuck?" Barry never swore unless he was talking dirty to her in bed. He wasn't very good at it, but he knew she liked it.

"Our will is eleven years old, when Chuckie was born. But I'm wondering if Tony made a new one with some other lawyer and didn't tell me about it."

"Why would he do that?" Connie could tell Barry was moving into accounting mode. He knew every trick in the book, so if Tony was squirreling money away somewhere, Barry could figure out how he did it. Which meant she was still in the game.

"I don't know, I called the lawyer, but naturally it's Sunday, he won't be in until tomorrow."

Chuckie and Patty slammed the car doors. Connie could hear the sugar in their voices.

"Connie, if Tony was stealing ..."

"But where would he hide it?"

"I don't know. Maybe he's got it in code on the laptop. The police said they found a whole bunch of names and bank accounts on there, maybe it tells where the money is."

"Well, if it's bank accounts, I can get into them can't I? I'm his wife."

"They might be frozen because he died. You might have to use your lawyer, get a court order. It could get complicated."

"But if there's money there, I could get it, couldn't I?"

Barry blew out his breath. "It would depend. If they can track that money back to somewhere, like wherever Tony stole it from—if he stole it—then it would be returned. But if the cops can't track everything down..."

"Is there any way that could be? Tony was a sharp accountant, Barry, almost as good as you. How could he do that?"

"Mom, mom, mommy!" Patty's scream was loud enough to reach Toledo. "Sam and Danielle have a new puppy, it's a cocker spaniel and it's sooo cute!"

Connie held up her index finger. "That's great, honey. Just a minute and you can tell me all about it."

"It's a boy, mom." Chuckie's voice was even louder than Patty's, but not quite as shrill. "He chases a ball and shakes hands and..."

"Just a minute, please, OK? I'm on the phone."

Both kids charged toward the stairs. Tobi was going to hear about the dog, too, whether she wanted to or not. Connie held the phone to her ear again.

"Say that again? The kids just came back."

"Yeah, something about a dog?"

"Yeah, whatever. What did you say?"

"Well, it's a long shot, but maybe Tony's got the money in cash."

"Cash?"

"Right. Cash is impossible to trace unless you've got the serial numbers of the bills, and if it's small bills—twenties or smaller—the banks won't have them. Hundreds, big bills like that, sure, but they trade zillions of the smaller ones."

"But if it's cash, where's he got it?"

"I don't know." Barry sounded like he was chewing something again. The kids screamed outside Tobi's room and Connie heard the door open and the voices disappear inside. *God bless Tobi.*

"The suitcases." Connie heard herself say it. "They're somewhere."

"Christ." Barry's voice sped up. "Tony might have been planning a trip, you know that?"

"What do you mean?"

"Len and I talked again this afternoon. That detective called him this morning, the same guy who talked to you."

"So?" Connie suddenly felt like she'd better sit down.

"The detective asked him if he thought Tony might have a girlfriend. He called me to tell me about it."

Connie's legs gave out and she collapsed onto the couch.

"A girl—that son of a bitch. That cheating motherfucking sonofabitch."

"Hey, honey, Len didn't know about one, so maybe it's not true. The detective was just asking. I think he was trying to find a reason Tony might steal. If he was, you know? It's all guesswork."

"No." Connie felt the truth roaring down the slope at her, too big to dodge, heavy enough to crush her. "He bought a guitar, he bought luggage. Someone killed him to find out where the money is. And now that luggage is gone. He was going away with someone."

The unfairness of it made her eyes burn. *How dare her husband cheat on her and her two beautiful children. That pig. That slimy disgusting pig.*

Her lover's voice sounded in her ear.

"Hey, I bet...if Tony was, uh, seeing someone, you remember...probably not. There was a woman at church. Tony's funeral. Dressed in black, she stayed in the back row. I saw her there, but I don't think she went to the cemetery and I know she didn't come back to your house."

Connie heard her blood pounding in her ears, almost drowning out Barry's words.

"What did she look like?"

"Blonde, young. Black dress, the skirt was kinda...short."

"Sweet holy Jesus of Nazareth." Connie squeezed her phone so tight it should have dripped memory. "My husband was seeing some slut. He was going to run away with her, with suitcases full of money. Now what am I gonna do?"

"Connie." Barry's voice brought her back down. "Listen. If those suitcases really have money in them, Tony must've hid them somewhere. Which means we can find them."

Connie heard him say "we." *Good. He was interested again.*

"Unless that bitch already has them."

"We can't think that." Barry's voice got softer. "Listen, I have to go now. I'll talk to you later. We'll figure this out."

Connie hung up and felt the whole house pressing down on her. Her husband was cheating on her. How could he treat her like that? Here she was thinking of divorcing him so she could be with Barry, but now she didn't have to divorce him. Then Barry, damn his eyes, started having second thoughts or a conscience or whatever. And now he thought Tony had money somewhere and he wanted it. Now she was a way for him to get that money.

Well screw that, Barry.

Connie went to the kitchen and finished pouring her glass of pinot noir. The kids seemed to have calmed down upstairs.

After she drank her wine, she'd go up and let them tell her all about the puppy.

Then she'd figure out where her dead pig of a husband hid the money that was hers and hers alone.

If Barry didn't want to marry her now, that was his problem.

With suitcases of money, she could buy another husband anytime she wanted.

42

Guthrie studied the keys, all in their little envelopes with a snap fastener and a bank logo. Four different banks. He wondered if Tony had the boxes under four different names and decided it was a safe bet.

Now what could he do with them? A good citizen would call Shoobie Dube to tell her what he'd found, but he still had the curiosity of a small boy awaiting Santa Claus. None of the banks were open on Sunday anyway, so there was no rush.

The more he thought about it, the more convinced he was that those safety deposit boxes contained cash, probably in small enough denominations—say, twenties—so the banks wouldn't have the serial numbers. He also managed to convince himself that because Tony was connected with the Detroit Mafia, the money was probably dirty. If Tony was stealing already tainted money, Guthrie felt less compulsion to make sure it returned to its rightful owner.

Everyone needs money, he thought. Someone needs it for a new mansion and someone else needs it for groceries. Valerie wanted to go back to college. Meg wanted to spoil her nieces and nephews, the children she couldn't have herself. Tony Fortunato seemed to be financing trysts and a possible flight from his wife with Jersey Girl.

Guthrie wondered what he wanted more than the impossible dream of making everything right.

Did Jersey Girl know about that money? Probably not. The woman struck him as one who swung the door wide open if she thought she heard opportunity knocking. Besides, if Tony was able to keep it secret from his business partners, he certainly was smart enough not to tell a stripper who was out to make a killing.

Bad choice of words.

But that brought up another line of thought. If Tony was stealing the money, the most likely source was an accounting client. Klein and Montesori were bringing outside help to audit everything, but maybe the Detroit PD should lend a hand, especially if the money was coming from the Mafia—a reasonable hypothesis—and hidden behind four layers of dummy corporations and fake names.

If Tony had been caught stealing from the Mob, that could explain his sudden death. But wouldn't a hit man have tried to find out where the money was before killing him?

Of course. The weird cause of death. Tony wasn't shot in the head and dumped in the river, he was hit in the mouth and choked on his upper plate. He wasn't supposed to die. Somebody killed him by mistake and dumped the body where Hot Rod found the car.

All this added more questions Guthrie couldn't answer. But now the money he couldn't even prove existed seemed to be the key. One of the few hard and fast rules from police work: follow the money.

Since he didn't know what name—or names—Fortunato used, he'd have trouble getting into the boxes anyway. Maybe he should call Shoobie after all, especially since Hot Rod Lincoln seemed to be off the hook. He'd earned his fee from Billable Hours Powers.

Was Shoobie at work on Sunday? He thought she was married, so maybe she and her husband were out somewhere or doing domestic stuff.

He stared at his phone, then had another thought. If Tony was stealing from the mob, the police would love to know, but might not be able to pin anything on the real culprits. Guthrie might be able to use that money—or, better still, the knowledge—to get a little leverage in places that could help more people. The more he looked at the keys, the more he thought he could put them to better use than the police could.

His phone let out a fast guitar run he recognized from Commander Cody and the Lost Planet Airmen: Hot Rod Lincoln.

"Woody…"

"Call me Guthrie. Or Chris."

"Sorry. I usually call cops 'officer' or detective.' That's what I called you before, but now you're not one of them anymore."

"Good point. What's up, Hot Rod?"

"Well, I was just wondering if you're getting anywhere. 'Cause I really don't want to go to jail, 'specially for this one. Yeah, I boosted the car, but I sure as shit don't want to go down for killing the guy. I never knew he was there, honest."

"I know, Hot Rod." Hot Rod's energy level felt like a squirrel munching a candy bar. "I don't want to get your hopes up, but—"

"Jeez, Musetta and I…"

"Musetta?" Guthrie asked. "Your fiancée?"

"Yeah. Musetta Saldano. She's why I called. We just found out. Well, she knew a few days ago, she just figured out how to tell me, though, so I figured I'd pass it on to you. I'm gonna call Powers later too, but…"

"What?" Guthrie felt the guy's energy revving up more and more, close to the red line.

"Um, I'm gonna be a daddy. Musetta's pregnant. She just found out."

"Well, that's…terrific. If you want—"

"You kidding? I always wanted kids. Teach 'em baseball and cars. Shoot, Musetta's a girl, girls can do cars, too. We could have kids that could fix anything on wheels, maybe open our own shop."

"That's an idea." Guthrie tried to focus on reality. "What would you call it? Fillmore and Family, something like that?"

"Actually, we were talking awhile ago. More like Mustang Sally and Hot Rod Lincoln. But that means I gotta stay out of jail. I mean, I want this kid, I want to be there with him. Her. And my wife. We're not married yet, but now I wanna do that, too."

Guthrie heard Hot Rod's excitement move into something bigger and warmer.

"Congratulations, Hot Rod."

He hung up and thought about Megan, who had four nieces and nephews but could never have children herself. He wondered if Shoobie had children.

He went downstairs and plugged in his guitar. He spent the next two hours re-tuning that new string and playing "Money," "Key the Highway," and every other song the case brought to mind. Except "Hot Rod Lincoln."

43

Danny finished his leftover General T'sao's chicken without taking his eyes off the phone lying next to his can of Guinness. Any second, someone would call back and tell him Jersey Girl's real name or address. He believed it less with every passing minute. He'd gone online, but she didn't have a web page like some of the strippers did. Or a Facebook page or a listing on Craigslist. Cherries Jubilee's so-called site was one page with the address, phone, hours, and a pixilated shot of a generic stripper on a pole.

He crunched the beer can and arched it into the basket near the door. Almost nine. He couldn't think of anywhere else to look or anything else to do. He hoped he could find the broad before he had to show up at work tomorrow night. Monday was slower than a morgue at the strip joints—most of them didn't even open—but he knew he was running out of time. By Tuesday, he figured he'd better have the girl or a full tank of gas.

He got another Guinness and flicked on the TV. The Tigers were up by two in the sixth, and both the White Sox and the Twins lost that afternoon. He sipped the beer and tried to figure out where to go next—besides Canada—if he couldn't find Jersey Girl.

The manager came out to talk to the pitcher and they went to a commercial. Danny flicked the set off and went back to his computer. Just for the hell of it, he clicked on the Expedia site. Good prices on plane tickets, but he didn't want to leave a credit card trail if he had to split. What if he booked a plane, then didn't show up for it? Whoever was after him would look for him at the airport, probably not figure out that he wasn't there for a day or so. An extra day, he could drive hundreds of miles.

Especially if he switched the plates on his car. Maybe he should go out and steal someone else's right now. There were shopping malls and movie theaters all over the place, he could find a car in a second.

He was digging through his tool drawer when his phone rang. He grabbed it and looked at the number.

"You got something?"

"Jackpot city, straight up. You remember I said I didn't think the guy was banging the nanny?"

"You were wrong?"

"No, he wasn't. But I found out today he bought a bunch of luggage a few months ago, and now the wife can't find it. Big suitcases, like he could stuff a lot of shit in them."

"The woman doesn't know where they are? What, is she retarded?"

"No, I think I know where the guy has them. You said something about a stripper, right? I think they're maybe going somewhere, and he had his stuff packed up, along with cash."

"OK, maybe. I'm still trying to find the stripper's real name."

"Maybe you don't need her. I might have a line on the suitcases."

"Where?"

"You know Belleville Lake?"

"Little pond a few miles this side of Ann Arbor?"

"Yeah, that's it. The family has a cottage there. They don't use it much, except for the girl. She takes the kids there and they swim and hang out on the beach. Most sunny days, they're there for hours."

"Does this guided tour have a point?" Danny opened the fridge for another Guinness.

"Yeah, listen. You remember the girl found a bed there, been slept in, or at least not made? I told you that, right?"

"Yeah." Danny popped the top and watched the draft ball block the opening. "So?"

"Well, this afternoon, we were back there. We were gonna check out that bed a little more, you get me? And before we really got into it, she rolled onto something. It's an ear-ring."

"Yeah? So maybe the wife dropped it."

"No, no, Tobi—the nanny—says she's never seen the mom wear it. It's not like her style, whatever. It's big and flashy. I'm no expert on women's jewelry except I like them pierced here and there, you know?"

"Yeah, yeah. Go on."

"Well, this sucker was big. I mean, humongous. And with a stone and dangly shit. It looked like something a Gypsy would wear to tell your fortune. Cheesy, you know?"

Danny began to catch up. "You mean like maybe a stripper might wear?"

"Ta-daah! Give the man a hand. Yeah. I'm thinking your dead guy was banging the stripper here at the cottage. So maybe he's got the suitcases there, too."

"Where?"

"I don't know. But the place isn't very big. We could probably check it all out, wouldn't take long."

"Where is it exactly?"

"Oh, nice try. Hey, they're here, I get my cut. I've earned it."

Danny took a deep breath. "All right. So where is the place?"

"Take the exit off I-94 and turn right. The cottage will be on your left a few miles down. There are about a dozen of them there, near the beach. A few trees in front, a few beat-to shit garages and driveways. There's a stone wall between them and the road."

"Which one is theirs?"

"I'll meet you there. Say, about two? I'll be working, but I can take a few minutes. I'll park my car there, you know my SUV, right? The Murano?"

"Yeah." Danny looked at his watch. "What's the name of the street, road, just to be sure?"

"Beachview. There aren't many signs, it's some piddly little route number, I don't even remember. Just take the ramp off the exit, turn right and you're on it. You can't miss it. I'll park on the road by the end of the driveway, you can pull in by the garage."

Danny ended the call and went on MapQuest. Sure enough, the directions looked right. From where he sat now, the driving time was thirty-one minutes. Well, tomorrow was his day off. He'd be there at one.

He went to his closet and found his gun and the extra clip.

Share, his ass.

44

Valerie Karr greeted Guthrie from behind her desk with her fingers interlocked so her soft pink nails seemed to stare at him. He could tell she had news.

"I think I've found a new church."

"Really."

"Well, I went yesterday and listened to the sermon. It's Episcopal, not Catholic, but the priest had more of a sense of humor than at St. Ladislaus."

Guthrie knew her former priest had pretty much encouraged the congregation to stone her when pictures of her taken hostage in a G-string and stilettos made the evening news. CNN obscured her breasts in the editing but not her face, so many parishioners recognized her, including Father

Krystof. Her grandmother—who shopped at the local market during the Detroit Riots—continued to stare down the detractors, but Valerie and her mother were made of softer stuff.

"What does your mother think?"

Valerie rolled her eyes. "At this point, I think she'd settle for my flossing twice a day. But God's...well. And thanks to you, I can go back to school in the fall."

Guthrie pondered the oxymoron of a stripper who seldom missed mass. Megan, who referred to Valerie as "Porn-Again," understood why Guthrie hired her, but in their rare conversations, she encouraged Valerie to make lots of friends when she returned to college, especially male. And she didn't even know about Valerie's coffee mug.

Valerie had unpacked it the first day she came to work.

"This was the last present from an ex-boyfriend," she commented. "In fact, it's part of why he's an ex."

Guthrie looked at an ordinary off-white mug with a large blue "D" that resembled the Detroit Tigers' logo.

"What's your middle name?" he asked. "Debra? Diane?"

She clicked her tongue. "Basia."

That caught him off-balance. "So why do you have a..."

"Men." Valerie stashed the mug in her top right-hand drawer. "They don't even check your sizes before they get you stuff."

Guthrie had known enough not to pursue the conversation.

He stepped into his office, draped his blazer over the back of his chair, booted up his computer and pulled out the envelopes with the keys from Tony's guitar.

He was pretty sure Connie knew nothing about her husband's affair—if he was even having one. That took away any motive she might have had for killing him, and he still thought that killing was an accident, anyway.

How did whoever Tony was stealing from find out? Instead of calling the cops, they kidnapped him and tried to make him talk, but ended up killing him instead. Then they dumped his body in the trunk and left the Mercedes in the Cass Corridor, where Hot Rod stole it. That suggested that the victims weren't entirely pure, either. Like maybe Connie's relatives? If Tony stole from his own connected in-laws, maybe he deserved what he got.

Guthrie found a web site for Fortunato, Montesori & Klein. It gave contact numbers, discussed their various services, and had a brief bio of each accountant, along with a few lame pictures. No list of clients, which didn't surprise him.

He searched the Internet for material on all three and came up with very little. Leonard Klein, the oldest of the three at forty-two, came from a family of accountants, going back four generations. One married into the Bernstein family in the twenties, which meant nothing to him, although it obviously did to whoever wrote the posting. Another worked for the IRS in the seventies. Barry Montesori came from a family of factory workers. Both he and Klein sounded boring as dust. Tony Fortunato had run track in high school—where he broke his teeth, according to Connie—but had nothing else to brag about.

The phone on his desk chirped.

"Mr. G, I've found a name for you. For the Jersey Girl."

Valerie appeared in his doorway and raised her arms in a "ta-daahh" kind of move, one hand still holding a highlighter. The pose made her look like she'd escaped from a game show. "Christine or Christina Something. I've heard Staples, Sable, and Chapel for the last name, too. Nobody's quite sure of that, but they recognized your picture."

"Christine Chapel?" Guthrie thought it sounded just wacky enough to be true.

Valerie's enthusiasm waned.

"Mr. G., I hate to speak ill of someone I barely know, but a couple of my friends say she'd sell her mother to a shark breeder if the price was right."

He remembered the woman's self-preservation instincts from Friday night.

"They say she's not very bright, either. She makes some...questionable choices."

"Like dating a married man?"

Valerie cleared her throat. "Not to be judgmental, but..."

Guthrie wondered if the Detroit police would have a sheet on her. "Does she have any other bad habits?"

"Nobody mentioned drugs, if that's what you mean. In fact, someone told me she's just stopped smoking and she's starting to bring in health foods for snacks. That just started a few days ago."

Guthrie wondered what to make of that.

"No address?"

Valerie shook her head. "Sorry."

He watched her face. "How's your reading coming?"

She held up the high-liter. "Three more books, and I should be through the semester. Unless someone changes his list from last year."

She twirled the highlighter between her fingers and vanished again.

The Detroit white pages contained dozens of Staples and Chapels with various spellings, but none was a Christine or Caroline. She probably used a cell phone. Guthrie checked the

Social Security records and found over a hundred women between 17 and 30 with those last names.

Motor Vehicles didn't help either. Guthrie was tempted to ask Megan if she could find an arrest record. It was a long shot, but if the woman was sleeping with Tony Fortunato, she might charge for it.

Then he realized that Carmine Diorio ran the prostitution in Detroit. Would he let a prostitute hook up with the husband of his own niece? Maybe he didn't even know. Guthrie remembered the man at the funeral, understated bodyguards with him, none paying much attention to Shoobie and her partner, whom they'd probably made as police instantly.

Guthrie thought about setting up an appointment with the man, but why? Even if the woman was sleeping with Tony, she probably knew nothing about the money.

He looked down and discovered his hands were playing an invisible guitar. He thought he'd broken himself of that habit when he was thinking. Apparently not.

He still didn't know the next verse, either.

He went back online and searched for the Bernstein family in Detroit history. Then he went back and looked at the accountants' web site again. Yes, he was reading it right. But if it was the same family, Leonard Klein certainly wouldn't have it posted, would he?

Not if he was really a grandson of one of the founders of Detroit's Purple Gang.

45

Shoobie Dube still felt last night's double chocolate fudge pushing against her waistband when she locked her car. Brian Trask was boffing some college bimbo—or worse—when they were supposed to be meeting a social worker to rescue their brittle marriage. She'd never doubted that they could figure out how to get it all back together, and now she saw for the first time that he didn't want to come back. He wanted to trade her in for a newer model, one with less mileage, better shock absorbers, and—most likely—better headlights. Shoobie tasted that ice cream again, burning with bile and hurt.

The air was already tried to glue her hair to the back of her neck and the sun wasn't blasting through the windows yet. Summer in Detroit. Nobody better give her any shit today. She'd tear his throat out and feed it to the rats along the river bank.

"Hi." Grady sipped from a coffee mug with the insides the color of crushed rock. It was probably older than both of them. The mugs here were so solid they wouldn't give one to a suspect because he could use it to fight his way out of the building.

Shoobie wondered if Grady was getting laid. Well, actually, he was married, so that was a distinct possibility. He wasn't bad looking, not Chris Guthrie, but not someone she'd kick out of bed. Of course, since Brian had walked, she hadn't had the chance to kick anyone out of bed. Maybe she should get a cat.

"The D.A. presented the applications for the search warrants first thing this morning." Grady smiled and held up the papers. "Fortunato's bank accounts. The judge is signing them even as we enjoy the lovely weather."

"Beautiful." Shoobie felt the first adrenaline kick in. The IT people were still digging, and the financial guys were trying to figure out how much money they were talking about. Twelve of those banks had safety deposit boxes, too. So far.

"You look tired, Ellie. You getting enough sleep?"

She looked toward the coffee and debated. Coffee always made her have to pee.

"Eleanor?"

"Oh, right. I'm fine. I'm just..."

Grady was the only person besides Brian who didn't call her "Shoobie."

"It just occurred to me, when we talked to the widow, she didn't mention these accounts, right?"

"Right." Grady seemed to follow her line of thought. "And she hasn't tried to get into them. So if she didn't know about them, she didn't have any reason to kill him, did she?"

"Right. And Fillmore's definitely not someone you'd hire as a hit man." Shoobie followed through. "So either we're doing laps on the wrong track, or everyone else is."

"Someone has to know about the money. Hell, we don't even know how much there is yet, but you don't stash this stuff without telling somebody."

"Or at least leaving information about it somewhere." Shoobie tried to figure out where the guy would have left it if it wasn't on his computer. Well, actually, the computer wouldn't be her first choice, either. Too obvious.

"Let's say he wouldn't tell anyone about this money. Assuming there's really some money out there, OK?"

"OK." Grady finished his coffee and looked at the residue in the bottom of the mug. "But he must've left word somewhere. I mean, here he dies suddenly, potentially serious chitlins out there, someone must know about it. Or will soon."

"'Chitlins?'" Shoobie cocked an eyebrow. "I love when you get all rural."

"Can't take the country out of the boy, missus."

"Don't call him 'boy,' either, right?"

"Got that right." Grady took a deep breath as if setting up to take a free throw on the basketball court. Shoobie remembered Chris Guthrie telling her he'd played basketball in high school and she tried to picture it. The guy wasn't even six feet. Wasn't there a law about that?

"Go ahead."

"I think the guy figured his wife or lawyer would be going through the safety deposit boxes after he died—like we're getting the warrant for, right? And I bet you every box has something, maybe a piece of a map, something like that. But when we check out all the boxes, we're going to find enough information to figure out where the money is."

"There's something else, too," Shoobie said. "If this guy was salting money away, it had to come from somewhere, but nobody's saying anything about money missing."

"So he's embezzling, nobody's caught on yet. That's why we told his partners, right? They'll do an audit, something's going to stick out for sure. Unless we're all crazy."

Shoobie picked up the carafe and poured sludge into another disgusting mug. Damn Woody Guthrie for bringing up all these questions. It was so easy when they had a car thief who killed a guy who caught him boosting the friggin' Mercedes Benz. She remembered telling Woody that fingerprints trumped everything. Except money.

"I just thought of something," she said. "If Tony wanted to let someone know about the money, maybe he's got something in his will."

"That's an idea." Grady started digging through the files on his desk.

Shoobie pulled out her cell and scrolled through her log for Fortunato. "Hi, Ms. Fortunato, it's detective Dube again. I'm sorry to bother you so early, but I thought of a question. Did your husband have a will? And if he did, has he made any changes to it lately?"

"Um..." Shoobie heard kids voices underneath the conversation. "He had a will, yeah. I don't know if he made any changes, though. I just called my lawyer to ask, he'll probably get back to me later today."

"Right, right." Shoobie realized that her shift started hours before banks or real people began working. "Well, could you call me back when you know?"

"Yeah, OK. You know, someone else asked me about that same thing. That's why I called him in the first place."

"Really? Who?"

"That other detective. That Guthrie guy."

Shoobie felt an awful premonition creep into her bones.

46

Chrissie dug through the coin bowl on her dresser and took her underwear downstairs to the community laundry room. The stairs smelled like piss and a wet dog, but the laundry room smelled like bleach. On the far side, storage bins obscured the small windows behind chicken wire where people kept the shit they couldn't fit into their apartments. All she had was three boxes of winter clothes, most of them so old she wondered if she could still fit into them. She wouldn't in another few months, bet your sweet ass on that.

Her head felt stuffed, frigging Detroit pollution, and she wanted more sleep, but she wanted to get her laundry done early, lots of her lingerie and stuff for work, and the old biddies on the second floor always looked at her funny when they saw the stuff. Women had to be seventy, and meaner than bill-collectors. Hell, they didn't need a push-up bra, they needed a friggin' wheelbarrow.

She filled both washers and fed them quarters. Thirty-five minutes, she'd use one dryer. The stuff was so thin, a lot of it she could put over her shower rod, especially with the sun coming through the window from about nine in the morning, brighter and hotter than the lights when she danced. She almost expected to see her panties steaming. She should be so lucky.

After her laundry, she had to get to the bank, deposit her tips to cover the check she'd post-date. Tuesday, she'd have enough to cover it. She hoped.

Then she had to scout out clinics. She'd looked up four walk-in medical centers, but two of them were in areas she wouldn't go near without Jack Splat along. The places were probably fronting drugs. She wasn't doing any drugs, especially not with the baby. But that was why she needed a clinic. She needed to get on the ball, or on the stick or whatever. She felt a little sick this morning, that's why she woke up early. Not enough to puke, though. Not yet.

But just for the hell of it, she pulled out the last test stick when she went into the bathroom. Her aim was even better and the little blue line was more distinct. Six for six.

She went back upstairs and looked in the fridge. The lettuce was the color of cat litter and probably less tasty. The tomato was more liquid than not. At least the milk was fresh.

She went back to the basement and tossed the "respectable" underwear into the dryer on delicate and thought she was good to go when the Polish witches showed up. She could feel their eyes on her back and forced a smile onto her face as she turned around.

"Good morning."

Two pairs of beady eyes zeroed in on the thongs and bras she clutched against her chest. "Guhd morhnink." The woman didn't quite make the forked devil horns, but Chrissie felt the vibe. Three hundred years ago, they would have burned the bitch at the stake. She was probably old enough to remember that, too.

"Iss bootiful day, yess." That was the other one, the older one. Hair the color of pavement and eyes two shades lighter. Maybe the white spot was a cataract. Or maybe she was part demon. Who knew?

"Yes. Well, enjoy it." Chrissie headed for the stairs. She felt the women staring at her ass and wondered why it bothered her more than when men did it. Maybe because the guys gave her money but these two seemed to be guessing how long to cook her.

Upstairs, she spread the thongs across the shower rod, over the taps, and across the rim of her bath tub, which was a neutral gray on the bottom. That needed cleaning, too.

She checked her phone. No messages. Like she expected any. She should print cards, give them to the men at Cherries Jubilee. Next week, she'd be at Fuzzy Arches, with that asshole who had the camera hidden in the dressing room. Everyone knew about it, but what could you do.

Damn you, Tony. Why'd you go and leave me like this?

And then Chrissie felt a beam of light soaring from the heavens.

Nine-twenty. When did accountants' offices open? Like Tony's? Probably ten.

She pawed through the junk on her kitchen counter and found the Yellow Pages. What was the name of the place?

Fortunato, Montesori & Klein, LLC. Two wops and a Jew. Yeah, she remembered that guy in the dark suit, looked like he'd been Xeroxed out of a recycling bin. He looked like a Jew.

Chrissie pushed the dust around her apartment for half an hour, then went down to check the rest of her laundry. The Polish witches were gone so she grabbed her stuff and fled.

At ten, she dialed the number and asked to speak to Mr. Fortunato.

"I'm sorry." The receptionist sounded like she almost meant it. "Mr. Fortunato isn't with us anymore."

No shit, honey.

"Mr. Klein is available, I can put you through to him if you like."

"That would be great, thank you."

"This is Leonard Klein." Chrissie waited for a click. The voice might've been a robot.

"How may I help you?"

"Um, I...I was hoping to talk to Tony...Mr. Fortunato, but he's..."

"Yes. Mr. Fortunato had a tragic...accident recently. We are still trying to organize his assignments, split them up. Were you one of his clients?"

No, I was just fucking him. Chrissie swallowed. "Well, we'd...talked a few times. I wasn't really working with him yet, but..."

"Ah. He might have your name in the computer."

Click, click, click. Speaking of computers. Chrissie wondered if they plugged the guy in at night to recharge.

"Um, well, maybe not. But Tony—Mr. Fortunato—may have some money for me, and, uh..."

"Your name please?"

"Chapel." It burst out before she could stop it. "He might have it under 'Jersey.'

"Ah. Is one your maiden name, Ms. Chapel?"

"Well, something like that. It's sort of...complicated, you know."

"I see." She thought she heard keys clicking, the guy on his computer. Or maybe him. Chrissie didn't have a computer. She knew some girls did, some even had web pages, stuff like that. She could get onto the Internet if she had to, but at the library. And all those books around, she felt weird. And not being able to download because of the library rules. She didn't like it.

"Um, Ms. Chapel, I don't see your name here. Could you spell it for me?"

More clicking.

"All right, I see two Chapels here. Your first name would be..."

"Christine." She spelled that, too.

"Um...no, I don't see you here. Had you initiated a project with Mr. Fortunato? It might be in his notes, not in his computer."

"Uh, no, not really. We were just..." Chrissie felt the weight of the building pressing on her shoulders. Tony hadn't left anything there, either. Where the hell else could she go?

"Well, let me have your phone number. I can check his memos, and if I find something, I'll call you back. How does that sound?"

"Uh, no, thank you. Never mind."

Chrissie ended the call and tried to swallow. Tears burned in her throat. Now what? She knew Tony wasn't bullshitting when he told her he wanted to go away. They even talked about where they might go, that last time in bed after they'd finished. That was the day she lost the ear ring, didn't even notice until she was halfway home.

Whoa. That cottage. What if Tony left stuff there? Sure, he said they didn't use it much. His wife was doing her own shit about three nights a week, he was meeting her here, but that was about it. Except for the nanny with the kids, but they only went out there to swim during the day.

The cottage. Where the hell was it? Lake Belleville? Sure, out off I-94, maybe, what, thirty-five, forty miles? She could go over to the library, try MapQuest, find it in two shakes of a cat's ass. She couldn't remember the address, but she thought she'd recognize the place if she saw it again.

47

Tobi watched Patty spoon corn flakes through the pout and into her mouth.

"Why do we hafta buy school stuff? It's not open for another three weeks. You make it sound like the summer's already over."

"Nonna Maria wants to get you stuff you really want." Connie already sounded tired. "Last year, you did nothing but whine about how much you hated your book bag. So did Chuckie—where is he, by the way?—so this time, we want you to be happy."

"Happy." Patty stretched the word out into a whole paragraph and wrinkled her nose. "School and happy. Yuck."

"No," Tobi said. "Your mom's right."

Patty went back to her corn flakes. Connie disappeared toward the stairs, probably to dump Chuckie out of bed.

"I hate school." Patty didn't pout often, but she made up for it with quality. Now her lower lip could hold another place setting for breakfast.

"No, Patty, that's not how to look at it." Tobi took a deep breath as though she were giving her monologue audition. She felt her diaphragm pushing up and started slowly.

"See, school is the start of a whole new year for you. And those first few days, you can make it all work. You come in smiling and ready to go, everything works out better. You'll like the teacher, she'll like you, and you can do stuff together."

"Together." Patty stirred her corn flakes. Tobi heard Connie pound on Chuckie's door.

"Yeah, I mean, you walk in with your cool book bag and your pencils and...and... and a calculator, you show her you're all ready to go, you want to learn. She's going to get psyched about teaching you, and it'll be fun. You'll be discovering stuff you never even knew you didn't know. It's like finding a new block you didn't know was right across the street."

Patty stared at her. Her pout faded a little.

"Remember that?" Tobi asked. She felt her energy spike, she'd found the character's center. "The first time your mom let you cross the street by yourself? And you found there were houses and yards and trees on the other side of the block? That you'd never even thought about before?"

"Yeah…"

"Chuckie, you open this door." Connie pounded upstairs and Tobi heard the door open.

"I'm sleeping." Chuckie's voice held the same pout as Patty's face.

"Get down here and eat your breakfast. Nonna and Nonno will be over in awhile."

Tobi turned her attention back to Patty. "And I'll bet you've even got friends you made then, don't you? Someone who lived over there? You didn't even know about her, and she didn't even know about you. And then you crossed the street all by yourself and found out about her."

Patty chewed slowly and seemed to think about it.

"Well," Tobi said. "That's what school is, like crossing a whole bunch of streets and finding a whole bunch of new blocks. And making a whole bunch of new friends, one at a time."

"The kids at school. I know them all now."

"But maybe someone new just moved in." Tobi realized that she actually believed what she was saying. It was true, like when she first read *Romeo and Juliet* and thought nobody really talked like that. But her ninth grade teacher showed her it wasn't the words, it was about how the kids felt. How people have always felt. They wanted more, and someone said they couldn't have it, so they went out to find their own way to get it.

"Maybe there's a new friend waiting for you. In a few more weeks. And she's going to see you with your cool book bag and your calculator and everything, and she's going to think, 'I want to know that girl.' And you'll learn other stuff together, history, and math, and—"

"Shakespeare?" Patty put down her spoon. "Like you tell us about? *Hamlet*?"

"Yeah." Tobi felt a jolt in her chest. The girl actually remembered she was reading *Hamlet*. "Maybe even *Hamlet*."

Chuckie slogged into the kitchen on cement feet. His hair stuck out over one ear and his eyes hid inside a squint.

"Stupid school."

"You know you love Nonna and Nonno," Connie said. "And they want to see you, take you shopping. The very least you can do is be ready when they come."

"Yeah," Patty said. "It's like crossing the street for the first time."

"Huh?" Chuck stared at her for so long his milk almost overflowed the cereal bowl.

Tobi went through her whole riff again, polishing it a little and loving it because it was hers. And because it was true. Even though she'd blown the audition, this summer teaching these kids had been one of the happiest times she could remember. Except for last week, of course.

Connie's phone rang. She picked it up and wandered into the living room.

"So that's why school is so cool," Tobi finished. "All those things you learn, and new friends. Maybe you'll go over and play with them a lot, or maybe you'll just see them on the playground or somewhere and wave. But you'll know them."

Chuck rolled his eyes, but Tobi could tell he was really thinking about it.

"I don't know if he made any changes, though," Connie said from the next room. "I just called my lawyer to ask about it." She wandered out of earshot again.

Tobi poured herself more coffee. If the grandparents were going to have Chuck and Patty for the day, she might

Steve Liskow

have lots of time to read. It would be a blessing, unwind after all the craziness of the last couple of weeks.

She returned to the table and found the weather forecast in the *Free Press*. Partly cloudy, ten percent chance of rain.

Maybe she'd take her book back to the beach to read. Since Chuck and Patty wouldn't be with her, Evan might like to rehearse a love scene with her at the cottage later.

48

The keys in Tony's guitar told Guthrie there really was money around somewhere, but even though those keys looked like they opened safety deposit boxes, he was pretty sure they didn't hold that money. At least not in cash, and the more he thought about it, the more logical cash seemed to be. Tony wouldn't put the money into stocks or CDs because even though they'd be easier to store, he wouldn't be able to liquidate them quickly. Not to mention leaving a paper trail he was too smart to risk.

Guthrie opened his door and watched Valerie's fingers fly across the keyboard the way he wished he could play guitar, her eyelids sagged in concentration. He knew she was re-designing all his forms and contracts because she thought they were "messy," her portmanteau word for "inefficient, unclear, or not aesthetically pleasing."

"Um, excuse me, Valerie?"

She didn't even look up. "What is it, Mr. G?"

"I need to pick your business brain for a minute, do you mind?"

"Of course not, a woman loves to be complimented on her mind."

She slowed down to what he guessed was about sixty words a minute.

"Um, suppose you had a large amount of money and wanted to stash it somewhere but still be able to get at it quickly. Would you keep it in cash?"

"How much money are we talking about here?"

"That's part of the problem. I don't know. I think it's safe to assume we're talking about a substantial chunk."

"Six figures?"

"I think so. Maybe even more."

Valerie stopped typing.

"Um, give me a minute."

She saved the document she was typing, minimized it, and went online. Guthrie watched her eyes narrow and her lips purse. She typed again.

"OK, to make it easy, I just checked the volume of a million dollars. The largest bill in circulation that banks will give people like you or me is a hundred. Ten thousand of those would make a million dollars."

Guthrie wasn't a math whiz, but zeroes were easy to cancel out. "How much room would that take up?"

"Ten thousand one-hundred-dollar bills would weigh slightly more than twenty-two pounds. You could carry it in a shopping bag."

Guthrie felt himself gaping. "Are you kidding?"

She shook her head and her silver ear stud glistened. "But a bank probably wouldn't have that many hundreds on hand, and they'd certainly ask questions if you asked for them. You're trying to be low profile about this, right?"

"Definitely."

"Well, nobody notices twenties, and you can get them out of an ATM. Go to a bunch of ATMs or several bank branches over a few days, you could get a million in cash and it would weigh about a hundred and ten pounds."

Guthrie thought Megan Traine probably weighed about a hundred ten pounds. He could carry her all the way up her stairs to her bedroom. A million dollars might be almost as motivating.

"How much space would that take up? In twenties."

Valerie clicked her tongue. "Five shopping bags. Maybe...a couple of large suitcases?"

Hello again. Guthrie thanked her and returned to his office, where he dialed Connie Fortunato's number again.

"Ms. Fortunato, I'm sorry to bother you again, but I think the key to your husband's death might be those suitcases. Have you found them?"

Stupid question. If she'd found them, she certainly would have opened them, wouldn't she? And if they held the money, she probably wouldn't be talking to him right now.

"Uh-uh. I looked everywhere I could think of last night. They aren't here." Her voice faded and she said something to someone else before returning to him.

"Listen, I can't really talk right now, we've got company."

"That's fine." Beyond Guthrie's office door, Valerie's keyboard sounded like popcorn on high heat. "Um, how about the lawyer, the will?"

"I called and left a message, but he hasn't called back." One of the voices got louder.

"Listen, I have to go."

Guthrie found himself holding a dead phone.

Two large suitcases. And a missing stripper.

49

Connie watched Chuckie and Patty dash upstairs to get the shopping lists Tobi helped them make. She told herself she was going to miss the girl in a few weeks, especially with the kids gone, too, but it meant she could have Barry over once in awhile. If the asshole would only dump that dried-out stalk of a wife. Christ, what was eating him? She rephrased that thought.

Chuckie and Patty blew back into the kitchen.

"Should you take a coat?" Nonna Marie wore shorts and her varicose veins looked like someone had gone crazy on her legs with a magic marker. Even though it was already ninety outside, she always worried about the kids being cold.

"I'm fine, Nonna." Chuckie evaded her kiss.

"Marie, leave the kid alone." Nonno Joe wore a red polo shirt and looked like he could still kick ass. Connie suspected he weighed pretty much the same as when he graduated from high school nearly sixty years ago. He had all his hair, too, a brilliant silver pompadour that set off his tan.

"Let's get this show on the road, whattaya say, kid?"

"Let's go!" Chuckie's sullen act disappeared. Connie knew both kids would return full of sugar and ready to bounce off the wall, but they needed a break. *She* needed a break.

"Now you listen to what Nonna and Nonno tell you." She turned to her mother. "Don't buy them everything they ask for, please."

"Constancia," Nonna Marie's smile would spread on toast. "What are grandchildren for if not to spoil?"

Before Connie could think of a snappy comeback, they were out the door.

Tobi seemed to be fighting for breath now that the Diorio tornado had blown away. She watched Nonno's old red Cadillac pull out, only a little younger than Connie and in better condition.

"They love the kids, don't they?"

"Their first grandchildren." There were seven first cousins, but Connie was the oldest kid and the first to marry, so Chuck was first out of the gate and could do no wrong.

Connie wondered how long Tobi knew that Evan guy from yesterday. Were they sleeping together? Hey, two college kids, who was she kidding? Tobi was probably getting more than she was. Maybe that would change now that she was single again.

Especially if she could find those suitcases.

"Listen, the kids'll be gone most of the day again. If you've got something you want to do..."

Tobi stared at her phone for a few seconds. "Thank you."

Connie watched her go back upstairs. She looked at her watch. In Rome, it was probably five o'clock. Close enough. She poured a glass of pinot noir and sipped slowly. The kids were gone, the nanny was going, the house was hers.

She went to her own room, the bed looking huge without Tony's stuff on the nightstand by what used to be his side. She still had to clear out his closet, though. Shoes, shirts, suits, slacks, enough neckties to gift-wrap the Renaissance Center and Ford Field combined.

She should get to Goodwill or somewhere, get some boxes and take the stuff all in. Actually, Tony wore good stuff. Maybe consignment instead?

She opened his bureau. The top drawer held about fifteen pairs of dress socks, all black except for two brown pairs for that one suit he didn't like because it made his face look pasty. She didn't think it was cut right through the shoulders, anyway. The next drawer held several white tee shirts and a bunch of others with band or movie logos. At least he didn't go in for ones with cheesy slogans and big-boobed blondes.

When she slid open the next drawer, she stared. She did the laundry, so how come she didn't recognize this stuff? Tony always wore boring boxers with her, but she saw some briefs here, and colors. She'd tried sexy lingerie awhile back, spice things up a little, but he hadn't been interested. They were still in her own bureau, maybe she'd try them out on Barry.

She picked up a pair of low rise briefs. Bright red. And turquoise? What the hell?

Connie forced herself to take deep breaths until her nails stopped digging into her palms. Now she knew where those fucking suitcases were. And if Tony was banging someone, planning to go away, he'd have all that money the cops and that PI kept talking about.

He was too smart to go to a motel, charge a room. He'd do it cash or somewhere free.

Like the cottage. Tobi and the kids used it during the day, change clothes there, go out on the beach, but as a whole family, they'd never been there since...

Shit. Tony was cheating on her. All the time she was telling him about her book clubs and her exercise class so she could meet Barry Montesori, her husband was doing some slut, maybe in their very own cottage.

How slimy was that?

Another thought burst into Connie's head.

If Tony was using the cottage, maybe the suitcases and the money were there?

Christ, what if that woman knew about them, and what if she got there first?

Connie grabbed her phone and punched in Barry's number.

"I can't talk right now, honey."

"Barry," her voice came out as a wheeze. "Listen to me. That money the cops asked you and Len about? I think I know where it is."

"What?" Barry put his hand over the phone and said something. "Look, let me call you back, OK?"

"No, listen, this is important. Tony was cheating on me, he's got the money in cash, in a bunch of suitcases. And I'll bet it's in our cottage, we've never gone there all summer, so he's probably stuck it there. That's where he's screwing this bitch. I'm sure."

"What? Wait—"

"No, I'm going to go out there now. You know where the place is? Meet me there as fast as you can."

"I don't know where it—"

"Shit." Connie tried to picture Barry in the red briefs from Tony's drawer and couldn't do it. "Finish up there and I'll meet you in...half an hour."

She hung up and grabbed her purse. She didn't want to cut Barry in, she wanted to have the money and use it to make him crawl across the floor to her, but if that bitch was out there, maybe looking for the money too, she might need Barry to beat the crap out of her.

50

The house seemed to echo now with Chuck and Patty gone. Connie's depression filled the halls and crevices, and Tobi felt like she was the mom and Connie was the adolescent. Tobi told herself she was too selfish to be a good mom, which was why she decided to go into the arts in the first place.

But she wouldn't perform in *Hamlet*, the showcase for her senior year. She spread all her research materials on the bed. Five different editions of the play: Arden, Oxford, Penguin, Pelican, and Signet. She'd even bought a facsimile of the First Folio a couple of years before after taking an intensive weekend workshop. Reading what Shakespeare really wrote before modern editors started screwing around with it was a revelation. But now she wouldn't get to use it.

The books and essays she'd downloaded or printed out about the play covered the rest of her bed like a beach made of paper. She must have put over two hundred hours of research into the role she wouldn't get to play. That was more time than she spent in classrooms for a whole semester, more than twice what she'd spend in rehearsal for a major role.

Much ado about nothing.

She could cross her fingers and hope they'd offer her an understudy, but wouldn't they have done that when they delivered that first palpable hit? King Lear's line to Cordelia came back to her: Nothing will come of nothing.

She picked up Cohen's *Acting Professionally* and put it down again. Then Berry's *The Actor and the Text*. Her concentration flew to the corners of the room. Back in the dorms, she and her roommate could talk to each other about times like this, whine when someone else got the role you wanted. Share nasty guesses about who the tramp slept with, wonder if she'd start puking to get the weight down to fit into that dress.

School would start in three weeks, just like it would for Chuck and Patty. Maybe she should go shopping, look at clothes, think about stopping by the bookstore, see if the course books were in yet. Big whoop.

Well, she'd told the kids it was a new chance, so maybe she should look at it that way, too. *You haven't lost a role, you've gained the chance to audition for others. To try something different. Learn about other plays and parts.*

If she couldn't act, maybe she could direct.

Are you serious?

Wait a minute. She made Evan understand her monologue, and he didn't even like Shakespeare. And the kids loved it when she turned Shakespeare's plots into stories. Wasn't that what directing was all about, making someone's ideas clear to other people so they could make them happen?

Tobi felt something shift, like the first time a boy dumped her and she didn't die. Maybe acting wasn't the goal, just part of the journey.

Yeah, she'd get to the bookstore later and look at books on directing, too. There wouldn't be anyone on campus that she could talk to, but maybe some of her acting teachers would give her a reality check in a few weeks.

Reality check. Among theater people. What was wrong with that picture?

She should talk it over with Evan. The guy was sweet, but he seemed to have less imagination than the average bulldog. He knew zilch about theater, so maybe he really would be a voice of reason.

Her phone rang, the generic ring, not a regular contact.

"Hello?"

"Ms. Loerner, it's Chris Guthrie again. Is this a bad time?"

"Oh. No. The kids are with their grandparents. I'm just kind of...floating around."

"I see. I talked to Ms. Fortunato awhile ago and now I've thought of a couple more questions and she's not picking up. Maybe you can help me."

"Uh...I don't know, but go ahead."

"All right. You said something about a cottage or cabin the family has?"

"Oh, sure. I take the kids there, we swim and hang out. Evan—you met him yesterday?—is a lifeguard there."

"Where is it exactly?"

"Lake Belleville. There's a row of cottages, most of them pretty old, and there's a beach behind them."

"How often do you go there?"

"Two or three times a week if the weather's good."

"Ms. Fortunato and I have been talking about some luggage, probably three or four suitcases, new, brown leather, expensive. I'm wondering if you've seen anything like that."

"Um, no. The whole family hasn't even been down there together all summer. I don't think either Ms. or Mr. Fortunato have been there at all, except the one time she gave me a key and showed me around."

"How big is the place?"

Tobi tried to channel her set design class.

"Just a cottage. The downstairs is a big open space with a kitchen and living room. Stairs up to two small bedrooms and a bathroom. That's pretty much it."

"No basement, no attic?"

"Uh. There might be a loft. I think I saw a trap door in the ceiling when I was checking the place out. No basement, maybe a crawl space."

"OK. What's the address? Or I could live with a couple of landmarks."

Tobi gave him the address. "There's a falling-apart stone wall along the road before the houses. It's...maybe waist high. And there's a faded red barn on the edge of some woods about...I don't know, maybe a quarter mile before that. I don't think anyone uses it, it looks like it's falling apart, too."

"Lake Belleville."

"Right." Tobi closed her eyes and saw the whole area, like a big outdoor set. "Um, there's a gravel parking lot down the road beyond the cottages. People use it for the beach. If you get there, you've gone by the cottage."

She ended the call, and the books on her bed stared back at her as if they were trying to tell her something. Shakespeare. Acting. Directing. Maybe she should go online and see what books were out there on directing. No, that might be jumping the gun.

She heard Connie's car cruise down the driveway.

Maybe meeting Evan was opening her up, taking her out of herself and making her look at the world more than her mirror. Like yesterday, when they were getting naked and she rolled over that ear ring. They both laughed about it, but the mood was blown to hell. Not long ago, that would have pissed her off, but now she told herself the delay would make him want her even more the next time.

There was going to be a next time, and damn soon.

How about this afternoon?

Connie Fortunato was outside practicing her cougar moves and she was in here feeling sorry for herself. Wrong.

She dropped her phone into her purse and headed for the stairs. Then she had a better idea. She tucked a big beach towel, her moisturizer and a thong into her beach bag. She'd hit the bookstore, then go out to the cottage without the kids. Evan was probably the lifeguard, so she'd get to talk to him, too.

She dug through the bottom drawer of her bureau, the one that held jeans and socks, the clothes she'd brought but hardly even looked at since the warm summer rolled in. There, in the back corner, was a box of condoms with three left.

She hadn't been with a guy since winter, the male ingénue who decided he had to stay free to maintain his artistic integrity. He'd probably slept with half the women in the theater program.

Six months since she'd been with anyone, the almost empty box a testament to that. Did condoms go bad once they were opened, like food? They didn't have an "enjoy by..." date on the box. It would really be her luck if these had gone moldy or stale or something, wouldn't it?

She dropped all three of them in her beach bag.

51

Dozens of lakes dotted Michigan's Lower Peninsula, some big enough for sailing, some barely big enough to soak your feet. Belleville was on the smaller side, about half-way between Dearborn and Ann Arbor, far enough from the city to be relaxing, but close enough to be convenient. Traffic on I-94 West was light enough so Danny had no trouble getting into the right lane for the exit. He turned right off the ramp and cruised down the road looking at the countryside: a few houses, but still some woods and open land that might have been farms once. A faded red building sagged in on itself, the roof ready to collapse any second. Animals probably took shelter in it, or kids who wanted to make out or smoke a little dope. Then a grove of trees, still pretty thick. Danny slowed down even more.

Ahead on his left, he saw a stone wall that looked like a tank had rammed it a few times. The cottages all had that fifties' look, sweet mom and pop and two kids but now only slightly less run down than that barn. Some yards were so overgrown Danny wondered if anyone used them anymore.

The fourth cottage down, a gravel drive led to the cottage, faded brown shingle siding, a few trees that needed trimming...and a black Nissan Murano in the driveway facing out at the road. But it had company, a little blue compact, a Saturn, not much bigger than a pimple.

"Shit."

Maybe it was someone stopping for directions, they'd be gone again by the time he got there. No. Nobody was knocking on the door or sitting behind the wheel. Someone was in the fucking cottage. Or maybe out on the beach. What did Evan say, the girl brought the kids down sometime? Between the cottages, Danny saw bright sky and dark sand. The lake shimmered behind the buildings.

If they were out on the beach, that might not be a problem. He could get in and out before they came back. Chances were they'd eaten lunch, maybe before they came and would be out there swimming most of the afternoon. Little kids, they'd do the beach thing till they were too tired to walk.

The stone wall didn't so much end as peter out a few hundred yards beyond the last cottage. Danny pulled into a lot big enough to hold a few dozen cars on crushed stone. Belleville Lake and the beach lay the other side of those cars, and he squinted against the bright sky.

A tower stuck out like a finger half-way down the beach, overlooking a few blankets. Danny guessed it marked the center of the twelve cottages, which made sense if the lifeguard was on duty. There were so few people on the beach he was surprised they even bothered. Weekends maybe, but now he only saw a handful of kids, and they all looked old enough to take care of themselves.

One-ten. Danny checked his pocket for the expired Sears credit card he used to open locked doors. He took the gun from under the seat and tucked it into the waistband of his jeans, unbuttoning his shirt so it fell over the gun. With sandals and a tee under the shirt, he looked like just another asshole from one of the cottages. He wished he had more of a tan to fit in better, but it would give him even more excuse to be out there. Business type trying to make up for lost time.

He still had almost an hour before Evan expected him, and a fifteen-minute walk back to the cottage if he stayed on the road, which he wouldn't. He crossed the pavement and entered a sorry patch of woods, like some nature freak looking for birds or squirrels. He knew a robin, cardinal, or blue jay if he saw them, and maybe a sparrow, but anything else was just a bird.

His phone vibrated and he pulled it out of his pocket. *Blocked number again, what a shock.*

"Yeah."

"Daniel, we are both having a lucky day. I have for you the name of Anthony's paramour."

What the fuck was a paramour? It sounded like a skin disease. But it had a name, so the guy must mean the stripper.

"Shoot."

"Christine Chapel. Given your connections, you may already know her."

Danny couldn't put a face to the name, but in a strip club, who looked at faces. Maybe she had a tattoo or a funky piercing. But that wouldn't make her very different, either.

"Look, I'm following up a lead right now. If things go well, I might not need the broad. But I'll check her out."

"I hope things do go well, Daniel. Wednesday, our agreement is null and void."

"No, wait, I'm definitely on to something. Any kind of luck, this will be wrapped up in a couple of hours. Give me a number where I can call you."

"Oh, I don't think so, Daniel. I will call you again at five-thirty."

Christine Chapel. It probably wasn't the broad's real name anyway. Even if they had a stage name, most of these women used another fake name too, just so you couldn't find out where they lived. A few of them had husbands or boyfriends who didn't like them out there sharing their stuff with other guys. Danny wondered how many of the women who turned tricks were married. Shit, that was really sick. Unless the guy liked her to talk about it when she got home, put another log on the fire, kinda.

He'd check out this cottage and split again. If he found what he was looking for—how many places could you hide suitcases in a little shack like that?—he'd be back in Detroit before the muscle-bound lug even came to meet him. And if it wasn't there, he'd still be gone. Maybe check out Cherries Jubilee tonight, see if Christine Chapel was Jersey Girl.

He told himself not to worry about the rest of the call, the "null and void" part.

The humidity brought out the mosquitoes. He swatted at them and kept moving until he saw the cottage ahead, the SUV and the compact in the driveway.

A car approached from Danny's left, two of them. He waited for them to pass.

The front one turned into that same driveway and Danny felt his eyes widen. A Mercedes, just like the one he left the dead guy in. The license plate was CONNI F. Fuck him gently with a chain saw. The wife picked today to come to the goddam beach?

The car following her turned in, too. What was this, a fucking convention? This one was an Acura, shiny as a new coin. A skinny guy got out, pasty face, half Danny's size and wearing a dark suit. He trotted over to hold the door of the Mercedes while the woman got out. She was wearing white shorts that showed off her great butt. Any tighter, you'd see her vaccination, too, unless she did it in her arm.

Danny tried to figure out what was going on, but was missing a few pieces. Well, that had been the way everything went since the night he grabbed Tony Fortunato on...8 Mile Road. *Shit, he'd been in the Cherries Jubilee parking lot.*

He watched the woman discover that the front door was unlocked and say something to the pasty-faced guy before they disappeared inside. Danny was still looking at all the cars when a guy in jeans and jacket appeared on foot from the other direction and stopped at the edge of the driveway. He looked at all the cars, then eased up to the window and listened. A minute later, he jerked open the door and strode inside. Danny counted to ten before he sprinted across the road and ducked behind Evan's SUV. He moved down until he could hear through the front door.

He wasn't going to need the credit card to get inside now, but he was glad he had the gun.

52

Tobi watched Evan look under the sink.

"Um, if you want sunscreen, there might be more in the bathroom, but you look like a hot dog already, so I don't think you have to worry."

"No, I'm...wondering about something." He stood up again, almost a head taller than she was so his pecs were almost at eye level. If their positions had been reversed, it would be like middle school all over again, her boobs where every seventh-grade boy could check them out. That was the only time she regretted getting her growth spurt early.

"What? I figured I had the day off, I want to spend it with you. And I..." she felt her face heat up. "I'm betting there aren't any more earrings or anything in the bed, and I-I thought maybe..."

"Yeah, upstairs." He looked her up and down in the white thong she picked because it showed off her tan. The contrast highlighted her assets, too, which she knew weren't huge, but heck, he saw them yesterday and seemed to like them. Now something else was on his mind, and she needed to get it out of the way.

She took his hand and led him up the steps, taking the lead so he could check out her ass.

"Tobi, you're really pretty."

"Thank you." She was afraid to keep talking because she knew she'd say too much. Just let him see her and touch her and then they'd get their clothes off in that bed and she'd show him what she could do besides act. She suspected she wouldn't have to fake anything when he got involved.

"How old is this place, do you know?"

"Um, I never thought about it. Probably sixty, seventy years. Why?" She leaned forward to draw his attention to her white bikini bottom again.

"Oh, nothing. I was just..." His fingers brushed the top of her thighs. "Wow. Nice."

Damn right, she thought. *And I want to share it with you right now, so get the hell up here.*

He followed her. "Um, there's no basement, right? And no closets down here?"

"You mean in the living room? No, just those coat pegs."

"Not even under the stairs? I mean, I didn't even look as we went by."

"Evan, what's going on here? I'm in the mood, we're alone, I thought you'd be a little happier to see me."

"I am, I am. Honest."

She felt an awful idea blossom and her throat turned to burning acid.

"Do you already have a girlfriend? Someone else, you're just playing me? You think you'll screw me here and go back to her? Is that it?"

"No, Tobi, no. Honest. I'm...I love you. There's nobody else."

He stepped closer and put an arm around her waist. He could probably lift her with that one arm and carry her up the rest of the stairs without even breathing hard.

"Honest?" She swallowed the bile back down. This was so not what she had in mind.

"Don't lie to me, OK? I know I'm not the most beautiful girl in the world, and I'm sure not the smartest, but I really..."

"Shh...C'mon, Tobi, let's get upstairs, all right?" He squeezed gently, then let her go, his hand brushing her thigh again as he released her.

"Yes, oh, yes." She danced up the last six steps and turned to look at him with her legs wide apart like some stripper queen. She didn't care how trashy she looked right now, she wanted the guy to make love to her.

"Like what you see, cowboy?"

His eyes slid up her legs, paused at the bikini, and moved up again. She swore she felt heat wherever he looked. *Damn, he was a hunk, and he was making her so so so hot.*

His eyes moved across her face and kept going, above her head.

"What's that?"

"What?" She looked up. Ceiling. She looked back at his eyes and tracked their gaze, past her head, through the door, to the bedroom ceiling. A hatchway.

"Is that an attic?"

"Are you serious? How the hell do I know?" She heard herself getting shrill, the Kate voice she used in the Taming of the Shrew monologue from last year. "Jesus, Evan, are we going to go to bed, or..."

"No, look." He brushed by her into the bedroom. The ceiling was only about eight feet, she could jump up and touch it, but he didn't even have to stand on his toes. His big hand reached up and pushed. The hatch lifted a few inches and he used his other hand to slide it over.

"Where's a ladder?"

"Huh?" All the energy drained out of her. The joy, the lust, everything. She couldn't decide whether she should get back into her car and drive back to Grosse Pointe, or simply go out the back door onto the beach and walk into the lake until the water rose over her head. Either way, she knew she was going to cry. At least underwater, nobody'd see the tears.

"A ladder, a stool, something. What's up here?"

"Evan, what the hell are you talking about?"

"No, listen. The suitcases. Are they up here?"

Tobi shook her head to clear her ears. "Suitcases? What suitcases? What the fuck is going on here?"

"Here, come here." He pulled her over under the hatch and put his hands on her hips. "OK, I'm going to pick you up so you can look up there. Tell me if you see any suitcases?"

"What—?"

Her feet left the ground and she brought up her hands to push the hatch aside before he rammed her head into it. Her head felt more heat, the low roof only a few feet above her and it was dark, but something brushed her face. Yuck! Spider web! She hated spiders. No, it was thicker and heavier than that. A string? She wrapped her fingers around it and pulled. Sure enough, a small light bulb clicked on above her.

"What's up there?" Evan's voice puffed on her back below her bra strap.

"Umm." She looked around, dust, a few dead flies, a few old newspapers, not much else. She turned her head and looked the other way, beyond the hatch.

Three suitcases, burnt sienna leather, gold buckles. They looked expensive, and they looked brand new. She could fit all the clothes she'd brought with her for the summer in those puppies with room to spare.

"Uh, yes. Suitcases," she said.

"How many?" His voice was moist on her back again.

"Three."

"Can you reach them? If I lift you a little higher?"

"Uh, wait a second." She felt herself shift in his hands. He lifted her a little higher and she felt his shoulder under her butt. "Oh, that's good. Step a little to your left?"

He did, and she stretched her arm out and found the handle of the biggest suitcase. She pulled it toward her until it tilted over the edge of the hatch.

"Here's one," she said. "It's heavy, I don't know if I can..."

"Let go of it. I'll put you down."

He did, then reached up and found the handle. A little maneuvering and he had it through the opening. He dropped it on the bed and turned back to her.

"Can you reach the others?"

"I think so, boost me up again."

When all three were on the bed, she could smell the newness, warm leather, really good stuff, slightly scuffed from her dragging them over the floor but that brought out the smell even more. The keys were still on chains around the handles. Evan grabbed the nearest one and unlocked the catch.

"Holy shit."

Money. Packages of bills, dozens of them. Tobi watched her hand reach out and take one. She riffled through the pack and Andrew Jackson stared back at her fifty times. A thousand dollars in her hands.

"Shit, can you believe this?" Evan picked up another package. "Son of a bitch, can you believe this?"

"But what is this?" Tobi felt her stomach clench. Something was rotten in the state of Denmark. "And how did you know it was...?"

"Come on, we've got to get out of here, right now." Evan stuffed the bills back into the suitcase. "Let's go."

"But what—?"

"Later, babe, OK? I'll tell you later. Right now, we have to shuffle off to Buffalo. Time's flying, and we've got to do the same."

"But I don't..."

She felt her lower lip wobbling. *He knew about this money, somehow, whatever it was, and that was why he'd been so nice to her. It was all about these friggin' suitcases and he didn't give a shit about her at all.*

"Come on, Tobi. Jesus." Evan picked up the two biggest suitcases. "Here, you take that one. My car's down in front. Well, sure, you know that, right? You saw it when you came in. Let's blow this popsicle stand."

Tobi watched him maneuver his load between the wall and the banister and followed three steps behind him. *When would she meet a guy who treated her like something more than a dog to fetch the paper?*

At least she hadn't fucked him.

They were half-way down the stairs when the front door opened and two people walked in. Tobi thought the man was one of Mr. Fortunato's partners, thin in a dark suit. She didn't remember his name.

And the woman leading him was Connie—Ms.—Fortunato. She wore a halter and white shorts to show off her own tan. When she saw Evan and Tobi, she stopped so quickly the man almost walked into her.

"What the fuck is going on here?" Her words flicked out and Tobi expected to feel her face bleed.

Evan didn't even break stride.

"Who the hell are you? This is private property and you're trespassing."

"Trespassing? I own this place, you asshole. You put down those suitcases right now and get out of here or I'll call the police."

"Bite me, honey." Evan didn't even break stride. "By the time the cops get here, I can be half-way to Chicago."

"You're not going anywhere." The woman's voice dropped to a pitch Tobi'd never heard before, a low growl that made her wonder what Connie was like under the full moon. Her feet froze on the stairs.

Evan looked bigger than both Connie and the man in the suit put together and he shifted his weight as though he planned to knock both of them clear through the wall.

"Hey, those are my suitcases."

Tobi looked to the door again. A woman with blonde hair tucked up in a bun and a tank top cut down to her navel. She wore strappy sandals and red hot pants that covered slightly more than Tobi's thong, and her nails matched the pants. Tobi tried to remember where she'd seen her before.

"Bullshit these are yours," Evan said. "Get your ass out of my way."

"Goddam you, Tony bought those for me, we were going away, then he got killed. They're mine, and I'm taking them with me."

"You cheap slut," Connie snapped. "You're not going anywhere with these. He was my husband and those are my fucking suitcases. You know what's good for you, you'll get out of here right now or I'll—"

The woman crossed the room in three strides and slapped Connie across the face. Connie shook her head and regained her balance, but the whole side of her face showed a red handprint.

"You fucking..."

"Ladies." Mr. Montesori stepped between the women, which turned out to be a bad idea. They leapt for each other and he got caught between them, teeth and nails, knees and hair-pulling.

"Those are mine, you bitch...Fuck you, you cheap whore... Give me those damn—I'll kill you, you slut...Those are mine...No, they're mine."

The front door burst open and that private detective stepped into the room.

"Stop it." His voice made Tobi think of a cracking whip. Everyone froze. The suitcase in Tobi's hand felt heavy.

Beyond Evan's shoulder, the two half-naked women wrestling on the floor looked up. The blonde girl had breasts to die for, and they were pretty much on display. Ms. Fortunato's weren't bad, but this woman...

The detective, Mr. Guthrie kept his eyes on the strange woman sitting on Connie's chest.

"Jersey Girl?" he said. "Christine?"

The woman turned her head toward him.

"Christ, you again?"

"Yup, me again. You were dating Tony Fortunato before he died, weren't you?"

53

"You slut." Tobi felt herself cringe at the rage in Connie's voice. "My husband. I'm gonna kill..."

Mr. Guthrie stepped over and grabbed the blonde woman's hands and pulled her straight up, off Connie. Her eyes opened wide and her mouth opened wider while he deposited her ten feet away, near the kitchen.

"Stay there," he said in that same whipcrack voice. He picked up her tank top and tossed it to her.

"Those are my suitcases." She tried to fit her arms through the sleeve holes, but the straps were torn. "Tony, he got them for me, we were going away."

"Bullshit," Connie snapped."Those cases match my own luggage, Tony and I got them together. He's my husband, they're my suitcases."

Connie regained her feet and adjusted her shorts. Her halter was a lost cause, but she tried to cover up the best she could.

"That money is mine," she continued.

"No," the detective said. "That money is stolen. I don't know from who yet, but—"

"Stolen, my ass." The girl tied her tank top's straps around her neck like a bib. It didn't cover much. "Those suitcases are mine."

"No," said another voice. "They're mine."

Tobi looked toward the door again. A man almost as big as Evan filled the doorway. His face looked both calm and mean at the same time.

And he had a gun.

54

Guthrie couldn't place the guy, but he was built like a bouncer, well over six feet with biceps the size of watermelons. He wore a black tee with a blue work shirt hanging open over it. The gun barely showed up in his huge hand but Guthrie could see it aimed at him.

"I know you're carrying." The big man's eyes seemed to take in the entire room. "Put your gun on the floor and kick it over here."

Guthrie did. Barry Montesori looked like he wanted to click his heels and find himself back in Kansas. Tobi Loerner's face lost more color by the second. Connie Fortunato struggled to make her shredded top cover her breasts again.

"You four all get over there by the kitchen."

"You're the woman who called us this morning about Tony and—" Barry Montesori's tenor sounded more curious than angry.

"Jersey Girl?" The giant tucked Guthrie's gun into his waistband. "You were fucking Tony."

Connie shifted her weight and Guthrie pulled her back. Christine pulled herself to her full height, which made her shredded tank top dance.

"Excuse me. Tony and me were in love. We were gonna go away from all this shit, he was gonna help me start over and I was gonna—"

"You bitch." Connie Fortunato's voice felt like a bowling ball.

"All right, we've been through that." The big guy spoke again. "All of you shut up."

"You tell that bitch she tries to start up with me again, I'll rip her face off."

"I said shut up."

The big man kept his gun on Guthrie, but glanced toward the stairs, where Tobi Loerner stood in the glowing white bikini that did wonders for her tan. Evan the lifeguard stood three steps below her in day-glow orange swim trunks and an open white shirt.

"Evan, put the suitcases on the floor at the bottom of the steps. Yours first, then the girl's."

"Danny, what the fuck?" Evan's face screwed up and made him into a kid discovering there was no Santa Claus. "I thought we were in this together."

"Hey, it's business, guy. Nothing personal."

"You fucker."

"You don't even know there's anything in them." Connie sounded like she didn't even believe it herself.

"Yeah, we do." Tobi's eyes widened and she almost clapped a hand over her mouth. For an instant, she looked even younger than the lifeguard.

"This isn't a panel discussion." The big guy with the gun—Danny—pointed to the bottom of the stairs. "Evan. Put them down. Now."

"What happens then?" Tobi's voice was almost steady. "What are you going to do to us?"

"Honey, if you do what I tell you, nobody has to get hurt. I'll just take your car keys and phones, leave you here. You can probably find another phone on the beach, but it'll give me a head start."

"You son of a bitch." Evan seemed to grow bigger and Tobi laid her free hand on his shoulder, like trying to hold back a pit bull with a kite string. "I'm trying to help you get this money back, and this is how you—"

Guthrie felt all the pieces falling into place. But now that he knew Evan Roenicke was working with the other side, he also saw that the kid was a loose cannon.

"Wait a minute." Connie's eyes widened. Her voice dropped an octave into a range that sounded feral. "You killed my husband."

The guy shrugged, but the gun never wavered. "Sometimes shit happens."

Evan slammed his two suitcases on the floor.

"Here, you sonofabitch." He turned and reached up his hands toward Tobi. "Give me yours, Tobi."

When she laid it in his huge hands, he looked up at her for a few seconds. "I'm sorry about this."

Guthrie didn't realize that he was taking those seconds to get a good grip on the handle of the suitcase until he spun again and hurled it straight at Danny.

55

Tobi had never seen anyone react so quickly. The big man shifted his weight and put up a forearm to brush the suitcase away. At the same time, that awful gun came up and flashed twice, the sound like hands clapping over her ears. She brought her own hands up to cover them before she saw Evan stumble back against the wall. He leaned against it for a second and she saw two red spots, no bigger than coins, appear on his chest, so small they couldn't possibly hurt him, but he sagged back and his knees folded under him. He slid down the wall into an awkward sitting position and she watched the light go out of his eyes. His head drooped and the weight of it pulled his body over on the bottom step.

"Evan." She wasn't even certain she said it aloud. All she felt was wetness running down her legs while her insides turned numb. She wanted to run to him, but her feet felt stuck to the stairs, standing in her own puddle.

The big man swung the gun back at the others. Mr. Guthrie's fists clenched and his eyes narrowed, but he didn't move. Both women screamed and the accountant's face turned the color of paste.

"No more heroes."

Tobi knew he was going to shoot her, too. His eyes flickered to her thighs and he shook his head like her older brother seeing his baby sister wet herself. She felt three years old again and even more helpless.

The detective spoke, his voice so soft she could barely hear him.

"You're in deep shit now, Danny—it's Danny, isn't it?—so don't make it any worse."

"You have no fucking idea how deep it is, chum. But these suitcases are going to make it a whole lot better."

He gestured with his gun. "You lay down on your stomach. Now the rest of you sit on him. That means you, too, pissy pants. But not you, Jersey. You're coming with me."

Tobi wanted to cry. She moved down the steps and over to the detective. She was sure everyone on the beach could smell her already. Mr. Montesori sat on the man's chest and Connie on his thighs. Good. She sat down on his feet.

"OK. Now, I'm taking the broad and the money. You wait fifteen minutes, I'll let her go down the road. You fuck with me, she'll end up like Dudley Do-Right here."

Tobi watched Danny drag Christine over by the suitcases. He picked up the smallest suitcase and pointed his gun at Christine.

"Pick them up."

Christine knelt and found the handles of each suitcase, her top hanging loosely. When she stood, Tobi had to admire her legs even though her knees were shaking. At least she hadn't peed *her* pants.

"I can't," she wheezed. "They're too heavy."

"The big one's got wheels, stupid."

They watched Christine figure out the handle and open it.

The man backed out the door and held it open for her, letting it slam when they were both outside. Tobi looked to her left and realized she was staring at Christine's purse. What did you want to bet her car keys were still in it?

Sure enough, she didn't hear a car start up. And Christine's had to be the last car in the driveway.

The detective shifted and she stood up. The others did too, and he got to his feet, his eyes narrow and his hands balled into fists.

"OK, everyone stay here. I'm going after him."

"Are you insane?" Mr. Montesori's voice was barely a squeak. "He's got a gun—two of them. We should call the police."

"In a few minutes. If they show up now, he's got a hostage. I want to get the girl away from him first. Then he's on his own."

His eyes turned to Connie. "I think I know who your husband was stealing from. And why this guy killed him. But unless we can get him alive, there's no way I can prove it."

He looked out the back door. "The good news is that the suitcases and the hostage will slow him down."

He disappeared through the back door. Tobi looked out the front door at all the cars. Evan's huge SUV made her think of a Saint Bernard.

Evan...

56

Guthrie plowed along the beach, sand filling his sneakers with every stride, the sun hotter coming off the water. The few bathers looked up to see a fully-clad man running by them, but nobody said anything. Guthrie knew the parking lot was only a few hundred yards away, but it felt like miles, especially with his inner voice urging him to move even faster.

He told himself that with Christine lugging two big suitcases, she couldn't go any faster than he could. She'd merit all of Danny's attention, too. Since Danny had the guns, Guthrie needed any help he could get.

He looked to his right, between the last two cottages, but didn't see anything. With luck, he was ahead of Danny and his prisoner. If not, he and Christine were both screwed. The parking lot loomed ahead, heat shimmering off the parked cars. He hurdled the split rail dividing the crushed rock from the regular beach sand, his re-built thigh throbbing and a sword stabbing under his ribs when he tried to breathe. Sweat poured down into his eyes, but he didn't see Danny and Christine yet.

Danny must have parked his car here and walked back so he didn't tip off the others, but there were over a dozen, and none bore a banner saying "Danny's Wheels." Guthrie moved over to a Honda CR-V and sank to his knees. It might not be the right car, but it was close to the road and offered him cover. Danny had two guns, so all he had going for him was surprise.

He heard wheels rattling on the uneven road and crouched to look under the car, between the front tires. He saw those suitcases, one on each side of strappy black sandals and white legs. Danny and Christine gradually came into view, her hair plastered to her forehead. He could see her eyes, too, round with terror.

Danny strolled two steps behind her, the smaller suitcase in his left hand and his right hand under his loose shirt so nobody saw his gun.

Guthrie watched the duo come closer and vanish behind the tire. A white Toyota blocked his view for a few seconds, then he heard feet shuffling in the gravel, along with a terrified whimper.

"Shut up." Danny's voice might have been a rubber hose clubbing the woman to silence. "Open the trunk." Guthrie heard a small jingle when Danny handed the woman his car keys. He risked peering around the CR-V's back tire and saw two sets of feet. Danny's were closer, and they faced the open trunk of an old Buick.

"Get in."

"What? I can't—"

"Get in the trunk."

"No." Christine's voice vibrated with terror. "No, I can't— I got—don't put me in there, Mister. I swear to God, I'll freak."

"It's only for a few minutes. I'll let you out when I get to the highway."

"No. I-I can't. It's small, it's dark. I won't be able to breathe, I'll die. Please."

Guthrie rose to a half crouch.

"Jesus." Danny stepped forward and Guthrie heard a gasp break off abruptly. "You stupid bitch. I don't have to shoot you. I can kill you with my bare hands, you won't even know it. I'm giving you a chance to live, so get in the friggin' trunk before I change my mind."

"Please, Mister. I'm—"

Guthrie lowered his shoulder and aimed at the middle of Danny's back. He covered the twenty feet in six choppy steps, enough time to see Danny's hand on Christine's neck. Her eyes looked ready to pop out of her face.

Danny heard him approach and started to turn, but Guthrie's shoulder caught him under his rib cage and drove him toward the car. One hand dropped Christine and the other dropped the gun into the trunk. His forearm pounded on Guthrie's back and nearly drove him to his knees. Guthrie threw a left hook with everything he had behind it and felt it sink into the big man's side. He heard a grunt and backed away before Danny could grab him. Christine struggled to all fours, wheezing and choking.

Danny kicked the suitcases away with a leg big enough to require bark on it and turned to face Guthrie, who watched his eyes for a hint. If the guy landed one good punch, he knew it was all over.

He feinted with a right and Danny shifted to block it. Christine scrambled out of the way over next to the suitcases. Danny took a step forward and Guthrie countered. He wished he'd let the others call the cops, not that they could get here in time to do anything except sweep up his remains.

"Fuck this." Danny stood straight and reached into his waistband, coming out with Guthrie's own gun. "Say good night, asshole."

Guthrie knew he was too far away to charge, but nowhere near far enough away so running would make Danny miss. A Cyclops could hit him at this range.

Then Christine swung a suitcase. Both her hands wrapped around the handle and she put her full weight behind the blow. It slammed into Danny's forearm and he reeled backward. Guthrie's gun sailed over the CR-V.

"Son of a bitch." Danny backhanded the woman and dashed between the cars. Guthrie turned the other direction. If he could beat Danny to the gun, he could finish this. They rounded the front end of their cars, Danny a step ahead, and looked at the sand ahead. No gun. Danny accelerated toward the beach. Guthrie hesitated long enough to be sure the gun wasn't masquerading as a beer can, then followed.

Running in sand was even harder now with so little breath, but Guthrie had less meat to move than Danny. His twenty-foot lead diminished when he almost ran over a girl in a striped bikini who was too busy texting to watch where she was going. Danny swept her out of his path as easily as breaking a spider web, but it cost him a step.

They pounded down the sand, zig-zagging through blankets and an occasional umbrella while the bathers gawked. Danny looked back and lost another step. Guthrie knew the big man was nearly into his reserve tank. Off to the left stood an empty chair on white stilts, Evan's station, abandoned for Tobi and three suitcases of money.

Guthrie put on a final spurt and dove, catching Danny around the waist and dragging them both down into the edge of the lake. He scrambled to his feet first and dug for footing in the shifting sand. When Danny turned with his hands still on his knees, Guthrie swung a right that caught the bigger man solidly on his left cheek. Danny tried to roll with the punch, but his feet slipped in the sand and he went to his knees. Guthrie dove on him and drove him into the water, but Danny clamped both hands on Guthrie's shoulders and lifted him straight up. His feet left the ground. Danny threw him off and struggled to his feet, still in the water.

Guthrie feinted and Danny threw a fist the size of a bowling ball. He missed and stumbled forward. Guthrie tried for an armlock, but felt the giant lift him off the ground again.

He got both hands on Guthrie's shoulders and threw him deeper into the water. Guthrie clamped his mouth shut and felt the water wash over him.

By the time he regained his footing, Danny was struggling out of the water, his sides heaving with every step. Guthrie dove on the man's back again and they collapsed at the water's edge.

"You..." Danny's voice was a wheeze. He reached for Guthrie's neck and Guthrie shifted forward onto the man's chest and shoved his head under the water. Danny's arms flailed, but he blocked them with his shoulders and held on. Danny's fists opened and he gripped Guthrie's biceps. Guthrie held on and the big man's grip weakened. His hands sagged into the water and his legs stopped kicking. Guthrie held on for another ten seconds, then slid off the man's chest.

He grabbed Danny's arms and dragged him onto the sand, his wheezing loud enough to drown out the seagulls.

"You bastard." Christine's scream almost burst Guthrie's ear drum. "You were gonna kill me, huh? Well now it's your turn."

Guthrie turned. Christine's eyes gleamed and her bare chest heaved. She held Guthrie's gun in a two-handed grip and pointed it more or less at Danny, who was coughing up impressive amounts of Lake Belleville.

"Christine," Guthrie said. "Don't do it. Give me the gun."

"You kidding? This bastard's gonna put me in the trunk, I don't do small places, I've got what-you-call-it, closetphobia. My boyfriend wanted to do it in the backseat, we were in high school, I was so freaked out I threw up. Ruined my whole evening."

"I'll bet. But that was a long time ago. Don't shoot him, OK? He's under control now."

"And dark, don't get me started about dark. If the light's off, I can't even—"

"TMI, Christine, TMI."

"Not even for an extra thou—"

"Enough." Guthrie thought maybe she'd respond to a cop voice. "Enough, all right? Jeez."

Christine lowered the gun. "I'm just saying..."

"Yeah, I get it. But don't shoot him. That's my gun. You kill him, the cops will think I did it, and that would really suck."

"Your gun." Christine looked at him and frowned. "Oh, that's right. He took it, didn't he?"

"Yeah." Guthrie put out his hand, slowly. "But I have to tell you, standing like that with the gun, you look seriously hot."

"Honest?" The woman lowered the gun to point at the sand and Guthrie took it out of her left hand. "Really? Hot? Maybe I don't need new boobs after all...?"

Guthrie thought he'd finished discussions like this when he hired Valerie.

Danny coughed up a mouthful of sand and Guthrie took the gun.

"Christine, why don't you get Connie and Montesori to help you bring back those suitcases. Then we're going to make things really easy for the cops."

Twenty minutes later, they re-convened in the kitchen. Guthrie put Danny's forearms between his thighs, then tied his wrists to his ankles with duct tape and sat him in a corner.

The metallic smell of Evan's blood filled the living room, and Tobi's eyes were two pink blotches in a pale face. Connie stroked her hair and hugged her tight.

Danny told them that Tony Fortunato was stealing from the guy who hired him. He was supposed to persuade Tony to return the money, but didn't know who the guy was.

"Don't worry about it." Guthrie looked at Montesori. "I think I do."

He looked at the others. "You know, so far they haven't passed a law making it a crime to be stupid. So I'm going to try to make this fairly simple for the police. First, we're all going to exchange phone numbers. Christine, you're going to call Tobi, Connie, and me. We won't pick up, but you're going to leave a message with your name, address, and email. If you've got a Facebook page or a Web site, give us that, too.'

"Why me?" Christine Chapel sat on the three suitcases, which brought her crotch level with Guthrie's eyes.

"Fine." Guthrie shrugged. "I was going to figure out a way you can have a share of this money. If you don't want it..."

Christine dug into her purse.

"Are you out of your mind?" Montesori said. "This money, it's got to be stolen. We could all go to jail."

"Of course it's stolen," Guthrie said. "From Connie's uncle Carmine. So we're going to give most of it back and call the rest a service charge."

They all stared at him.

"Oh my God," Connie finally said.

"Yeah," Guthrie agreed. "So now, let's make this easy. Christine, after we exchange numbers, get in your car and drive home. One of us will call you either tonight or tomorrow and let you know what's up."

"Don't I get a share of the money?"

"Eventually, but Carmine Diorio has to give it to you. When you get a call from one of the numbers you're going to put into your phone, pick up."

"But..."

"Your car is blocking all the others," Guthrie said. "You need to go. We'll all follow you in a few minutes."

They listened to her car start up and pull away, then Guthrie looked at Connie and Montesori.

"Tobi, give Connie your keys. You two put the two bigger suitcases in her trunk and come back in."

Guthrie turned to Danny. "Danny, you're screwed no matter what happens. If you go along with the story I'm going to tell the cops in awhile, I won't tell Carmine Diorio you were trying to steal mob money. But if you say a word about Connie or Montesori being here, you can measure your life in hours."

Danny glared at him. Guthrie glared back. Danny looked at his taped wrists and ankles. Then he nodded.

"Good." Guthrie looked at Tobi. "I'm sorry, but you're going to have to stay here with me. You and I are going to tell the cops we saw Danny shoot Evan."

Tobi's eyes drained tears again. "Why do I have to...?"

"Because you're part of the motive." The others returned and Guthrie held out his hand for Tobi's keys.

"You two go home or wherever. Mr. Montesori, don't go back to work and don't say anything about this. Ms. Fortunato, I'll call you later tonight."

"What about the other suitcase?" Montesori nodded toward the smaller case, the one Christine used to disarm Danny. "It's full of money, who even knows how much?"

"I need it to sell my story to the cops."

Tobi looked at Evan's body at the foot of the stairs. Guthrie wanted to go over and hug her, but nothing would help her much except time.

He watched Montesori back out of the driveway and turn toward Detroit, Connie close behind. When they were out of sight, he turned to Tobi.

"Whatever you're thinking about him now, he tried to protect you."

She buried her face in her hands and he dialed 911.

57

Shoobie watched Woody Guthrie escort the college kid toward the elevator. She'd be back at the Fortunato place and he'd be back in Ferndale long before she and Grady finished typing. Guthrie and the girl and the big guy shared a story that was less secure than a house of cards in a hurricane, but it hung together and nobody was changing anything.

Danny Hammersmith saw Tony Fortunato dropping big bucks on the strippers where he tended bar and followed him one night. The guy resisted and Hammersmith killed him and dumped the body in the trunk of his Mercedes. He left the Mercedes where Hot Rod Lincoln found it. She guessed that part. The big guy figured Tony had money somewhere, and finally found out about the cottage when his buddy Evan Roenicke tipped him off. Then Evan and the girl found the suitcase and Danny tried to take it from them. Evan tried to stop him.

Shoobie watched Grady type. "Do you buy any of this?"

Grady didn't look up. "No. Because most of it works."

"But why did it take Hammersmith and the lifeguard two weeks to figure out the guy stashed the money in the cottage?"

This time Grady looked up. "That part doesn't work."

Shoobie checked Hammersmith's record, a former boxer, bouncer, and now bartender with two arrests for assault, but no convictions. He looked like low-level muscle, which would make sense. But Hammersmith—"Danny the Hammer"—waived his right to a lawyer and told the same story, not quite word for word, but close enough so it sounded like he'd practiced.

"Seventy grand in that suitcase," Grady said. "For all the bank accounts, that's a piddling little stash, isn't it?"

Shoobie's feet hurt. She'd been on them most of the day, first at banks, then trying to break the song and dance Woody Guthrie started and the girl and the ape followed. "I wonder who the girl was Fortunato tipped at the strip club. Or if it was more than one."

"You think she knows where there's more money?" Grady finally looked up from his typing. "Or they?"

"Well," Shoobie said, "like you said, seventy grand's not much for all the work the guy did hiding it."

The clock across the room said ten-ten. It seemed to have specks on the glass, or maybe that was Shoobie's eyes.

"*Cherchez la femme*," Grady said. "Or maybe not."

"Not," Shoobie said. She wanted to get home to that lonely bed, but another thought struck her. "Grady, do I look old?"

Grady's eyes widened. "What do you mean, 'old?'"

Shoobie remembered that bubble-gum voice at Brian's two nights before.

"You know. Like...old."

297

Grady shook his head. "I wouldn't put you at a day over...you look great. Why?"

"I was just thinking." If they left now, they could reach Brian Trask's bachelor apartment in Warren by eleven. A week night, but maybe it was worth a shot.

"Want to do a little field trip before we call it a night?"

*　　　*　　　*

They pulled to the curb by a brick apartment building at eleven-five. Shoobie counted windows and felt a warm glow of malice. Her husband's window was the fifth one from the left on the third floor, and it was lit.

They flashed their ID at the door, got the landlord to buzz them in, and walked up the stairs at the far end of the hall. The carpet was worn, but clean. The paint on the walls looked fairly new, too. Shoobie looked at unit numbers on the doors and meandered down the hall. When they reached her hubby's door, she unbuttoned her blazer so her gun butt showed.

She pounded her fist on the door and held her badge up to the peep hole.

"Police. Open up."

She was about to pound again when the door swung open and there was her husband, boxer shorts and a Taylor Swift tee shirt. *Taylor fucking Swift, for Christ's sake.*

"What the hell? Eleanor, do you know what time it is?" His hair stuck up on one side and his breath made Shoobie clench her teeth.

"Detective Hall, do you smell something suspicious here?"

Grady knew enough to follow her lead. "I think we need to check it out."

They both stepped forward.

"What the hell?" Brian's eyes widened, but he stepped back before Shoobie walked right up his chest and stomped his nose out the back of his head. "What the hell do you think you're trying to—?"

"Keep him here," Shoobie snapped. To her left was dark, but light streamed from a door to her right. She kicked it open the rest of the way, her hand going to her Sig Sauer.

"Police," she barked. "Put your hands on top of your head and don't make a sound."

The girl's squeak made Shoobie's fillings vibrate. She yanked the sheet up over her chest, eyes the size of golf balls and hair sticking up in all directions. Red, green, purple, orange. She could have been a bag of jelly beans. Shoobie stomped over to the bed.

"Police," she said again. "Keep your hands in plain sight."

She yanked down the sheet, clear to the foot of the bed. The girl was naked, a Celtic ring tattoo on her right ankle and a piercing in her navel. She didn't look a day over eighteen.

"Let me see your ID."

"Who are—?"

"Police. Where's your ID?"

"In...in my purse. It's over..." The girl's eyes rolled toward the dresser.

"Keep your hands on top of your head." Shoobie watched the kid's hands hover over her breasts first, and cleared her throat. When the girl obeyed, she turned the purse upside down and watched everything spill on the carpet. She sorted through it with her foot, scattering keys, cosmetics, a cell phone, assorted tissues and a small baggie all over the room. She picked up a wallet and flicked it open.

"Joanie Bublewicz." She glared at the girl. She had nice breasts, round, high, no sag. Her stomach was ironing board flat, and she had tan lines that showed the outline of a thong. Her legs were a little thin, but not bad. Shoobie hated her.

"This your current address? Southfield?"

"Yes, ma'am."

"Yes, Detective."

"I'm sorry. Yes, Detective. I didn't—"

Shoobie waved the baggie in the girl's face. "You tell me this is for medical purposes, I will drag you down Woodward Avenue by that sorry little piercing. It is marijuana, isn't it?"

"Uh, well..."

"Yes or no?"

"I...yes. But I don't..."

The girl started to cry, which made Shoobie feel both wonderful and shitty at the same time.

"He brought you back here and you smoked a little dope, and he suggested you go to bed, didn't he?"

"Well, actually, we're—"

"Don't interrupt." Shoobie gave the kid her best glare, the one that bounced off real bad guys. "You met him tonight for the first time when he sweet-talked you back here, didn't you."

"I...yes. Um, uh-huh. I don't...have you been watching him? I don't know him...I just..."

Shoobie weighed the baggie in her hand, maybe an ounce. She handed it to the girl.

"Come with me."

She made the girl walk in front of her, naked, down the hall past Brian and Grady to that dark bathroom. She had a butterfly tattoo above her butt, too. Monarch tramp stamp.

"Detective." Shoobie turned on the light. "You didn't see this part."

She pointed at the toilet. "Dump it all. If you're slow, I'm doing a full cavity search, right here, right now."

"Please," the girl whimpered. "I'm sorry. I'll never..."

"Pour it in the toilet."

The girl emptied the baggie and pushed the lever. They watched the stuff swirl around the whirlpool and disappear before Shoobie took her by the arm and marched her back to Brian's bedroom.

"Joanie Bublewicz. Have we ever arrested you before?"

"No, ma'am. I mean, no, Detective."

"Good." Shoobie looked at the girl. Pretty, but lousy taste in men. "This man is a predator, so don't you ever come near him again. I'm going to let you get dressed, then you're going to leave here. We'll run your name through the computer downtown. If you're not in there, you're going to be fine. If you've lied to me, you can't begin to imagine the nightmare that will become your life. Do you understand?"

The girl nodded, tears shiny on her cheeks.

"Get dressed."

Shoobie watched her climb back into her clothes and sweep everything back into her purse. She had a cute butt, better with jeans on.

"All right," Shoobie said. "Is your car parked down in the lot?"

The girl nodded, her keys rattling in her hand.

"Go home."

The girl dashed past Grady and Brian and slammed the door behind her. Shoobie looked at her husband and tried to remember why she'd been busting her ass to get him back.

"Really, Brian. The kid turned twenty-one three weeks ago. Why don't you just cruise Toys R Us?"

"You fucking bitch."

Shoobie felt her rage fade and a warm rich glow replace it.

"No, I've been trying to get you back, change who I am so an asshole will love me. Well, enough of that shit. It's over. Tomorrow, I'm filing for divorce."

Brian's eyes narrowed.

"Yeah," Shoobie told him. "For desertion, mental cruelty, adultery, and anything else I can think of."

Grady cleared his throat. "Maybe the haircut?"

"Yeah. A really crappy haircut. And alimony. And if I find you within a hundred yards of a virgin sacrifice again, I will shoot your balls off and make you eat them."

Shoobie watched her soon-to-be ex-husband swallow.

"Detective, our work is finished here."

58

Carmine Diorio looked even less lethal behind his desk than when Guthrie saw him at Tony Fortunato's funeral five days earlier. Liver spots gave his small head definition on a thin neck that made him resemble a flesh-colored balloon, and his polyester suit—was that salmon???—might have been fashionable when Guthrie was learning to walk. A cloud of thin white hair surrounded his bald pate. Carmine was the undisputed head of drugs, prostitution, gambling, loan-sharking, and probably a few other enterprises the Michigan State Legislature frowned upon.

"Constancia," he wheezed. "So good to see you again. I'm so sorry about Anthony. How are the children handling it?"

"They're OK, Uncle Carmine." Connie seemed to be debating between kissing the guy's ring and touching her forehead to the floor. She wore a discreet dark blouse and black skirt that took ten pounds off her. "Um, thank you for seeing us."

"Family comes first." Carmine flicked his eyes across the others and Guthrie felt his cheek burn. He wondered if it would leave a scar. "You, you're Guthrie, right? You called me last night."

"Yes, sir."

"And you said you had an offer."

"Well, sir, what I said was a proposition. Since it involves your family, I thought I should discuss it with you personally."

Carmine had to be pushing seventy, but he looked like he could jog twenty miles uphill carrying a beer keg. He spread his arms, palms up in a move he might have learned from the Pope.

Guthrie sat with Christine Chapel on his left and Connie to his right, Tobi beyond her, all three women wearing predominately black. The two larger suitcases lay on a table to the left of Diorio's desk, and large men in expensive suits had already opened them and found no bombs, guns, or other dangerous weapons. Money was deadly enough.

Guthrie took a deep breath and began.

"About two weeks ago, your niece's husband Anthony disappeared, as I'm sure you know. He was found a few days later in the trunk of his car. He'd been punched in the mouth and swallowed the bridge he'd worn since he broke several teeth in a high school track meet."

Carmine's eyes flickered toward Connie. Guthrie took that as a cue to keep going.

"The police found a fingerprint from a gentleman named Lincoln Fillmore in the car and arrested him. Lincoln told me he'd 'found' the car in the Cass Corridor with the keys in the ignition and the door unlocked. He didn't know at the time that Anthony was dead in the trunk, but it looked pretty clear to me that someone had set him up."

Carmine stretched out his arms across the arms of his chair. "And you followed this up how?"

"Well, before I could do anything, someone tried to break into Tony's accounting firm. The security scared him off, but both the police and I thought it was too much of a coincidence."

Guthrie cleared his throat and Christine stopped digging at a cuticle. Her black skirt showed miles of thigh.

"The police took Anthony's computers to check them out. I have a...contact in the PD who told me they thought Tony was hiding money under several names, and he'd embezzled it from the accounting firm. Neither of his partners had noticed."

"Shocking," Diorio said. "How could they be so lax?"

"Because one of them didn't know those accounts existed," Guthrie said. "And the other set them up himself, and he was stealing from someone else, someone who works with some of your...enterprises. I'm guessing either a chop shop over on 6 Mile or some of the clubs on 8 Mile."

Christine whimpered on Guthrie's left and he made eye contact just long enough to shut her up again. Connie shifted and Guthrie realized yet again that this was news to her, too.

"That person and one of Anthony's partners were hiding money and somehow, Anthony found out. He figured he could steal from that account and the people involved couldn't go to the police because the money was already...um, questionable."

"Smart," Carmine Diorio said. "And also very, very stupid."

"Tacky, too," Guthrie said. "What kind of person steals from his own family, especially when he's married into it?"

"You understand these things, Mr. Guthrie." The old man raised his eyebrows, the thickest hair on his head.

"I try, sir," Guthrie said. "Anyway, when Tony's partner figured out that Anthony was stealing, he hired a man named Danny Hammersmith to get the money back. Danny's not big on subtlety, and he accidentally killed Anthony before he got the account numbers—or learned about the cash in the suitcases." Guthrie gestured toward the luggage.

"Danny thought maybe Anthony had a girlfriend. He and I both suspected Ms. Loerner over here, who actually knew nothing about what was going on. But Danny's partner, Evan, became friends with Ms. Loerner and tried to find out from her where the money was."

"But I didn't—" Tobi's voice reminded Guthrie of a baby lamb.

"I know. You were completely innocent. But Danny and Evan and I all thought maybe Tony was cheating on his wife with you. Your niece, Mr. Diorio."

The man looked stern. Connie sat up straighter and pouted, just enough to look righteous.

Guthrie saw almost the same look from Shoobie Dube and Grady Hall the previous afternoon. They'd found the gun that killed Evan Roenicke in the trunk of Danny's car. Guthrie said he'd chased Danny away from that car and kept Connie, Christine, and Barry Montesori out of the story. Danny understood what would happen if he offered a different version.

Guthrie could tell that Shoobie wanted to throw him in a cell but couldn't find a reason to do it. Tobi admitted to losing control of her bladder when she saw her boyfriend killed. Shoobie had enough sisterhood in her to let the girl clean up in the bedroom and change out of the stained bathing suit before taking her downtown.

The police had the smallest suitcase full of money, which sold everything.

Fourteen hours later, Guthrie and the women looked bright and contrite for the head of the Detroit mob. Guthrie's ribs and leg didn't hurt any more, and he knew Shoobie would give his gun back once they confirmed that it hadn't been fired.

Carmine Diorio cleared his throat. "You said something a few moments ago about someone stealing. The person Anthony was stealing from."

Guthrie nodded. "Leonard Klein, Anthony's partner. He was helping your associate skim from you. It's probably been going on for quite awhile, just a little at a time, not enough to notice. But when Klein realized Anthony was dipping into it, he knew he had to get it back before someone *did* notice. I think Klein's accomplice may have already known Danny the Hammer, which is how he got involved."

He glanced at Christine. "You called him yesterday, didn't you? That's why Barry Montesori knew you. And Klein called Danny, which is why he knew you at the cottage."

Tobi dug in her purse. "Um, then I'll bet this is yours, isn't it?" She held up a dangly earring with a large dark stone.

Christine's eyes widened. "Yeah, I was wondering where..."

Tobi's face glowed. "I...we...found it in the bed when we..."

Connie's face turned even redder than Tobi's and Guthrie reached over to grab the ear ring and stay between Connie and the stripper. Tobi took Connie's near hand and everyone watched her slowly move from a full boil back to simmer. Christine dropped the jewelry into her own purse and looked at Carmine Diorio again as if he fascinated her.

Carmine shifted everyone's attention back to the suitcases. "So this is the money."

Guthrie shifted in his chair. "Well, there's probably a lot more. This is what Anthony had in cash, minus the suitcase the police have. I had to give them enough so they thought they'd closed the case. I'm guessing there's around three-quarters of a million dollars there, but it's a wild guess. Klein may have stolen several times that."

"And I get that back, how, exactly?"

Guthrie met Carmine's stare. "If you have someone who knows computers, you take Klein's machines and check them out. I called him last night and told him you knew what he was doing, so he's already left. I doubt that he took the time to erase the files."

He reached into his pocket. "And here are four keys to Tony's safety deposit boxes. I'm guessing you'll find more keys or directions to more money in them. The police need search warrants, but you probably have people who can show the right forms of ID. Besides, the police are looking at Tony's stuff. Klein's may be in different banks."

Carmine Diorio stared at Guthrie. Then he looked at the women, one after the other. Connie flinched less than the other two.

"Mr. Guthrie, I appreciate, but I know how the world works. Nobody does favors anymore, not like you're talking about."

Christine's voice sounded about twelve years old. "I'm gonna have a baby."

The room fell silent except for the whisper of the central air conditioning. Guthrie remembered Valerie's findings.

"That's why you gave up smoking? And started bringing healthy snacks to work?"

The woman nodded and tears worked their way down her cheeks. "I tried one of those tests, you know, from the drug store? Six days in a row, every single one a winner."

Tobi Loerner clamped onto Connie Fortunato's arm and watched the woman's face turn bright red. Guthrie pointed at the suitcases.

"Maybe you could see your way to help her out a little, Mr. Diorio? I mean, indirectly, she is one of your employees."

Christine flinched. Guthrie turned to Tobi.

"Ms. Loerner was perfectly innocent, but a man killed her boyfriend and put her own life in jeopardy. She's been taking care of your grand-niece and nephew all summer during a tough time when they've lost their father. I think she deserves something, too. At the very least, enough to pay for her last year of college."

Carmine turned and stared at Tobi, who seemed torn between laughing, crying or crawling under her chair.

"Where you going to college?"

"Wayne State," she whispered. Then she shook her head and Guthrie watched the stage presence bump up. "I'm a theater major."

"College. That's good." Carmine rubbed his palms together as if applying lotion.

"Lincoln Fillmore is going to be a father soon, too," Guthrie said. "I'm hoping you can see your way to helping him out a little, too. Since he actually helped your niece by stealing the car."

"How you figure?"

Guthrie ignored Connie, sitting next to him with her mouth open.

"Well, if people figured out that Anthony had a lot of money, she'd have a motive to kill him, especially since he was cheating on her. So when Hot Rod—"

"Who?"

"Hot Rod Lincoln," Guthrie said. "We've called him that for years because he usually steals high-end cars. Like Anthony's Mercedes."

"I see."

"Well, with that money, your niece had a motive to kill her husband. But Hot Rod stole the car and hid it so Connie had an alibi for the time when he died. She was never a real suspect, which protected the family from lots of stress. And, of course, scandal."

Guthrie omitted the other scandal. Barry Montesori probably wouldn't marry Connie, but he was now the remaining owner of an accounting firm.

Carmine steepled his bony hands under his chin.

"I notice you haven't mentioned anything for yourself, Mr. Guthrie. Or my niece."

Guthrie held his gaze.

"Your niece is family, sir. And she's still an attractive woman. I'm sure she'll meet men who can take care of her— and her children—in the manner she deserves."

God, he felt like an old aristocrat.

Carmine cocked an eyebrow. "I'll say it again. And for you, Mr. Guthrie?"

Guthrie glanced over at Connie.

"I'd like Tony's electric guitar."

59

The following April, Valerie handed Guthrie a plain white envelope with a Daytona Beach postmark. He tore it open and found a color photograph of three people, the man with long sideburns but shorter hair than before. He didn't recognize the woman, but she held a shapeless pink bundle. If his math was right, the child was no more than two weeks old. Both parents seemed to glow.

"I'm surprised he could find a place that still develops film." Valerie wore her honey-colored hair short, brushing her collar. Guthrie suspected she'd picked the look up from the newly-divorced Shoobie Dube. "Everyone I know uses a digital camera and downloads to their computer."

"But you're ahead of the curve, Valerie."

"Men used to tell me that."

Nobody had seen Leonard Klein since he left his house an hour after Guthrie called him, but police found his car at the airport. Diorio's experts found even more names on his computer than on Tony Fortunato's.

The manager of several strip joints on 8 Mile Road died a week after Klein disappeared. His car apparently went off the road and slammed into a tree. Christine Chapel told Guthrie about it. Neither of them believed that was what happened, especially when Guthrie learned that Danny Hammersmith was one of his bartenders.

Christine Chapel took her money and moved back to Kentucky somewhere. Guthrie wondered if she was still not smoking. And about the baby.

Shoobie was talking to Guthrie again now, but she still had a look in her eyes that he was smart enough to fear. She didn't see the whole picture, but she lacked the right crayons to fill in the rest of it.

Tobi Loerner changed her major to elementary education the previous fall, but she sent him two tickets for the production of *Hamlet*. He took Meg, who didn't think much of the actresses playing either Gertrude or Ophelia.

Guthrie wondered if Connie Fortunato was still seeing Barry Montesori. Somehow, he doubted it.

He was up to about an hour a day on the Les Paul.

#   #   #

Acknowledgments

Anyone who tells you he wrote a book all by himself is lying or has produced a book that could have been much better. This book had several sets of eyes looking at different parts of it, and it gained from every single one of them.

The following members of Sisters in Crime shared anecdotes and information to help me with Chrissie's pregnancy dilemma:

Laura Mitchell, Mary Feliz, Corilynn Arnold, Michelle Markey Butler, Deb Auten, Clea Simon, Robin Burcell, Kimberly Garnick Giarrantano, Meg Opperman, Jennifer Adolph, Diane Schultz, and Sarah Zettel.

Kelly Cochran of the Guppies Chapter spotted some inconsistencies in the final MS, which I hope I corrected.

Frank Breen let us take dozens of pictures of his Mercedes...which we ended up not using on the cover after all.

And, finally, my wife Barbara, who knows that titles are one of my many weaknesses. Without her, this book might have been called *Hyundai, Bloody Hyundai*.

About the Author

Steve Liskow is a member of Private Eye Writers of America and serves as a mentor and panelist for both Mystery Writers of America and Sisters in Crime. A former English teacher, he now conducts fiction writing workshops throughout Connecticut to satisfy his teaching Jones.

His short stories have earned an Edgar nomination, the Black Orchid Novella Award, and two Honorable Mentions for the Al Blanchard Story Award. *Blood On The Tracks*, the first "Woody" Guthrie Novel, won Honorable Mention in the Writer's Digest Self-Published Novel Awards for 2014.

He lives in central Connecticut with his wife Barbara and two rescued cats.

This is his ninth novel.

Visit his website at
www.steveliskow.com

Like his Facebook Author page at
www.facebook.com/#!/steveliskowcrimewriter

Made in the USA
Middletown, DE
19 April 2015